Kay Mellor, the creator of the ground-breaking TV drama series, *Band of Gold*, is an award-winning writer whose recent West End play, *A Passionate Woman*, starring Stephanie Cole, achieved huge success. Her ITV series, *Just Us*, won The Writers' Guild and The Royal Television Society awards for Best Children's Drama.

John Burke is an acclaimed writer whose novelisations include *The Bill* and *London's Burning*. He lives in Scotland.

The novelisation of the first series, *Band of Gold: Ring of Lies*, is also available from Headline.

Also by Kay Mellor
and novelised by John Burke

Band of Gold: Ring of Lies

BAND OF GOLD:
Chain of Power

Created by
Kay Mellor

Novelised by
John Burke

HEADLINE

First published in 1996
by HEADLINE BOOK PUBLISHING

10 9 8 7 6 5 4 3 2 1

All characters in this publication are fictitious and any resemblance to real persons, living or dead, is purely coincidental.

ISBN 0 7472 5406 0

Typeset by Palimpsest Book Production Limited,
Polmont, Stirlingshire
Printed and bound in Great Britain by
Cox & Wyman Ltd, Reading, Berks.

HEADLINE BOOK PUBLISHING
A division of Hodder Headline PLC
338 Euston Road
London NW1 3BH

BAND OF GOLD: Chain of Power

1

George Ferguson had never been much of a one for the open air, but today he took in great gulps of it. It wasn't country air – he was more used to the polluted town stuff anyway – but it tasted sweeter than the atmosphere inside Wakefield prison.

He looked along the street. They had told him the general direction of the railway station and the bus terminal, but he was still dazed and unsure whether they had said left or right. Lugging the holdall with the few possessions he had reclaimed on leaving, he didn't fancy walking back to Bradford; but automatically he began moving away from the prison entrance, moving just for the sake of moving.

There were footsteps behind him. George quickened his pace. They couldn't be trying to re-arrest him, not after he had served his few months for petty fraud and been let out on parole, but still it was going to take time to get over that humiliating routine of being watched, followed, ordered about.

'Wanna lift, George?'

It was no use. He had to stop. Smiley's voice was unmistakable. So, when George turned round, was his vicious grin, no more than a narrow gash in that thin face.

'Going my way?' He had meant it to sound light and matey, but it came out with a nervous gulp.

Smiley said, 'Alfie'd like a word.'

Most men released from prison might have enjoyed the prospect of being driven off in a Rolls Royce. George

Ferguson wasn't one of them. But one of the back doors was being held open, and Alfie was waiting for him – Alfie in a fine cashmere coat, a gold tiepin gleaming at his throat, polished shoes at the end of impeccably pressed trousers. George climbed in. Smiley closed the door and went round to the driver's seat, still grinning as Alfie considerately slid the glass panel open so that he could hear what was going on in the back. Alfie often liked to make sure that everyone within hearing range could be suitably impressed.

'George, me old mate, how yer doing?'

'Good to see you, Alfie.'

'Likewise. You owe me two hundred grand, sunshine.'

The Roller slid away from the kerb and purred its way through the traffic on to the Bradford road. The interior was maintained at a steady, mild temperature, but George felt the sweat gathering in the folds of fat round his neck. He had lost some weight in prison, but not a lot. All that had really been lost in his absence, with no one to trust and no one to wheel and deal with, was money. He didn't have two hundred grand or anywhere near it. Alfie must know that. Alfie knew every damn thing that went on, and couldn't possibly suppose there was still that much left.

'It'll take me time to get on my feet again, Alfie,' he stuttered. 'You know how it is.'

'I know how it *was*. As I remember it, the money was put offshore and you channelled it back in through Klensit.'

'That's right, yes. But I thought we could make even more by investing in that loan company.'

Alfie picked thoughtfully at his teeth. 'If I'd wanted a shark, I'd have gone to the Atlantic. I came to you 'cos you were a small fish. A small clean fish. And do you know what happens to small fish when they try swimming against the tide?' He extricated a bit of gristle from somewhere between his back teeth. 'They get hooked up,' he said, 'battered, and served up on someone else's plate.'

He seemed so pleased by this little fancy that they

covered several miles along the motorway without him saying another word. It was not a companionable silence, though. Silent, Alfie could be even more menacing than when he was talking. He was capable of breaking a man's neck without even flinching. When at last he spoke again, it was quiet but deadly. 'It was a deal, George. I'd like my investment out now, please.'

George Ferguson looked out of the window as they came off the motorway, trying to feel reassured by the sight of familiar streets opening up around him. But there was nothing reassuring in the way Smiley glanced up into his driving mirror and smirked again.

'Right to your door,' said Alfie. 'What more could you ask?'

They were drawing up outside the garage where George's prized Jaguar had been stored.

Desperately he tried to explain how his treacherous bitch of a wife had double-crossed him, gone in with that rival cleaning company of scheming hustlers to snatch the Leisure Centre contract, and on top of that started divorce proceedings which would clean him out. There was simply nothing left.

Alfie heard him out, and sighed. 'Now don't tell me you haven't got a secret little stash somewhere.'

George had no intention of telling him about the little bit set aside where not even the Fraud Squad had got a whiff of it. 'Honest to God,' he lied, 'if I had it, you could have it. But I'm stony broke. The loan company's gone, and it'll take time to get my cleaning company back on its feet again. It's just been marking time while I've been away.'

'Sell the cleaning company. It's not worth a fart now you've been done for fraud. They're gonna be watching you like a mother hen.'

'It's all I've got,' George protested. 'If I sell that, I've got nothing.'

A mechanic was wheeling the Jag out on to the forecourt.

It was a lovely sight. George wanted to get out of the Roller, settle himself behind his own wheel, and drive off the way he used to, with profitable deals waiting for him and people eager to lick his boots.

Alfie said, 'You could start by selling that car.'

It was like being kneed in the guts. He'd had that car since it was new, years back; and even if he could bear to part with it, he'd be lucky to get a grand.

He leaned closer to Alfie so that even the attentive Smiley couldn't hear. 'Look, I'll tell you what. I might be able to lay me hands on sixty by the end of the month. I'm not even supposed to have that. If they find out, they'll have me back inside.'

Alfie stretched and yawned, then leaned forward to speak through the open panel. 'Right, Smiley, we'll have a little trip up Brampton Moor.'

'No.' George knew what that could mean. Alfie wouldn't hesitate to leave another corpse up on that cursed bloody moor. 'Hang on a minute.' He was plucking ideas wildly out of the air. 'Look, I know this other cleaning company you can put your money through. It's nothing to do with me, really – it's up and running, and it's kosher – but they owe me a favour or two. You can keep my cut. I know them, I can do a deal. First thing tomorrow morning, honest . . .'

The light of dawn was beginning to show through the flowers on the hotel bedroom curtains. Tracy Richards tried to turn over, but was pinned down by a heavy arm lying across her. The punter was a large man, and a pretty rough one. She hadn't much cared for the sight of him, but the idea of a night in a comfortable bed had been too tempting. Since she'd come back to Bradford from London, things hadn't been the way they used to be. Rose had got too bloody puffed up to be believed, giving up hustling so she could get down on her knees and scrub floors, and making Tracy feel she wasn't really wanted about the place. So a whole night with someone who could afford to throw his money about ought to have been a nice change from lonely wanderings and cheap, quick shags off Lambton Lane. Only that comfortable bed had turned out uncomfortable right from the start, and was even more so now. The man was a slob, he stank, and he was snoring.

Tracy carefully eased the greasy arm away. The punter grunted, turned over on his side, and rolled away from her. Tracy slid out of bed and groped in the uncertain light for her clothes.

Suddenly he had grabbed her arm. 'Where d'you think you're going?' Before she could fumble an answer, he had dragged her back on to the bed and was holding her down with all his weight, snarling at her but starting to enjoy the struggle. 'I paid for a night with you,' he growled into her face, 'and I want a whole night, not part of a night. Understand?'

'I was just going to the toilet.'

'I say when you go to the toilet. You ask me, you say "Please, Daddy, can I go to the toilet?"'

Tracy struggled for breath. 'Please can I go to the toilet?'

'Daddy,' he prompted.

No, she wasn't going to say that. No way. It was because of her father and those games and pawings of his that she had run away from home in the first place. She wasn't going to start playing them again with a slob like this. The word *daddy* didn't exist in her head or anywhere else any more.

'I don't want to go after all,' she said.

'Let's make sure of that, shall we?'

He was treating her like dirt, angry yet enjoying himself. He had reached out to the table on his side of the bed and clutched his tie. Before she realised what he was up to, he was forcing her wrists together and tightening the tie round them, cutting into her flesh.

'I'm not going to run away,' she sobbed.

'That's right, you're not. I'm making sure of that.'

'Let me go.' The more she struggled, the more he shifted his weight on her, and she felt that he was getting an erection again. 'I'll scream,' she wailed. And he laughed.

Tracy bit his hand.

'You do that again, and I'll kill you.' He swung his injured hand round and was squeezing her face between his thick, splayed fingers and thumb. 'You little whore.'

When he let go, she sagged back on the bed. It was getting brighter. Time to get out of here. He couldn't want much more: surely he couldn't want to go on much longer? When he heaved himself away from her, she was sure he'd had enough. But he was reaching for something else. Dimly she could see that he had grabbed a large roll of sticky tape out of the bag by his side of the bed. He bit off a length, and to stop her leaping away from him put a hand firmly on her stomach.

'What yer doing?' She was trying to raise her hands in terrified appeal, but he had tied them too tightly. 'What's that?' Willing to make any plea now, she said, 'I'm sorry . . . Daddy.'

It was too late. He had other ideas. The tape came down across her mouth. And the man came straddling across her thighs, gasping with joy, then eased himself back to get a better view, and wanked himself off.

There was a tap at the door. He went still immediately, slamming his hand down across her face, though with the tape nearly suffocating her, he didn't need to do that.

'Tracy?'

He stared down at her, whispering, 'Who the hell is that?'

Stupid question, when he knew she couldn't speak. Tracy tried her best, but could only summon up a choking, mumbling sound. It was her new mate, Colette: someone she had started with since Rose was no longer so interested. Trust Colette to come to the rescue.

'Tracy, are you all right in there?'

Sure enough she was in here. But not all right. Her head was fit to burst. She forced sounds up from her throat, writhed under the man's filthy fat hands, and tried to wriggle her way to one side of the bed. There was a phone on the table at that side. Tracy made a wild jab with her head, and knocked it to the floor.

'You stupid bitch . . .'

By the time Colette had been alerted by the clatter of the falling phone and forced a chambermaid to use her key on the door, he was on his feet, getting dressed and managing a look of pained surprise as if he might at any moment summon the manager to register a complaint. With a disdainful shrug he tossed a small wad of notes on the bed, offered the chambermaid a fiver, and went out, leaving Colette to tear the tape agonisingly off Tracy's lips.

Tracy dressed with difficulty, her fingers trembling as she fumbled with buttons and her bra strap. 'Bastard,' she muttered obsessively. 'Bastard. Shit.'

They found their way down the back stairs and out into the alley at the back. Colette knew what was needed. She was on her mobile phone to her dealer right away. Half a six, and fast . . . meet him in the Lane.

'Bastard,' said Tracy again. 'I thought I were gonna suffocate. And it's all your fault.'

Colette raised her eyes to the pink and yellow smears in the morning sky. 'Oh, I might have known I'd get the blame.'

'It were you that set me up with him.'

'Well, I didn't know he were into bondage, did I? He said he was straight. Anyway, you should just have kneed him in the bollocks. You're too soft sometimes, y'know. You bring out the worst in 'em with that baby look of yours. *You're* the one who's got to call the shots.'

'Don't tell me how to hustle,' said Tracy indignantly. Colette looked super and domineering in her tight black leather trousers and vest, big chunky belt, and studded leather wrist bands; but she was a fairly recent newcomer on the Lane, and Tracy knew a whole lot more about the local scene than she did. 'If it hadn't been for me,' she pointed out, 'you'd still be paying yer twenty percent to that slimy Sid.'

'Did you ever do him?'

'No.' Tracy was mildly curious. 'Did you?'

'Smallest dick I've ever seen. No kidding, it were like the end of me thumb. Some bloody escort agency *he* ran!'

They both laughed, mates again as they reached the end of Lambton Lane. They were halfway down, moving slowly in the cool morning air, when a man in his late twenties came round the corner at the end. He sauntered towards them, looking too tired to quicken his pace even when he recognised Colette. He was half asleep, half stoned, and his hair was a mess. Tracy had heard about Rabbit before – difficult not to, with Colette around – but this was the first time she had met him. His name would have been right if he hadn't looked more like a weasel, with sharp but bloodshot eyes blinking from side to side as if to fight off any other animals that might fancy a taste of him. 'Got a light?' He focused on Tracy as Colette fished her lighter out of her bag. After the light he waited for the money, and then handed the crack over. He was still watching them both as they went off in the direction of Rose's place.

Tracy had hoped to creep in unobserved, but Rose was already up. They could hear her voice on the telephone as Tracy eased the back door open. 'Thirty pound an hour should be all right. Yeh. So I'll be there about twelve, then. You won't be late, will you? Just that I've only got a little time to . . . yes, right, well then, I'm about five foot seven, I've got long wavy blonde hair, and I'm—' Rose became aware of the two others coming along the passage. 'Must go. See you later.'

Thirty quid an hour? It couldn't be scrubbing floors. Rose

wasn't going back to the other kind of scrubbing, was she? As if to fight off any questions along that line, Rose snapped: 'Where've you been till this time?'

'On me holidays.'

'Well, aren't you the lucky one? Ring in future if you're staying out.' Rose glared at Colette. 'What does *she* want?'

'Nowt you've got, love,' said Colette.

Tracy felt a tug of loyalties. She loved Rose so much really, depended on her, couldn't see how she'd have got on without her this last year or so; but she'd had so much fun with Colette, and was coming to rely on her as well, and wished she and Rose didn't have to prickle at each other.

Rose decided to ignore Colette's snappish retort. 'I bought some milk and toilet rolls. Eat something, will you? Get yourself some breakfast.'

'I hope your meeting goes all right.'

There was a touch of the old Rose in that smile: pleased that Tracy had remembered about the meeting. As if to force herself back into the picture, Colette ran her hand very slowly down Tracy's bare arm. When Rose had left, she said: 'She thinks she's yer bleeding mother, her.'

Tracy waited for the slam of the outer door. 'Are we gonna do this rock, then, or what?'

They settled side by side on the settee. Tracy was the first, touching her lighter to the rock and beginning to draw the smoke in steadily through the Biro casing of an improvised pipe. Colette's fingers found her arm again and began to stroke her in a slow, hypnotic rhythm, stopping only when Tracy passed her the pipe. Together they sank into a trance of contentment. Everything in the room was becoming incredibly clear and beautiful, with a reality like a wonderful dream from which you didn't want to wake, didn't have to wake ever.

Anita Braithwaite didn't want to wake up. She had taken

more than her usual ration of Malibu and Coke last night, and it hadn't given her any wonderful dreams, but still she didn't want to open her eyes. Something was shaking her arm, and she had to push it away. She dragged the duvet over her head, but somebody pulled it down again. Anita opened her eyes, staring at the ceiling and wondering where the hell she was. The bed didn't feel like her own bed, and when she moaned and turned on her side, the bedside table wasn't hers.

'Auntie 'Nita, it's quarter past nine.' A clock from the table was thrust into her face. 'You slept in.'

Reality flooded over her. Anita pushed herself off the bed while Carol's daughter, Emma, stared up at her reproachfully. Of course this wasn't her own room. That had been taken away from her by George Ferguson months ago. Here she was in Carol's spare bedroom, supposed to be getting Emma to school on time. Anita groaned again. Carol would kill her if she found out.

Bits of last night's makeup were still tacky on her face, but there was no time to fix that now. She grabbed her denim jacket from the wardrobe, found a slip that had somehow gone under the bed when she was undressing, and ten minutes later was trying to catch up with Emma, whose little dark brown face kept turning impatiently back to urge her on.

Stupid, really. Anita could never understand why Carol was so insistent on Emma going to school every day and getting there right on the dot. Most kids skived off for a day or two. It wasn't normal going every day.

'Do *hurry*,' Emma was insisting. A red car slid alongside the kerb beside Anita. She took one quick glance at it; then another; then looked away and made a real effort to speed up her pace.

George Ferguson leaned over as he coasted slowly along, keeping level. 'Anita, I thought it was you. I recognised the jacket. It's nice to see you. You're looking really well.'

'Liar.' She wasn't going to let herself look at him. 'I look a bloody mess.'

'You couldn't look a mess if you tried. You've got a bonnie face, you always had. But then you don't need me to tell you that. Do you need a lift up to the school?'

In spite of Emma's dismayed expression, Anita stopped. 'Look, what the hell do you want?'

'Nothing. Just that I was thinking about you last night.'

'I thought you were inside.'

'I'm on parole. Model prisoner, you see. I've been thinking about you a lot.'

A likely story, she thought. Ditching her after all those years, chucking her out of the flat he had got for her, taking up with another woman, trying to block every move their cleaning team made towards respectability and profit, going to prison because of his dirty tricks and expecting her to greet him as if nothing had happened . . .

'Thinking about me?' she said sarcastically. 'I wonder what your *respectable* lady friend would have to say about that?'

'Maxine and I split up three weeks after you and I had finished.'

'And how's your dear wife?'

'Busy screwing me for all she can get.'

'Good. I'm glad to know she's doing something worth while.'

He had never been good at keeping his temper under control. He glowered, and as she walked on he began to wind the window of the Jag up again.

'Sorry I stopped, if that's how you feel.'

Anita felt a sudden panic. No matter how he had behaved in the past, she couldn't help feeling in a confused sort of way that a lot of things in the past had been a bloody sight better than what she was lumbered with today.

'I'm not stupid, George.'

'I never thought for a single second that you were.'

Emma was growing more and more apprehensive. 'Auntie 'Nita!'

Anita stopped once more and went to the half-open window. 'What the hell do you want?' she asked again.

He grinned. She remembered that lopsided, shifty grin of his all too well. But it was part of George, and they had laughed such a lot together; she had fallen for his lies so often and been happy enough to believe them.

'To make friends, that's all,' he said with glowing sincerity. 'To talk to you. It wasn't all that bad, you know. Some fun times we had, right? Look, I know I've been a bastard in the past, but, Jesus, I've paid for it. I've lost everything. I'm not a young man any more, Anita. I need some sort of stability.' Oh, it was the old George all right; but then, she had never been able to resist the old George. 'I'll tell you something.' He was more earnest than ever. 'Sometimes you don't realise what you've got, till you lose it.'

Anita took a deep breath. 'Emma, come on, we've got a lift.'

Emma came doubtfully back. 'Mam says I'm not to get in strange men's cars.'

'He's not a strange man.' Anita exchanged a glance with George. 'Well, no stranger than the rest. Come on, get in.'

They got in. George smiled briefly at Emma, meaningly at Anita, and went on smiling as he concentrated on the road ahead.

After they had dropped Emma at the school gates and watched her scamper across the deserted playground, he turned the Jag around and said, 'Just as a matter of interest, how's your Scrubbit International team getting along nowadays?'

2

Rose could hear them arguing as she approached the door of the ladies' changing rooms. Empty at this time of the morning except for the cleaners, the corridors of the Leisure Centre echoed with every raised voice. And Brenda had a particularly piercing, whining voice.

'All I'm saying is that when I worked for George Ferguson, I used to get paid cash in hand, that's all.'

Carol, in her red-and-white Scrubbit overall, had her head down over the toilet, scouring away with a lavatory brush. Without looking up she growled, 'Yeh, but you got less money at Klensit, didn't you?'

'I could still get me soch, though.'

Carol scrubbed even more vigorously. 'Tell you what, you try hustling. You'll get your soch then, won't she, Rose?'

'I don't want to hustle.'

Rose glanced at Brenda's plump legs and ankles, and at Carol's slim, dark legs. The idea of Brenda waddling along Lambton Lane looking for punters was laughable.

'And you'll get plenty of cash in hand,' Carol went on angrily. Maybe she was beginning to regret quitting the Lane. 'Go on, Rose, tell her.'

Rose reached for a cloth and began wiping down the inside of the shower cubicle. She could do without this useless gabbing. She had come in this morning only to help Carol finish early, in time for the meeting.

'Come on, get cracking. I ought to be back at Joyce's sorting out next week's rota instead of—'

'And *I'm* here with me hand down the bleeding lav doing Joyce's shift for her.' Carol shot a glare over her shoulder at Brenda. 'Last thing I need is her moaning on.'

They finished in a sullen silence.

It took an effort to assume relaxed smiles when they hurried round to Mrs Minkin's office. Rose and Carol had had no time to change. Joyce, stepping out of the lift just as they reached the landing, had taken advantage of her free time to dress in her best, putting on the airs of a company representative with a bulging briefcase. Carol scowled but held back what she wanted to say.

Behind her imposing desk, Glenys Minkin looked pleased with herself. She had always been unfussily friendly towards them, smoothing their way into the cleaning contract and fighting off some of George Ferguson's cronies who had tried to block their application; but Rose had never seen her quite so bright and happy. She hoped it was a good omen.

Mrs Minkin waved for them to sit down.

'I've brought all the files,' said Joyce briskly.

'What for?'

It didn't take much to throw Joyce off balance. She had come prepared for questions on wages, expenditure, timekeeping, and anything else the Leisure Centre manager might want to throw at her. A question as unexpected as this left her fumbling for words.

Rose stepped in. 'We thought you'd called us in to go through them.'

'No.' Mrs Minkin leaned back in her chair, smiling broadly. 'I just wanted to see you all personally, to tell you I'm leaving the Leisure Centre.' Before any of them could get their breath back, she added, 'There's a new manager starting. Name of Gavin Ward. He's a bit of a whizzkid.'

'Shit,' said Carol instinctively.

They had got on so well with Mrs Minkin through the most difficult patch. No change could be for the better. The idea of some bossy whizzkid blasting in through the department and turning everything upside down wasn't a comforting one.

'I've told him all about you,' she tried to reassure them, 'and he's dead fair. I don't think you'll have a problem.' She looked along their dejected faces. 'Anything the matter?'

'Nothing,' mumbled Joyce.

Rose said, 'We'd sort of got used to you.'

Mrs Minkin looked even more pleased with life. 'Well, you're not getting rid of me that easy. In fact, you may be seeing even more of me. I've been asked to be General Manager of the whole thing – Civic Health and Leisure.'

'That's nice,' Carol managed.

They left in a jumble of good wishes and handshakes; but the brief, phoney cheerfulness soon ebbed. Glumly they went their different ways: Joyce back home, Carol off to do some shopping, and Rose to get to The Hustlers' Arms in good time for her appointment.

She had never before felt her heart in her mouth when she walked into the pub. There had been a time when she had made herself boss of the Lane, decreeing which hustlers could operate on her patch and which ones had better clear off before they got the lash of her tongue. When she strode up to the bar, there was always someone who would hastily slide off one of the stools for her. Today she hesitated in the doorway.

There were a few familiar faces, but several empty tables. A new girl was chatting up a possible punter: a droopy sort of sweeties girl Rose would never have allowed on the Lane for more than five minutes. But she dragged her mind away from that. It was none of her business now, and wasn't going to be again.

She thought of Gina Dixon, who she'd tried at first to drive off the patch. If she'd succeeded, Gina might still be alive today. Best not to think any more about that. Never. Just concentrate on the future she was going to make for herself.

A quite attractive man in his forties was sitting on the far side of the bar, eating a sandwich and scribbling notes on a jotter. This could be the one. But if he wasn't, and he thought she was trying to pick him up . . .

He glanced up, obviously trying to make up his mind about her, too.

She risked it. 'Excuse me, are you Brian Roberts?'

'I guess you must be Rose.' He was on his feet at once. 'Can I get you a drink?'

She saw that Jan was already pouring her usual half of lager. She sat down, and Brian settled back on to his bench. He was serious-looking, with a rueful mouth, but his eyes were deep brown and friendly – the sort of eyes that could coax you into offering confidences which you wouldn't let anyone else near. But that was his job, anyway.

Rose said apologetically, 'I couldn't think of anywhere else we could meet.'

'That's all right. Nothing wrong with this place. Don't do a bad sandwich here.'

There was an awkward pause. He was waiting for her to go on. 'I'm sorry it was so early when I rang,' she faltered, 'only I had to go out and—'

'Not a problem.' His voice was as encouraging as his eyes. 'Now, don't look so worried. First of all, shall we talk about how much this is going to cost?'

'Anything. Whatever.'

'And make sure you've really thought about it.'

He was too bloody patronising. The tightly wound spring inside Rose snapped. 'Oh, for Christ's sake. Why do you think I'd go to the trouble of . . . no, let's forget it, shall we?' She began to get up.

'Whoa! Hang on a minute. What's the matter?'

Jan lifted the bar flap and bought the glass of lager over to the table. 'So how's tricks? I tell you, it's been dead in here.' As Rose was fumbling for her money, Brian held out the coins. 'It's all right,' Jan said, 'have it on the house.'

Brian watched her go back to the bar, and then looked at Rose with a faint, questioning lift of his eyebrow.

She said, 'Look, I want you to get started. Right away. No hanging about.'

She took out the photograph of the baby, reluctant to hand it over for a moment, yet not knowing where else to start. Brian took it and laid it flat on the table, having made sure that there was no dampness or crumbs there. She liked that. It calmed her down, and she waited for his verdict.

'Just how long is it since you last saw . . . er . . .?'

'Hannah.'

'Hannah. When did you last see her?'

'Then.' Rose nodded at the photograph. 'They took her off me when she were two months old.'

He whistled faintly. 'That's a tall order.'

'You mean you can't—'

'I don't mean anything of the sort. What I do mean is that it may take time. You've had to wait all these years. Please be patient now.'

'So you do think there's a chance? You *can* find her?'

He handed the photograph back, and touched her wrist soothingly. 'It's my job. But, seriously, you do have to consider the cost. Shall we sort that out first?' He flipped back the top page of his jotter.

He kept it impersonal and businesslike. It was what Rose needed. He had already stated his rate per hour; now he briskly explained the likelihood of necessary expenses, and a bonus if he succeeded. It would be no use her badgering him for news every day, he stressed: he wasn't going to waste her time or his on vague telephone calls. When there was news, she would hear from him. Right now, he wanted every date and place and detail she could offer, no matter how apparently insignificant.

It was wonderful to pour it all out, and to see how carefully he listened and made his notes. Rose went home uplifted, ready at last to believe in miracles.

The sight of Tracy lowered her spirits again. The house reeked with a cloying, smoky smell. Tracy's eyes were sunk within dark rings. She had been deteriorating over this last couple of months – ever since she met Colette. Rose didn't want to provoke a row by banning Colette from the house; but sooner or later there was going to have to be a showdown.

'What shall we have for dinner tonight?' Rose kept her question level and ordinary.

'I don't want no dinner.'

'Oh, come on.' Rose couldn't hold it back a moment longer. Tracy was great at spoiling everything. 'All right, then, I'll eat by myself.' She sniffed an exaggerated sniff. 'I suppose you and Madam Leather-Knickers have been busy shoving stuff up yer nose, blowing yer brains to smithereens?'

'Don't start,' said Tracy sullenly. 'I'm not hungry, that's all.'

'Let me tell you something. That one'll go right down the pan in a couple of years, and she'll take you with her if you give her half a chance.'

'I don't care. I like her. Anyway, what's she ever done to you? She's been in children's homes since she were twelve, screwed up by everybody.'

Rose thought of her baby, taken from her; and her father calling her a whore and throwing her out. 'What do you want me to do, weep?'

Tracy drifted aimlessly to the window and back again. She picked up her mobile phone, looked at it as if willing it to ring with a proposition, then put it down again.

Rose said: 'That reminds me. Someone called Brian Roberts might ring. If he does, I want to know, right?'

That at any rate jolted Tracy. She was immediately jealous and possessive. 'Who is he?'

'He's doing some work for me.'

'What kind of work?'

'Looking for someone.'

'Who?'

Rose was sorry she had started this. 'Someone called Hannah.'

'Hannah?' There was no shaking Tracy off now. In spite of the new attachment to Colette, she still clung to Rose – they had been to London together, they had come back, and she took it for granted that somehow, in spite of everything else and everybody else, they would always be together. 'Who's Hannah?'

'My daughter.'

'What? You haven't got a daughter.'

'They took her off me—' how often had Rose said this, to herself and other folk, over and over again? '– when she were two months old. I've been saving up to find her.'

'Oh, that's great. That's friggin' brilliant. Why didn't you tell me before? Rose and Hannah, Hannah and Rose, that's fantastic. Well, I hope yer find her. I hope yer'll be really happy with her.'

Tracy had grabbed up her phone again. She stabbed wildly with her fingers. Rose felt frightened of such intensity. For all her time on the streets, Tracy was still only a kid, but couldn't she understand: understand what it meant, giving birth to Hannah, carrying her inside her for nine months when she was just Tracy's age? As Tracy's frenzied fingers misdialled and she had to start all over again, Rose tried to distract her. 'Tracy, listen—'

'Colette, it's me. Where are yer? I'm coming round. Right now.'

'Tracy, will you talk to me. Listen to me. Tracy . . .!'

The door slammed.

It should have been a hopeful day, the first day of a new beginning. It looked more like ending up the last day of something that had gone very, very sour.

Carol put the plates in the oven and automatically wiped the top of the cooker even though there had been nothing on it to make it greasy. She made herself put the cloth to one side. She didn't want to get into that old obsession again. Least of all did she want another spell in that psychiatric unit. But the thought of Curly arriving any minute set her on edge. She ought to have said no, and certainly she ought never to have let him have a spare front door key; but he had crept into her life and persisted on staying in it even after she had poured boiling water over his dick. Maybe cold water would have been better.

She heard the click and thud of the front door, and then Curly's eager, insinuating voice. 'I'm here!' He came along the hall with a white carrier bag bulging with an Indian takeaway. 'Got some of them nams you like.'

Emma appeared at the top of the stairs. 'Can I have some curry, Mam?'

'You've only just had your tea.'

Curly fished a large bar of chocolate from his coat pocket. 'Now then, Emma, look what I've got for you.'

Emma reached through the banisters.

'Say thank you,' snapped her mother.

'Thank you.'

'Uncle Granville,' Curly coaxed.

'Uncle Granville.'

It came out with difficulty. It was just as difficult for Carol to get herself into the habit of calling him Granville. She wasn't sure she wanted to try. And she was getting more and more uneasy about his simpering glances at Emma. With those weird tastes of his, he might have other notions as well. Or else it was just that he would never be able to force himself to go about shooting his sperm into any woman and giving her a kid – he had other personal uses for it – so he liked the kids readymade. Either way, Carol didn't like it. But she didn't like the idea of giving up his regular payments, either.

'That's my girl,' he was cooing. 'She's such a poppet,

she's lovely, she's going to break all the boys' hearts, aren't you? Do you know—' he summoned up what he must have thought was a roguish grin at Carol '—I think she's going to look just like her mum when she's older.' He was reluctant to quit Emma. 'Did you have a good day at school, pet?'

Emma shook her head. 'Mrs Meadwin told me off for being late again.'

Carol stared through the banisters. 'You didn't tell me that.'

'Nita took me in a big red car with a man.'

'She did *what*?'

By the time she had dragged the full story out of Emma, Carol was in no mood for a curry or for sitting at the table with Curly. She wanted to storm out and find Anita and tear the treacherous bitch apart. But Curly was making soothing noises, managing to stop Emma bursting into tears, and then saying, 'The curry's going to get cold.' He steered Carol through to the kitchen, and took the plates out of the oven. This was enough to distract Carol. She wasn't going to have anyone else messing about in her kitchen or taking charge of any of the arrangements.

When they had dug into the rice and ladled chicken satay on to it, Curly said, 'Look, I can see you get tired and upset. That job of yours, that's what's doing it. Why don't you tell them you can't do the cleaning any more? I'll put your money up a bit, and you can tell them they can stick it. How much do you get there?'

'Sixty.' She had come out with it too quickly. Maybe if she played it clever she could get a bit more. 'Sometimes seventy if I'm covering for someone.'

'Well, how about I give you an extra fifty a week – round it up to a flat two hundred?'

'What do I have to do for it?'

'Nothing.'

She was not so sure about that. But since he was in such a good mood, simpering at her across the table like some drooling teenager, she thought maybe she could push it further – two hundred and twenty, maybe . . . two hundred and thirty? 'It's just that Emma's getting bigger. I have to buy her a new pair of shoes every four weeks. I've got the rent, the electricity, and some fines are still hanging over from when I was doing the Lane. *And –*' it was a good time to blame him for pushing her into paying things she had dodged until he got all uptight with her '– now I've got my council tax, and my TV licence. After all the shopping, there's nothing left. If our Emma asks to go on a school trip, I have to say no.'

'You should ask me. I don't mind giving you an extra couple of quid now and again, especially if it's for Emma. It's going to be yours one day, so—'

'Y'what?'

Curly appeared to be concentrating on mopping up curry sauce with a fistful of nam. 'I'm thinking of changing my will.'

Carol felt a leap of excitement in her stomach – half hope, half disbelief.

'I've been talking to my solicitor. Well, who else have I got? There's only my nephew, Vincent, and he's hopeless. Always on the scrounge, wanting to know when I'm going to hand over some of the business to him and pay him as some sort of executive, so he can chuck it away on booze and horses and fancy gear. There's no point letting him have any of it. Besides, you're the only one who's ever done anything for me.'

'Am I?' She was too dazed to find anything else to say.

He pushed his plate away and looked straight at her. 'And anyway, I love you.'

Helplessly Carol said, 'Really? That's nice.'

A naughty smile crept over his face. Obviously he felt that after all this he was entitled to a treat. 'I've brought the stockings. I'll just go out to the car and get them.'

She cleared the table swiftly and angrily. It was only the

thought of a rise in the money that persuaded her to start on the familiar routine, when she would much rather have been getting the washing-up out of the way. But there he was, pulling his marigold gloves on and putting the towel ready; and here she was, pulling the stockings up and trying to make them rustle the way he liked it. Hadn't he agreed she didn't have to walk for him any more; that they could just be friends, and that was what he was paying her for? She was letting him talk to Emma, letting him bring curry in for supper, and that ought to be enough. Surely he could remember that time when she had tried to finish it with that kettle of boiling water?

'Can you go just a bit slower?' he said,

'Look, you can't have it both ways. You lied to me. You said I didn't have to do this any more.'

'But I haven't asked you to do it for months.'

'You said we could just be friends. You said you'd give me the money as long as you could still see me.'

'But I'm changing my will and everything now,' he wheedled. 'Go on, start at the beginning again. Say "I'm putting them on", and say about them being all soft and silky.'

It was no use. She was going to have to dash to the kitchen and get one of her tablets. He was doing her head in. She wanted him out of the way so that she could concentrate on something important: what she was going to say to Anita when she came back in the morning, which she'd have to do because she had nowhere else to go. And then Anita was going to be told that she had better find somewhere else to stay and get the hell out of here.

3

Anita had never expected to set foot in this expensive club, with its plushly carpeted floor, its intimate lighting and huddles of posh men and women at tables with crisp white tablecloths. Posh, everything about it. Even without overhearing a word, she knew that if they weren't actually talking about money, the conversation was loaded with it. She had put on her best pink suit and lipstick and nail varnish to match. From the way people were glancing curiously at her as she passed, she began to wonder if she had overdone it a bit. But to hell with them. She was with George Ferguson, and in this sort of place wasn't that recommendation enough?

'I could eat a bloody horse,' she said. 'I'm starving. Haven't had a bite to eat all day.'

'How come?'

'I've just started this little part-time job, and—'

'Part-time job?' She couldn't imagine why he looked so startled. 'I thought you were a director of the company.'

'Yes, well . . .' She had no intention of telling him what the little job on the side was, so rushed on, 'Of course I'm a director. It's just that we're not making any money yet, it's only our first year.'

George steered them towards a table in a corner alcove, half shielded from the main restaurant area by a curved panel with a mirror up to the ceiling. Pulling out a chair for her, he said, 'Who told you that?'

'Told me what?'

'About not making any money so far.'

'Rose. Why?'

George settled himself opposite and leaned confidentially across the table. 'Just make sure you see all the accounts, that's all I'm saying.'

Anita shifted uneasily. This wasn't how she had expected the evening to begin. 'What's that supposed to mean?'

'I'd hate to see them put one over on you, that's all. Though really it's none of my business.'

'That's right.'

'Well, if we wanted to be absolutely accurate about things, I suppose you could say it *is* part of my business.'

'How do you get that?'

'Because Kathleen,' he said venomously, 'is another director of that company of yours, and British law dictates that when it comes to divorce, half of what belongs to the husband belongs to the wife, and vice versa. She owns half of Klensit, and through her I have a part share of Scrubbit. Not that I'm bothered for some two bit company, it just happens to be a fact, that's all. I mean, who knows . . .' He was staring intently, right into her eyes. 'It might all work out in both our favours.'

The waiter arrived with two huge menus in gilt-embossed folders. George at once ordered two Daiquiris without bothering to ask Anita what she wanted. She didn't mind. George had always been masterful. But she was going to make her own choice from the menu, determined not to let thoughts of cleaning contracts and finance spoil her digestion.

When they had ordered, George sat back and took another long look at her. She liked the way he did that. If he had brought her here just to soften her up with food so that she would go to bed with him, that was wonderful, but he need hardly have bothered. Already she had only to look at his face and his hands, and remember the times they had had together, and she was all prepared to be led wherever he wanted.

Through most of the meal he seemed to have caught her mood. He kept harking back to some of their little private jokes, and the memory of one lovely summer afternoon when he had risked being seen out of doors with her, strolling through the park beside her; though the park *was* a long way from any main road. Once more he was the George she had first met and known.

Over coffee and brandy he became more serious. 'I've always known you've got a good brain in there. You've just never had the opportunity of using it properly.'

She wasn't going to argue with that.

'And behind that brain,' he went on earnestly, 'you need good solid money. So I've been wondering. How about me coming into Scrubbit? Injecting a little capital and helping to get the thing properly organised, ready for expansion? Your friends may be all right for scrubbing –' for a moment she thought she could detect a snide note there '– but you're not telling me you can sort out their financial messes single-handed?'

'It hasn't been easy, no.'

'Look, put it this way. . .' She was sorry to have the conversation steered away from things she had been enjoying; but even on this sort of thing George was a hypnotising speaker, and she listened obediently. 'It's not just a case of what I can do for you, Anita. I have to be perfectly honest about this: it's what you can do for me as well.'

She tried to repress a faint returning flicker of doubt.

'I mean, you know me,' he went on earnestly. 'I wouldn't be offering this if I thought you couldn't do it. I'm a businessman, and a bloody good one, and I know what's going to work for me. And for you. All you need is confidence. And from what you've already learned at Scrubbit, I reckon you'd be a useful manager of my

Klensit operation – get it back on its feet. We combine forces, we make a fortune. You see, I think you're not just a pretty face – well, to be perfectly accurate, a beautiful face . . .' He reached across the table and laid his hand on hers. 'I've really missed you, Anita.'

Anita blinked back her tears. 'I thought you'd gone off me.'

'How could I go off you? I was hurt, that's all. I wasn't thinking straight.'

'And when you threw me out of the flat—'

'I can't believe I did that. There's nothing I can say, Anita. I feel terrible. I was a complete bastard. Do you think you can find it in your heart to forgive me?'

She knew exactly how she could prove that she had forgiven him. 'Shall we go?' she whispered.

She left their destination entirely in his hands. He would know a hotel, or maybe he had already taken another flat somewhere – she wasn't going to consider it might have been occupied by that Maxine of his – and they would both settle in without him ever having to dash back to his wife again. She was aching, deep down in her stomach, for him to start those slow, insistent caresses and then come in hard and heavy.

It was a disappointment to find them stopping outside Carol's house.

'Don't you want to sleep with me?'

''Course I want to sleep with you.' He put his hand on her knee. 'I don't think you realise how difficult this is for me. God, there's nothing I want more, but we've got to take things slowly. It's got to be for real this time, Anita. We're not playing at it, we've got to plan things properly, take one step at a time.' Before she could argue he kissed her fiercely. She clung to him and responded passionately, hoping to make him change his mind. But he broke the kiss, and said, 'Think this over, Anita. Ring me at the office as soon as you've decided what you want to do – about that business, I mean.'

She watched his tail lights disappear round the corner, and let herself into the house. She had walked dreamily into the sitting room before she realised that something was going on there. Curly was sunk into an armchair, his marigold-gloved hands working away like mad, with a towel ready over the arm of the chair; while Carol in her long black stockings and high-heeled black shoes was saying, 'No, it's no good, I'm not going on, I'm not—' She was brought up sharp by the appearance of Anita. 'I thought you were out for the night.'

'So did I.'

'I was just . . . she was just . . .' Curly grabbed for the towel, and shrank deeper into the chair.

'I'll put the kettle on,' Anita mumbled. Then she remembered what had happened to Curly months back from Carol's kettle of boiling water. 'Er – I mean, I'll make a cup of tea.'

She stayed in the kitchen until the front door had closed and Carol came storming in. Anita tried to get her excuses in first. 'I didn't know you were still seeing him, after what happened.'

'Well, I am, but I haven't been walking for him.'

'Oh, yes? And I'm Cindy Crawford.'

'It's the bleeding truth. And anyway, this is my house and I can do what the frigging hell I like in it. Besides, I've got a bone to pick with you. Our Emma were late for school again this morning, and I want to know whose car you took her in.'

'I don't know what you're talking about.'

'Don't give me that crap,' Carol blazed. 'I let you have a room here, I don't ask a lot, I trust you to do one frigging thing, that's all, and you can't even do that. You're worse than useless.'

Anita wasn't going to stand for this. 'Let me tell you,

there's others that think I'm very clever. There are other people – ' she emphasised every single word ' – that believe in me, so you'd better watch what you're saying.'

'What the bloody hell are you on about?'

'George has offered to make me a manager of Klensit. I'm going to sign cheques, and everything.'

'George Ferguson?' Carol was gobsmacked. 'You've been talking to George Ferguson?'

'And what's wrong with that? I used to have a . . . a relationship with him, and if it hadn't been for you lot warping my mind I still would have. And on top of that, he wants to put money into Scrubbit as well.'

Anita hadn't wanted to come back here tonight. But neither did she want to be dragged out again and marched down the street, up Lambton Lane to collect Rose, and on towards Joyce's house. Carol and Rose were more used to stepping out than Anita was, in her best shoes. She tottered behind them, too proud to ask them to slow down, trying to explain things to Rose, who might have altered in some ways but was still as forthright as ever.

'What sort of money?'

'I don't know. I mean, we haven't gone into details yet. Investment money.'

'Sounds a load of bollocks to me. I thought he were broke.'

They reached Joyce's door, and Carol played a tattoo with the knocker vigorously enough to push the door open a few inches. They marched in to find Joyce on the phone in the hall.

'Bring 'em over on the coach? Don't think I can manage that, Steve. We've got a lot on at work and—' She broke off to survey the three who had just arrived. 'Come in,' she said sarcastically. 'Steve, I'll have to go. God knows what's going on here.'

She put the receiver down and led the way into her front room.

A corner of the room had been laid out like an office. A small wooden table was littered with papers, and a noticeboard had been hammered on to the wall in front of it. On a large chart Joyce had stuck coloured dots denoting the various shifts to be worked.

Carol waved Anita forward as if she were a schoolteacher delivering a troublemaker up to the headmistress's desk.

Anita was out of breath, and her nerve was failing her. 'I'm not telling her. It's up to you to tell her.'

'Tell me what?' asked Joyce.

'Tell yer,' said Rose, 'that George Ferguson thinks we're doing so bloody brilliant that he wants to put his hard-earned brass into Scrubbit.'

'Tell me another.'

'It's not a joke. She says he means it.'

Joyce stared hard at Anita. Her face had become careworn over the years, and more deeply lined since her daughter's murder; but it was the first time Anita had seen it harden into real hatred. 'It bloody better be a joke.'

'It's no joke,' said Anita.

'Hang on a minute. I don't think we can be talking about the same George Ferguson. I'm talking about the corrupt piece of slime that killed my daughter—'

'I might have known you'd say that. He didn't kill Gina. That nutcase killed her. Why do you always blame George?'

'Because,' said Carol, 'Gina were selling her body to pay off Ferguson's bloody heavy.'

'But George didn't know that. It's not a crime to have a loan company. And anyway, he's packed it in now.'

Joyce took a menacing step towards her. 'It's a crime to frighten young mothers shitless, it's a crime to drive someone on to the street selling their body. And it's a bloody shameless crime to have to look at those three babies' faces up there, upstairs, and know that come six months' time they'll have forgotten what their mother looked like.'

'All right, Joyce.' Rose put a hand on her arm. 'Don't upset yourself.'

'Don't upset myself? Christ, I'm not letting that corrupt evil bastard anywhere near this company, so don't even think it.'

'He's been to prison,' Anita pleaded. 'He's served his sentence. He's not like that any more, he's changed.'

'He's got corruption stamped on his forehead.' There was no holding the torrent back now. 'It runs through him like a stick of Blackpool rock. For Christ's sake, Anita, how can you stand there and think of setting up his backhanders for him again?'

'I'm just telling you what he told me. Anyway, he can do what he likes, because he owns part of the company.'

'Which company?'

'Scrubbit. He said that when two people are getting divorced, like him and Kathleen, half the husband's property goes to the wife and vice versa – so she owns half of Klensit, and he owns part of Scrubbit.'

'Not while I breathe, he doesn't. This isn't some two-bit fiddling set-up like Klensit. This is a proper company. We might not be making a lot of money yet, but we're respectable, we can hold our heads up and say we're doing summat with our lives. So you can go back to George Ferguson and tell him he's not getting his filthy fingers anywhere near our business.'

'Yeh, well, there's more than just you in this company, Joyce.'

Joyce took the last step to bring her up to Anita, seizing her shoulders, shaking her to and fro, pushing her back towards the door. 'Get out of this house. Go on, get out! I don't want you anywhere near this house, you stupid bitch. Get your face out of my sight – and keep it there.'

Anita's shoulder jarred against the door jamb. She looked from Carol to Rose, waiting for them to come to her rescue and say something sensible. There was not a word. After all she had tried to do for them . . . after all George had been ready to do to back them up . . .

She stamped out of the house. Nice to know who your friends were. Now there was only one thing for it. She would have to look after her own interests, and go in for that job on the side, fixing appointments for Tracy and Colette, as they had suggested. It probably wouldn't be for long. George would soon see her straight on Klensit, anyway. She would have to work out some way of breaking the news about Scrubbit gently over the phone, and then arrange to meet him and talk things over: lots of things.

4

Ten quid an hour, Tracy had promised. That was a whole lot more than Anita had got out of Scrubbit so far, or was ever likely to get if George wasn't allowed in to straighten the whole business out his own way. It wasn't quite the sort of part-time job she would have chosen, but it wouldn't really be all that different from what she had done in the past, letting the girls use her flat any day except Thursday when George came around. Just a matter of being a front woman, taking phone calls and fixing times, and sniffing any trouble in advance.

There was one worry, though. 'You mean letting them in *here*?' She glanced apprehensively around Rose's living room.

'Yeh, sure. Unless they've got a place of their own, or it's a hotel job.'

'Does Rose know about this?'

''Course she knows. We pay for this place between us, and where does she think my share comes from?'

'Anyway, she owes me plenty.' Anita's indignation at the way they had treated her bubbled up again. 'I wouldn't have to do this if they hadn't turned against George and me and maybe thrown away the chance of us all making some money. None of them know the George I've known. They think of him as a ruthless loan shark, and that's just ridiculous. I mean, it's like saying Carol's this mad woman who never does anything but pour boiling water over men's private parts, or that Rose is still a hustler—'

'And what's wrong with that?'

'Nothing,' said Anita hastily. 'What I'm saying is that she isn't any more, is she? She's changed. And so's George.'

The mobile phone began ringing. Tracy, busy moisturising her right leg, glanced up and nodded at it. It was time for Anita to start on her act.

She reached for the phone. 'Tracy's massage parlour. How may I help you? Yes, she's here, but I'm her personal secretary and I take all her calls. Would you like an appointment?'

The caller was hoarse and stumbled over his words, but he certainly did want an appointment for a massage, only he wasn't quite sure what was on offer. Anita ran through the menu: fifteen-minute hand relief shoulder massage, or a thirty-minute full-body massage, or the whole stress management massage, which was – she enjoyed making it up as she went along – an hour up and down, every little nook and cranny massage, with a cup of tea thrown in. Did he want it or not?

Oh, he wanted it; something in the sound of her voice on the phone had made him want it very much.

'Let me look in the book.' A ring at the doorbell brought Tracy to her feet and out into the hall as Anita, allowing a few seconds' pause, went on, 'Yes, you're in luck. We've just had a cancellation. Now, then, what's your name?' She was not surprised when she learnt it was John Smith. They had just settled the time when Colette and Tracy came into the room, arguing furiously.

'But I've got Lionel outside in the car,' Colette was pleading. 'I can't just tell him to piss off. We've rung round every frigging hotel, but there's a bloody convention on and they're all full. Come on, let us use yours.'

Anita waved the phone at Tracy. 'You've got a punter coming in an hour.'

Colette wasn't going to give up. 'I thought you'd got two bedrooms.'

'You can't bring him in here,' cried Tracy. 'Rose'd freak.'

'How's she gonna find out?' Colette studied the room. 'Come to think of it, we could manage well enough in here. Might suit him better – more natural.'

By 'natural', Anita discovered, Colette meant that Lionel liked to be bullied into doing his housework in a realistic setting. He came into the room as a solid, slightly balding businessman complete with charcoal grey suit, silk tie, briefcase and furled umbrella; but within minutes had transformed himself into a frumpy charwoman with a pleated skirt and tatty sweater, stuffed with false bosoms. Tights stretched taut across his buttocks, bulging up as he crawled across the carpet with dustpan and brush.

Colette kicked him hard with the pointed toe of her black boot, producing a gratified wince.

'You've missed a bit,' she squawked.

'Sorry, mistress.' Along with the scruffy gear he had put on an affected, effeminate voice.

Colette turned back to Anita. 'You were saying . . .?'

Lionel did not seem to mind in the least having another woman in the room. Perhaps this, too, was making it more 'natural' for him: the daily woman going about her work while the suburban housewives chatted over an afternoon cup of tea. Anita had already poured out her woes to Tracy. It was good to be able to go through them all again with Colette.

'Well, it sounds like a good idea to me. Can't see what they're being awkward about. Mind you, that Rose, it doesn't surprise me.' Colette paused as Lionel shuffled back towards her on his knees, and took a swipe at him with a rolled-up newspaper. 'But if he owns part of the company, can't he have his say just like the rest of you?'

'You can't tell them that. All he wants to do is invest some money, for God's sake, but—'

'Maybe you should just dump that lot and stick with

him. If he says he's gonna make yer a manager, then . . .' She broke off again and threw a rubber ball at Lionel's backside. 'Faster. You've got all them kitchen cupboards to clean out.'

'I'm going as fast as I can.' Lionel was allowing himself to sound irritated.

Colette produced a gasp of mock horror. 'What did you say?'

'I said I'm going as fast as I can.' He was trembling in eager anticipation of a shower of blows.

Colette glanced at Anita. 'Fancy a go?'

'No.' Then the idea suddenly appealed to her. She got up, poised herself, and booted him hard, as satisfied as he was by the howl of pain. 'Mistress!' she snarled.

'Not so hard,' muttered Colette. 'It'll leave a mark.'

'He forgot to say "mistress".'

Lionel grovelled. 'Mistress.'

'That's better.' Anita settled herself back on the sofa, feeling more cheerful.

When Lionel went out to change back into his usual clothes, Colette started laughing raucously. 'God, you're a natural! You booted him like you was born to it.' She was glad when Tracy sauntered back into the room so that she could report on Anita's unsuspected talent. 'Born to it,' she repeated. 'And you bloody loved it!'

'I don't know what came over me,' said Anita demurely.

Tracy was looking her up and down. 'Fancy coming to a party with me tonight?'

'What kind of party?'

'It's these businessmen. They like a few of us around, that's all. Yer get seventy quid, and all yer have to do is chat a few blokes up, have a drink or a line, and maybe watch a video.'

'I don't have to take my clothes off or anything like that?'

'Not unless you want to. Anyway, I'll give yer the address, and if you turn up you turn up. Right?'

Lionel reappeared as the sober businessman. His voice had dropped to a manly baritone. 'Thank you very much, ladies.' He handed Colette five ten-pound notes. 'Keep the change.'

'Thank you.' It was her turn to be deferential. 'Everything all right for you?'

'Perfect.' He was looking approvingly at Anita. 'The change of location was rather nice.'

'Do you want to do the same next week, then?'

'I'll ring you.' He hesitated in the doorway, again turning to Anita. 'I hope you don't mind, but . . . about your friend, he's talking complete and utter bullshit. And as for the money he wants to invest, if he's fresh out on parole then do yourself a favour and check out where that money's coming from. I hope you don't mind me telling you this, but I do deal with these matters every day. I'm a corporate solicitor.' He smiled sympathetically. 'Good afternoon.'

Anita sat frozen for a moment; then pushed herself up and chased after him into the street. 'Hang on a minute!'

It was quiet in The Hustler's Arms at this time of the afternoon. Carol looked round the familiar bar and found herself wondering if it had been such a good move to quit the Lane and dedicate herself to an honest life cleaning up after other people. Sometimes when she had her hand down the bog, scrubbing away at a piece of shit, she would think to herself how much easier and cleaner it would be to do a wank for some punter and get double the money in half the time.

She was going to say something about it to Rose; but Rose, her drink untouched, had that faraway look of hers, thinking about something else that would probably never come true.

Joyce appeared without warning in front of them, flourishing a letter and slapping it down on the table.

'We've got it! We've bloody got it!'

Rose woke up and grabbed the letter. Then she let out a whoop that made two drowsy men in the corner choke over their beer, and tossed it to Carol.

It was true. They had got the Health Centre contract. Glenys Minkin hadn't let them down. They all three started talking at once. There was a whole new load of things to sort out. They would have to advertise for more staff, and get a proper accountant instead of leaving it to Joyce. And they'd better consult a solicitor about George Ferguson's interests, and see about kicking him out. But anyway there would be more money, there was bound to be better money for all of them. Which was a good excuse for getting more drinks in right now, and settling down to celebrate.

Carol vowed that now she was going to do what she had always promised herself one day: set about buying her house from the council. Rose was talking about taking driving lessons. Joyce was smiling brightly for the first time in long, wretched months.

So of course there had to be a cloud. It came in the shape of Anita, edging awkwardly up to the bar, looking dead miserable and afraid to come near them.

Joyce's smile faded. There was no telling whether she would scream at Anita again to get out of her sight. But whatever bloody stupid ideas she had let herself swallow from George Ferguson, Anita was still one of the directors. She had to be told. As she sat down warily on the bench, as far away as she could get from Joyce, Carol handed the letter over.

'The Health Centre!' Anita marvelled. 'How did we do that?'

'Bloody hard work,' said Joyce. 'By some of us.'

Anita went on staring at the letter, not meeting any of their eyes. 'I want to tell you all something.'

Whatever it was, she couldn't get it out until Carol prodded her. 'Yeh?'

'I know I'm a bit thick sometimes.' Anita ignored Joyce's

snort, and went on with her head bowed. 'I can't help it, I suppose. You were right about George, all of you. You were right.' When she looked up at last, there were tears in her eyes.

'All right,' said Rose. 'What the hell's happened? What's he done *this* time?'

'I'll tell you.' Anita dabbed at her eyes as Carol got up silently to fetch her the usual Malibu and Coke. 'And this time I'm going to fix him once and for all. I've got a plan.'

George Ferguson made a last check in the office mirror, twitched his tie a fraction of an inch straighter, and went off towards the Town Hall. He was a bit surprised that Anita and her pals had set up this crucial meeting there; but maybe the Leisure Centre didn't have a suitable room for this kind of discussion, and of course any of their own homes would be too cramped and shabby to offer the proper atmosphere. One of the first things when he joined the group would be to channel all administration through his own office.

He marched confidently up the Town Hall steps and up to the first floor. He remembered very well where the conference room was: he had been there often enough when Councillor Baker had been in his pay, and done many a profitable deal in there. Now another profitable deal was coming up.

He rapped on the door and strode in.

The scene was not quite what he had expected. The four women were dressed in their Sunday best, putting on one hell of an act as smart executives, with files, pens, blotters and water glasses on the huge mahogany table before them. It looked more like a court of inquiry than a small gathering of which he was going to take charge, which had been the whole idea. That Minkin woman must have lent them the use of the room. And that wasn't a good omen.

'I think you know everybody,' said Rose Garrity.

'Do sit down, Mr Ferguson,' said Joyce Webster.

He wasn't keen on Mrs Webster being here. Not at all keen. She was the one who had ratted on him: working for him all those years, then going behind his back and joining this Scrubbit crowd with all the know-how she had acquired from her job with Klensit. But she was one of them now, and he had to force a polite smile as he looked about for a chair.

There was only one, at the far end of the table, set very low.

They were all staring at him, waiting. Well, if they wanted him to set the pace, so much the better.

'Let's be frank,' he said breezily. 'Things all got a bit silly before, and seeing as we're going to be working side by side, I suggest we start some sort of dialogue right now. That's how we do things in the contract cleaning business – no back-stabbing, it's all open and above board.'

'That's why yer ended up in the nick, is it?' asked Carol.

'I'm not here to talk about that.' Evasion was the only possible response to that sort of comment. 'I'm not here to defend myself.' He smiled at Anita, and felt more confident when she smiled back. 'Right, then. I've got something interesting to put to you. You're a new company, a successful company, and I think I've got something I can offer.'

'Like what, exactly?' asked Rose.

'Like free advice, for a start. I've got twenty years' experience in the cleaning business. I'm not blowing my own trumpet, but I think I know a thing or two. I'll be perfectly honest with you: I've heard that you're struggling a bit financially, but in a couple of years' time, with the right capital injection and a bit of expertise I can see Scrubbit going all the way. You've got everything it needs, you've got drive and commitment and—'

'Both Health Centre contracts?' Rose enquired sweetly.

This took him completely off guard. There had been no hint of any such thing. It just showed what could happen when his back was turned. It wasn't going to be turned again if he could help it. He smiled at Anita; and again she smiled back.

'Libraries next year,' added Rose.

'Why not? So now's the time to start expanding, earning yourself a bob or two with a sound investor behind you.'

'Like yourself? And what do you get?'

'Nothing. You run the company your way,' said George expansively, 'pick my brains if and when you want. I can advise you on equipment hire, purchasing and accounts, all that sort of thing. Of course I'd have to have some small input into the financial side of things, but that's all.'

'I'm not sure what the Council'd have to say about that.' Rose seemed to have appointed herself spokeswoman for the four of them. Pushy, but better than the Webster woman might have been. 'What with you having served time for corruption.'

'There'd be no need to come out with too many details about that. Any more than they have to know too much about some of your own past activities.'

'Come again?' said Rose.

So he had got them where it hurt. Now was the time to put on the pressure. George sat back as comfortably as he could on this hard, low chair. 'I don't think the Council would like the idea of prostitutes in charge of their Health Centre cleaning contracts. But nobody's running to tell them that.'

Anita's fixed smile was beginning to make him uneasy. He had not expected her to chip in here. Yet she was saying: 'And I don't suppose they'd like the idea of a brothel keeper out on parole investing in the company, either. But we'll not go into that. What I'm interested in is what you said about owning part of Scrubbit.'

'What I actually said was—'

'What you actually said was legally a load of complete and utter bullshit.' She sounded as if she was quoting. Where the hell was she getting all this from? 'And as for your money, in the papers it was reported that in court you stated you didn't have any left.'

'Yes, well.' George tried a conspiratorial grin. 'I've got plenty tucked away, don't you worry about that.'

'Well, we are worried about it.' He couldn't imagine what had got into Anita. 'For all we know it could be dodgy.'

'What're you talking about – dodgy? I've got plenty of money that I deposited offshore. Money that came from my company. Years of hard graft. I've got bank accounts I set up just in case—' He saw Anita ducking down under the table, and broke off. 'What're you doing?'

There was a sharp click. Anita fished up a gaudily coloured cassette player and set it on the table. She pressed a button, waited a moment for a part rewind, then pressed again. George heard his own voice crackling out of the speakers. 'I've got plenty of money that I deposited offshore. Money that came from my company. Years of hard graft. I've got bank accounts I set up—' Anita switched off, ejected the tape, and dropped it into her bag.

'In case you ever try to pull a fast one on us again,' she said, 'this goes straight to the police station. I'm sure they'd like to know you've got all this money. And so would a few other people, maybe.'

'You bitch. You set me up.'

'That's right.'

George grabbed the edge of the table and hauled himself to his feet. 'I'll see you in hell,' was all he could find to say as he stormed out of the room.

Anita enjoyed being the centre of attention, with the girls offering her drinks and congratulating her. But the more she drank, the more gloomy she felt about the other side of what she had done. The prospect of spending her life without a man was a dismal one. Even a man like George. She used to think that one day she would be married. Didn't have to be anyone handsome, because then somebody might take him off her. She would be happy with any ordinary feller. Her father had always said what a lovely wife she would make for some lucky man. She had looked after him when her mother ran off with the Corona pop man. And then her father had died, and when no husband came along she had thought that as long as she'd got someone it didn't really matter about being married.

She sniffled.

'Come on.' Rose set another drink in front of her. 'That was a nice bit of work you pulled off back there. Terrific.'

Anita perked up. 'Yes, I did get us out of the shit, didn't I?'

'Didn't think you had it in you,' said Joyce admiringly.

'Well, you see, I'm not as thick as you all think. As soon as Colette's punter said I shouldn't trust George, I knew straight away what I had to do.'

Rose tensed. 'How come you know any of Colette's punters?'

'We were round at your house, and he heard me telling Colette about all this carry-on with George, and it turns out he's only a bloody solicitor. Just good luck, really.'

'Colette were doing a punter in my house?' Rose was on her feet, heading for the door. 'I'll bloody kill her.'

Too late Anita realised what she had said. 'Look, there was a convention on, all the hotels were . . .'

But Rose had gone.

'Christ, you've done it again,' said Carol. 'You know she bleeding hates Colette.'

'She seemed all right to me. Her and Tracy, they . . .' And now she remembered something else. 'Oh, bloody hell, I'm supposed to be joining Tracy for some sort of party.'

She followed Rose out into the evening and hurried down the Lane towards the bus stop. She ought to have nipped into the toilet to have a proper look at her makeup, but had to make do with a quick dab of lipstick as she teetered on the pavement, waiting for a car to pass before she crossed, and having a glance under the street light at the slip of paper with the address on. If only a taxi would come along, she'd treat herself. Seventy quid at the other end, Tracy had said.

When there was no sign of any cab or anything else, she stepped slowly out, shoving the lipstick back into her bag. The noise of another car didn't register for a moment; and then she realised it was approaching at a hell of a lick. Lights blazed into her face. She put up a hand in protest as the full force hit her. She felt herself flying into the air, and the whole world going round. She landed on the road with a sickening thud. After that there was nothing but blackness.

5

George Ferguson groped his way out of sleep, his hand sliding off the edge of the sofa and knocking over a bottle on the floor. With his head pounding, he managed to heave himself upright. The whisky bottle was empty: he had finished the lot in the small hours of the morning. A tumbler lay on its side a few feet away.

George clutched his head. It would have been impossible to sleep the whole night through on this cramped office sofa if he hadn't been pissed out of his mind. The whisky had dulled everything, including his fear. Now the fear was coming back with the sickness after his night on the booze.

He took the telephone directory from its shelf and narrowed his eyes to get names and numbers into focus. He would try St Katherine's Hospital first. They seemed to have some difficulty in making out what he was saying, and he had to make an effort to get his questions into a sensible shape. In any case, they knew nothing of the accident he was talking about.

By the time he had dialled the number for The Royal, he had got more of a hold on himself, and spoke slowly and clearly. 'I believe you may have had a woman involved in a road accident brought in last night. Anita Braithwaite.'

He waited, his right hand shaking uncontrollably, until a competent, impersonal woman's voice confirmed that yes, they did have someone in – the victim, apparently, of a hit-and-run driver. They were glad to have confirmation of the name, as the victim had not had a handbag or any other means of identification. He knew that, all right. The handbag had held one deadly item he had to dispose of: the incriminating cassette that was now stuffed into the bottom drawer of his desk. At least he hadn't been too far gone to shove the bag out of sight. But maybe he shouldn't have blurted out her name so quickly. They might start wondering.

'I'm her brother,' he said quickly. 'How is she?'

'A couple of nasty cuts, and she's still not fully conscious.'

'She'll be all right?'

'Oh, yes, we're pretty sure she'll be all right. If you'd like to check again, later in the day—'

'Thanks. Yes, I'll do that.'

George scraped his hand worriedly along the bristles of his unshaven chin. At least he wouldn't have her death on his conscience. But that might almost have been safer. When he drove at her in a rage last night, he had wanted just that one thing: to shut her up for good and get his hands on the cassette. Now there was no telling what that pack of women might get up to next.

He took his electric shaver out of the top drawer of the desk. Within minutes he felt a whole lot better. Amazing how thoughts sorted themselves out in your head while you were shaving.

He reached for the phone again, dialling directory enquiries. He was impatient to get cracking on his idea, without having to peer down columns of print again. It was still early, but there would surely be someone on the *Daily News* awake enough to know a good story when he heard one.

George was put through to a bored man who sounded as if he had already had a bellyful of improbable news items this morning; but he perked up and began to ask brisk questions once George got going.

'The new Council Leisure Centre, yes.' George repeated it slowly so there should be no mistake. 'And both Health Centres. Contracts for all of them awarded to Scrubbit . . . International.' He let the listener make what he would of the sneer on that last word. 'And what I'm saying is, at least two of them are known prostitutes. I think we're on very dodgy ground here. I mean, who knows what diseases these women have picked up along the way? Yes, exactly.' When asked for his name, he finished quickly, 'Let's just say I'm a concerned member of the community.'

He sat back, beginning to think the day might turn out not so badly after all. Anita wasn't going to die; but she would surely be too dazed to know what had hit her. 'Never knew what hit her,' he sniggered aloud. That was one nasty little scheme of theirs he had managed to clobber in time. Now he would have to think of some way of putting Klensit back on its feet, and fast, before Alfie began asking what had gone wrong with his other promises.

Rose hadn't heard Tracy come in last night; but by morning her anger hadn't dimmed. She stared at the clock, rolled out of bed, and stormed into the spare bedroom ready for a scene.

Tracy's bed had not been slept in.

For a moment Rose felt a pang of remorse and worry. She still felt half responsible for the silly little bitch, in spite of all the rows they had had recently. Then she went downstairs, to find Tracy sprawled on the sofa, out to the world. It was enough to bring back all the things Rose had wanted to say last night. She went to the kitchen, filled a bowl with water, and came in to throw it all over that slack face and gaping mouth.

Tracy spluttered, coughed, and struggled up. 'What yer doing? Why'd yer do that, yer stupid thing?'

'I'll tell you why. Because you've been letting that tart use my room, haven't you?'

'I don't know what yer talking about.'

Rose dragged her bodily off the sofa and began shaking her. 'Colette,' she raged. 'Madam Leather-Knickers. And don't lie to me, I've been told. It's a bloody good job you weren't in last night, 'cos I'd have killed you. If you ever let that slag on two legs use this house again I'll give you the biggest hiding you've ever had – d'you hear?'

'You've got it all wrong.' Tracy wiped a wet strand of blonde hair out of her eyes. 'Who told you all this?'

'If you lie to me, I'll knock your bloody head off.'

'She didn't use yer—'

'Liar!' Rose smacked her hard across the face.

'I'm not lying.'

The phone rang. Rose was in no mood for polite conversation at this time of the morning. She snatched up the receiver and snapped, 'Who is it?'

'Me. Carol. What's up wi' you? I can't do my shift, 'cos Anita's not here.'

'Where's she got to?'

'I don't bloody know. Changed her mind yet again and gone off shagging George Ferguson probably. What else does a woman do that's got no brain? Anyway, I've got nobody to look after Emma, and she's got the day off school.'

'Well, what d'you expect me to do? It's not my problem, Carol.'

'I just wondered if there's some way you could—'

'Just make sure you get to that Leisure Centre. Take her with you if you have to.'

Carol's voice at the other end of the line was getting aggressive. 'No, I won't. And don't get your knickers in a twist with me. It's not even my shift, it's Joyce's. How come I'm expected to cover for her while she goes off with the kids to see that creep Steve, when there's never anyone to cover for *me*? Try telling *her* to take those kids along with her. I'm sick of this, I'm not bloody going in.'

She must have slammed the receiver down. Rose did the same. So Carol was sick of it, was she? She wasn't the only one. Rose was sick of the whole thing, of all of them. Tracy backed away and made a dash for the stairs before Rose could take it out on her.

It was no good. Somebody had to go in and get the work done. When she had cooled down, Rose set off grimly to the Leisure Centre. She wouldn't mind a bit of leisure herself.

This was going to be one of those days. The first thing she ran into was somebody else's fit of the miseries.

'I can't manage without me income support. It's impossible.' Brenda was wiping the mirrors in the shower cubicles, without much energy and not looking at her own reflection or Rose's. 'I don't want to go back to Klensit, 'cos everyone knows he's a bastard, but I've got no choice, I have to live.'

'But if they found out you've been taking the soch and working for him as well, you'll be in big trouble. You'll have to pay it all back – what's the good of that?'

'I'll have to take me chance,' said Brenda stubbornly. 'I'm sorry, but that's how it is.'

Rose tried to keep it calm and reasonable. 'Look, we're trying to do things properly, Brenda, and it's working. We're doing it right. We've just landed both Health Centre contracts, we're moving into the big time. I know it's not a lot of money, but we're paying nearly two quid an hour more than him.'

'Two quid's nowt if I can't get me soch.'

It was no good. No bloody good at all. 'Please your bloody self what you do. You don't know a good thing when it's staring you in the face. Go on, piss off back to George Ferguson – go lick his bum!'

Before she could get even more steamed up, she went off to the storeroom to do a stock check on the disinfectant and cleaning materials. Strictly speaking this was Joyce's job; but Joyce was off with her grandchildren to Scarborough or

Blackpool or wherever, so somebody else had to step in, and Rose was beginning to think that that somebody was getting to be herself far too bloody often.

She was checking off the last five items on her clipboard when Glenys Minkin appeared in the doorway.

'I've been looking for you.' Mrs Minkin's voice was colder than usual, and the familiar easygoing smile wasn't there today. 'I've rung everywhere. There's nobody at the Scrubbit office.'

'I'm sorry. I had to come in, one of the women has taken sick, and—'

'Where's Joyce?'

'She's . . . er . . .' Rose hastily summoned up a smooth lie. 'She's gone to see about a new disinfectant. We're a bit down on stock, that's why I'm . . .' She realised that Mrs Minkin was hardly bothering to listen. Her face was set and unyielding. 'Is there anything wrong?'

Mrs Minkin closed the storeroom door. 'I've had a telephone call from the Council. It seems they've had a newspaper reporter on the phone asking questions.'

'What about?'

'About . . .' Mrs Minkin was finding it difficult. 'About the . . . the previous occupation of some of your employees. He said that two of you are known prostitutes. And have criminal records for soliciting. I said that to my knowledge the reporter's information was incorrect. There was nothing on the tender application form suggesting any criminal record, and you had shown yourselves totally honest and trustworthy.' She looked hard at Rose. 'That is the truth, isn't it?'

Rose felt colder inside than she had ever felt in her life. Should she come out with the truth to someone they had always got on well with; or fudge the whole thing until they could all get together and decide what to do . . .?

Carol had expected to find a rather ramshackle little factory in some grotty back street. In spite of all the things Curly had said about having plenty of money, and the things he promised for her and Emma, she hadn't really believed in anything more than a small-time business in some old converted warehouse. It was a shock to see the imposing modern frontage with its large, bright lettering: DURKIN'S CHICKENS.

Even more of a shock was the painting of Curly smirking out beside it, as if just the sight of his face would persuade people to buy more chickens. She hadn't wanted to come here, but after the muck-up this morning she had to get right away from Scrubbit's problems and work out how to stay away from them. Curly wasn't the most attractive escape route; but if he meant everything he'd been saying, he might come up with enough money, one way or another, to ease things for her and Emma.

'There, Mam!' Emma had spotted the painting. 'That's Uncle Granville.'

Carol had dressed Emma in her best, half ashamed as she did so. And now Emma hadn't needed any prompting: she had called him Uncle Granville straight off.

'Now don't forget, if he asks if you enjoyed yer school trip, you just say "yes, thank you very much, Uncle Granville".'

'But I haven't been on a school trip.'

It was no business of Curly's how she used his money, even if he had actually said some of it was for Emma's school trips. But right now Carol wanted to play everything carefully. 'He gets mixed up sometimes, like when it was your birthday, remember? It's like that when you get old. Best not to confuse him, just tell him what I've been telling you to.'

They went in through double plate-glass doors, to be greeted at a small reception desk by a girl too tidy to be believed: black suit, white blouse, not a hair out of place. Carol tried to picture her in black stockings and high heels, walking for the boss in his office somewhere in the building as part of her job; and tried not to laugh at the implausibility of it.

A phone call brought Curly hurrying down from the first floor. At the last minute Carol had worried that he might be upset by them showing up at his factory, in front of his staff. Maybe he wanted to keep her well away from the rest of his life. But he was beaming with pleasure, putting his arm round Emma and saying: 'This is a treat! Come and have a look round. Come on, let me show you how it all works. You'd like to see that, wouldn't you, Emma?'

'Yes, Uncle Granville.'

A conducted tour wasn't what Carol had had in mind. Serious talk about money came before that. While they were waiting in his office – three or four times as large as she had expected – for his manager to bring protective gear for them to wear, she started saying how fed up she was, and what did he think she ought to do about the cleaning contract? These surroundings were beginning to persuade her that, whatever kind of freak Curly was in his private life, he must be pretty hot stuff as a businessman.

'I've told you.' His tone had much more authority here in his own surroundings than when he had offered her advice in her house. 'You don't need to do it any more. I'll give you a bit extra so you can manage.'

A woman almost as trim and starchy as the one downstairs came in with white overalls and hairnets over her arm.

'Thanks, June. This is Carol, who I was telling you about.'

June said: 'Pleased to meet you.' But she wasn't pleased. Maybe at some stage she'd had her own eye on Curly. Or on his money, anyway. Looking at Carol – dark skin, long legs, dangly earrings – she couldn't disguise her shock. 'I've heard a lot about you.' Her smile was as false as her voice.

'Right, then.' Curly had his arm round Emma's shoulders

again. 'Want to see how we do things?' He led the way through doors with a screen of chill air behind them into a long room where women in white coats and hairnets were rhythmically plucking away at rows upon rows of chickens. After the plucking, he explained with an earnestness that showed he had never got fed up with his job, no matter how many thousands of identical birds went through the same treatment, day after day, that the final stage would be through into the next department where they would be stuffed and wrapped. And then he could take them to see the giblets being packed.

Emma didn't much like the look or the smell of the place, and she fidgeted under the hairnet, but was fascinated enough to watch every detail of the process.

Curly made a big thing of rolling up the sleeves of her overall to make them more comfortable. 'Did you enjoy your school trip, poppet?'

'Yes, thank you.'

'Good. It's nice, is Whitby. Did you see the whale-bones?'

Emma glanced worriedly at her mother. 'Yes.'

They were both glad to get out into the open air, with Curly fussing over them. A taxi was waiting. He had ordered it while they were still inside, and you had to admit his timing was perfect. As Emma settled happily into it, Curly shoved two five-pound notes into her mother's hand. 'For the next school trip, right?'

'If there's any change, I'll give it you back.'

She meant it while she was saying it, though there was no telling how soon she would need the money for something.

'That's all right.' Curly was waving to Emma. 'Listen, I'll come straight round from work and we'll talk it all through.'

'Yeh, 'cos I were better off working the Lane. At least I could please myself then.'

'Now, don't think that. You go straight home, and this evening I'll fetch us a takeaway, right?'

'I'm not walking for yer,' Carol whispered fiercely.

He looked disappointed, but said, 'I didn't ask you to.'

'Right, then. And get a Chinese, I'm sick of Indian.'

'Chinese it is.'

She glanced back at the factory. 'And no chicken.'

'Right. Now, don't you go worrying and thinking a load of rubbish. This is easily sorted. And I've got a little surprise for you.' As she wondered suspiciously about this and turned away towards the taxi, he said, 'Hey, just a minute.'

'What?'

'Come here.'

She took half a step towards him, and he lowered his head to try kissing her. She jerked aside so that he could only dab at her cheek.

'It was nice of you to come to the factory and surprise me like that.'

As the taxi drove off, Carol automatically wiped her cheek where his lips had been. It would be all she could do to prevent herself having an obsessive wash when they got home.

Waiting outside the house was a police car. And a uniformed policewoman was knocking at the door. What the hell could it be now?

She helped Emma out of the taxi. 'Are you looking for me?'

A plainclothes policeman beside the car said, 'Detective Constable Barstow. Do you know if Anita Braithwaite lives here?'

'She don't live here, she's only staying here. Why? Who wants to know?'

'I do. We're trying to trace her movements last night.'

'What the hell for?'

'To account for her being run down by a car and near killed, that's what for.'

* * *

George Ferguson liked to have women sitting on the other side of his desk like this, trembling, their livelihood in his hands. He liked to let them crawl, making it last as long as it suited him, and then making a decision. It was specially nice to have this one come crawling back. Another weak link in the Scrubbit armour. The more the merrier.

'You were with me how long, Brenda? Nine or ten years?'

'Yes, Mr Ferguson.' Brenda looked humbly down into her lap. 'Never missed a day.'

'Cash in hand every week, and you just walked out on me like that, with not even so much as a thank you. Not a word. Here one minute and then gone to work for a set of whores the next. You don't seem to have much loyalty, Brenda.'

'They made me do it, Mr Ferguson. They said I didn't owe you anything.'

'Did they, now? Well, they got it wrong. You owed me plenty. And now you want your old job back. Well, what do you think I'm likely to say?' She was squirming. It would give him the greatest pleasure to tell her to get out and close the door behind her. But there were other more important things than a few moments of self-gratification. 'I was very hurt, Brenda, losing four of my best cleaners just like that. I was hoping that you were going to take over from Mrs Webster as manageress.' He saw the gleam of hope in her eyes, and let her stew for a full half-minute. 'Anyway, no good harping on that. You've come here to see me, and . . .' He was still keeping her guessing.

'Mr Ferguson, I just wanted things back how they were, that's all.'

'The problem is, Brenda, I haven't got the contracts I used to have. I've lost the Leisure Centre, and now it looks like I'm losing the Health Centres. Seems to me that what you need to get on in this business is to be a criminal –

preferably an ex-prostitute. Hard-working people like you and me, Brenda, get our noses pushed right out.'

'It's terrible, is that.'

'I mean, I've lost so much you wouldn't believe it, and all the time God knows what *they're* up to. Once a whore always a whore, they say. And there's children going to that Leisure Centre, that's what worries me. You've got children of your own, Brenda—'

'Yes.'

'And you wouldn't want them to come across anything like that without even realising . . . Not that I know quite what they're actually doing, of course . . .'

He saw that she was gradually getting his drift. 'Maybe,' she said uncertainly, 'they stay on after the evening shift.'

'Maybe. I never thought of that.'

'They could go into the sauna or the steam room.'

George Ferguson looked suitably shocked, and waited for her to dream up a few more titbits just to please him.

6

The ward sister had drawn back the curtains from around the bed to reveal Anita lying prone with her neck in a brace, her face a riot of coloured bruises against the white pillow. One eye had started to blacken.

Carol stared in horror. 'Jesus, what the hell hit yer – a combine harvester?'

The sister pushed two chairs into position beside the bed. Emma climbed into one, looked into Anita's face, and turned away. Carol sat down and listened. She had heard plenty of Anita's stories before, but this one turned out to be one of the most startling – and true, just for once.

'Must have been drunk out of his mind.' Anita had enjoyed drawing the tale out as long as possible. 'Just came swinging all over the road at me. Mad. I was unconscious when they brought me in. Man that found me thought I were dead.'

'Well, you did race off from the pub like yer arse were on fire. Maybe he couldn't avoid yer.'

'It wasn't like that. I was just making my way across the road towards the bus stop, and he came on like a bat out of hell. I don't know why things always have to happen to me.'

'Because you're bloody gormless sometimes, that's why. Look, I'd better get off and let the others know. I'll try to get Julie to babysit, and then I'll come back tonight. Aw, shit.' She had just remembered Curly. 'I've got *him* coming round.'

'Can't you get rid of him?'

'I'm trying to be nice to him at the minute.'

A nurse came in and leaned over Anita. 'Now then, how are you feeling? You gave us all a scare.'

'I'm in bloody agony.' Anita wasn't going to miss a chance of self-pity. 'I want some more painkillers.'

'Sorry. It's another half-hour before you can have any more. Can I just take your temperature?' Emma turned to watch, fascinated, as the thermometer went into Anita's mouth. 'Oh, yes. Your brother rang earlier asking about you.'

'What brother?' Anita mumbled round the thermometer. 'I haven't got a brother.'

Either the nurse hadn't heard, or had put it down to the sort of rambling she was used to hearing from patients. She took the thermometer out and studied it. Anita's gaze met Carol's. It wasn't hard to guess what was running through their minds. Who would pretend to be her brother and ring the hospital when nobody even knew she was here?

Emma was getting fidgety. 'I'll see if I can switch things and bring Rose in to see you tonight,' Carol promised, leading Emma off for ten minutes in the park.

One of the swings had lost a chain, and the carousel had been vandalised and hung lopsided; but the other swing was still usable, and Emma deserved some fun after the mixed-up day she'd had so far. After ten minutes, Carol said, 'Come on, we've got to go and see Rose. And your Uncle Granville's coming round later.'

'Aw, we've seen him already today.'

'Well, I've got to see him again.' She was still not sure what she wanted from Curly. It had to be settled one way or the other this evening. 'Come on, we'll see if you can go round to Julie's. She'll be home from college by now.'

Rose had made a dozen attempts to ring Carol and break the news about Glenys Minkin's accusation. She couldn't afford to budge from the phone until she had got through. She had made two more attempts in the early afternoon when the door opened and Tracy reeled in, her eyes blurred with the crack she had been taking, and with a punter pushing in behind as if to make sure he wasn't seen by anyone in the street.

Tracy stopped. 'Oh. Didn't know you'd be in. I thought—'

'Well I am,' snapped Rose, 'and I'm staying in, so you'll have to find somewhere else to go.'

'We'll only be half an hour.'

'You heard what I said. You'll have to find somewhere else. I don't want him in here.'

Tracy hesitated, but was too far gone to have the strength for a row. She turned to the man crowding into the hall behind her. 'You'll have to go.'

'What d'yer mean, go? I waited half an hour for you.'

'Tough.' Tracy edged him back on to the step. 'Get someone off the Lane. Karen's on the corner, she's good. Go on – piss off.' As he shambled off, muttering under his breath, she began a high, hysterical laugh, inviting Rose to join in.

Rose was not amused. She could only look at the dreary, swaying wreck of the girl with disgust. 'What's up with you? High as a kite, are you?'

'He thought he'd got me,' Tracy giggled, 'and he hadn't.'

'You're going off your head, d'you know that? We're going to have to have a different going-on from now on. I can't stand it any more.'

Tracy tried to steady herself against the wall. 'Stand what?'

'This. I don't want punters in this house any more, and I don't want to go to the toilet and find used rubbers floating down the pot. I want rid of the whole lot.'

'I'll tell him to flush it next time.'

'It's not funny, Tracy. I mean it. I'm sick of it all.'

'And me as well?'

Rose couldn't look at her any longer. 'Yeah, you and all.'

'Aw, that's great. Think you're a cut above me now, do you, with your cleaning company? Scrubbit International – more like Scrubbers International! Just a load of slags trying to do summat else, 'cos there's not one of yer could pull a punter if he had the clap. Yer make me laugh, going on and on about your stupid Council contracts.'

'Get out. Go on, get out.'

'I'm not going nowhere.'

'Right, then. If you're not gonna go, I will. As far away as I can get.'

Tracy was swinging back to become a pathetic little girl again. 'You wouldn't? Look, I'll pack in the hustling. Rose, I don't want you to go, Please don't leave me. Please.' She groped shakily for Rose's shoulder. 'Is it because of Hannah?'

'Nothing to do with it.'

'I need you.' Tracy was beginning to cry. 'You're the only good thing in my life. If you left I'd have nothing to live for. Say you won't leave me, Rose. Please say it.'

Rose put her arms round her, stricken by her grief. 'Hey, don't be so daft. You're such a kid.'

Tracy lifted her face and kissed Rose on the lips: kissed her intensely, clinging to her. Rose pulled away.

Tracy said, 'I love you.'

'Not like that.'

'Yes,' said Tracy fervently, 'like that. Like I love you properly.'

Rose retreated a couple of feet. 'Tracy . . .'

'Don't you love me, then?'

'Not like that I don't.'

'Well, how *do* you love me?'

'Like . . . well . . .' Rose struggled to find the words. 'Like family. Like you were my daughter.'

'Yes.' Tracy was suddenly jubilant. 'That's how it is.

You can do that.' She tried to writhe closer to Rose again.

All at once it clicked. 'No,' cried Rose. 'I said family. Not like your father. What he did was nothing to do with love. He warped your brain, Tracy. I'm not gonna do what he did.'

'You hate me, really.' Tracy had plunged into childish temper. 'You do really, I know yer do.' She flung herself at the door, yanked it open, and swayed down the pavement.

Rose called after her. 'Tracy, don't be so stupid.' But it was wasted breath. She was about to turn back towards the phone when she saw Carol and Emma coming towards her. About time, too.

Emma came out straight away with, 'Auntie 'Nita looks awful.'

Carol made no attempt to soften this, and didn't wait for Rose's news, but launched straight off into the story of Anita. She wouldn't be offering much help to Scrubbit International for a week or two yet. Not that she'd ever pulled much weight, apart from trapping George Ferguson in his own twisted plans. And even that, thought Rose bitterly, hadn't lasted long.

When Carol paused for breath, Rose moaned, 'Jesus, anything *else*? I've had a bloody lovely day. Ferguson's gone and done what he said – shopped us to the papers, and Minkin knows all about our past.'

'You're joking.'

'She asked me straight out.'

'So you told her it were a pack of lies?'

'No, I told her the truth. And she said she'd stand by us. Square it with the Council. Admires us for our – what was it? – attempts at rehabilitation. Mind you, she were just a bit pissed-off that we didn't own up in the beginning.'

Carol shrugged. 'Well, I'm thinking of packing it in, anyway.'

'Packing it in? This company's about making summat of our lives. Isn't that what we've always said?'

'Oh, yes,' said Carol tartly, 'that's what we've always said. Making summat of our lives. Sounded fine. But what does it really amount to, when you get down to it? Getting up at the crack of bloody dawn, worrying about who's going to look after Emma, and having your hands down the bog for six frigging hours a day. It's hard graft, that's all. There have to be easier ways of making a living.'

The phone rang. Rose stalked impatiently towards it. 'Yes?' It was a challenge rather than a question. 'If you're looking for Tracy, she's not here.'

The voice at the other end was suddenly wonderful. 'I wonder if we could meet?' It was Brian. 'I'm in the pub down the Lane. I don't want you to get too excited, but I think we've had a bit of a breakthrough.'

'Oh, Brian. Hiya, sorry.' She listened, only half-believing. 'Fantastic. I'll be there in ten minutes.'

She took a step one way, then another, then peered at herself in the mirror over the fireplace and began patting her hair.

Carol looked amazed by the change. 'Who was that?'

'God, me heart's nearly bumping out of me body. I've hired this detective to find someone for me, and that was him.'

'A detective? You're having me on.'

'I'm not.' She couldn't wait for them to get out of the house so that she could be on her way.

'And who's he looking for?'

'My daughter.'

Vinnie Marshall had enjoyed his lunch. Claudia had been impressed by his new Armani suit and his Rolex, and by the facts he had told her about his position in his uncle's firm, his prospects, and the lifestyle he could share with any woman who fitted in and appreciated the finer things of life. He reckoned one more lunch and a candlelit dinner would fix it.

Approaching the entrance to the chicken factory brought him back to reality. That miserable old bastard in there knew nothing about the finer things in life, and didn't want anyone else to know. It was time they came to an understanding about his own future. But Vinnie was in pessimistic mood as he entered his uncle's office.

He was met by just the sort of drivel he had learned to anticipate. 'What time d'you call this? We've done half a day's work before you've even shown your face.'

'I've been checking out a new supplier. I told you about that free-range farm: well, that's where I was all morning.'

It was not entirely untrue. He had driven out to see the farm and had a cup of coffee with the man running it, before heading for his date in the city. Weren't executives entitled to that sort of programme? It was good for the firm's image.

'Why didn't you ring in and let us know?'

'I'm supposed to be the assistant manager. I've got a right to take important decisions when an opportunity presents itself. I'm supposed to be taking over this place next year, so I should be able to—'

'Yes, well, that's something else I want to talk to you about.' Granville Durkin looked even shiftier than usual. He prided himself on making all the key decisions that kept the business prosperous; but he had a slippery way of handling things. 'I know I said I might be taking early retirement, but I've . . . er, well . . . I've been having second thoughts.'

'How d'you mean, second thoughts? You promised me I could take over the business next year.'

'I said you *might*. Listen, Vincent, if I thought—'

'No, you listen. I've worked my bollocks off for this place. I've bagged giblets, I've fixed machines, I've scraped chicken shit because you said I had to work the shop floor before I could take over. All that, so—'

'Mm, yes.' His uncle looked through the glass partition into June's office next door as if sending her a secret appeal for help. 'But I can see your heart's not in it.'

'My heart? What's my heart got to do with it?'

'Everything. That's where you go wrong. When you love something, you treasure it. You nurture it with everything you've got, and you want to be with it, watching over it.' Vinnie had never heard such sickening crap in his life. And there was more to come. 'You see, you should be here because you want to be here, not because you have to be. It's like a marriage, Vincent. It's like being with someone you love.'

That was the bloody end. 'You'd know all about that, would you, you sad bastard?'

'Get out of this office.' The puffy face was wobbling in pathetic anger. 'Go on – out.'

'No, not until I've got an explanation. I worked that shop floor for three bastard years—'

'I don't want to talk to you, Vincent.' But he still had things to say, like a besotted lover who simply had to talk. 'I know more than you think about women. In fact, that's part of the reason I want to keep going for a couple more years. I'm thinking of settling down.'

'Y'what?'

'That's surprised you, hasn't it?' Curly was smirking away to himself. 'If you'd come in earlier, I could have introduced you to her. So you're going to have to look out for yourself now. I'm going to have other responsibilities.'

'Like getting your end away, you disgusting pervert?'

June nudged the door open with her elbow and came in with two mugs of tea. 'We're out of biscuits, I'm afraid.'

Vinnie brushed past her, out of the room and out of the building. He had never liked his uncle. He'd had to put on an act, but had always detested the man. Now it was ten times worse. He hated him. Hated everything about him and his cheap, grubby mind.

When he crept back to the office it was after he had seen Granville Durkin leave. It was June he wanted to talk to. She was his uncle's right-hand woman, often disapproving of Vinnie; but he had usually been able to get round her, playing the hard-done-to younger relative, needing a bit of sympathy.

'Uncle Granville not around?'

'He left early,' said June coolly. 'He was quite upset.'

'Where's he gone?'

'As far as I know, he had an appointment with his solicitor. And then I think he was making a . . . well, a social visit.'

The mention of a solicitor alarmed Vinnie, especially with what might follow. 'To see his woman?'

'It's not my place to say.'

'Come on, June, you saw her this morning. What's she like?'

She softened slightly. He got the impression that she was worried about his uncle, but wasn't going to spell it all out. 'She's . . . younger than I expected. Her name's Carol. She has a daughter, and your uncle's besotted with the pair of them.' She drew herself up sharply. 'Will you make sure the lights are turned off before you leave?'

He made a pretence of sauntering along the gallery above the deserted packing floor, and returned slowly when he was sure June had gone downstairs. There was a large plastic-covered address book on his uncle's desk. He flicked through it, trying to guess at surnames; but then had another go, and found simply the name Carol and an address.

He waited until dark before driving his Porsche slowly down the street and parking a few doors away from the house. There was a light through a half-festoon of lace drapes in a ground-floor room. He pretended to fumble for a cigarette and lighter, stooping against the breeze and squinting through the narrow gap in the curtains. He couldn't see the top half of the woman; but could see black stockings pacing up and down, to and fro, pausing and turning, pacing back again, to and fro; and a man's elbow jerking rhythmically away over the arm of a chair.

The filthy old bastard! Some sly bitch angling to have him hand over every bloody penny in return for cheap thrills . . .

Vinnie dug his nails furiously into his palms and went away cursing to himself.

Brian was explaining that he had a contact in Social Services who had looked through the records. It had taken time, but now he had come up with the names of foster parents who looked like the ones who had applied to adopt Hannah. Dates fitted, names seemed to fit. That was all he could say until tomorrow, but he had wanted to let Rose know that there really was the hope of good news. He had a meeting planned at which he was sure he would find out more.

'Can I come along?'

'Not at this stage. Just be patient. It looks like it won't be for long.'

'You'll ring me?' she urged.

'No, I'm going to keep it to myself.' He laughed. 'Of course I'll ring. But like I said, only when there's something to report. Don't go building your hopes up too high, because even now I might find I've come up against a brick wall.'

'And then what?'

He finished his beer. 'And then I kick the bastard down.'

She liked his tough voice and his blustering act. Behind that front there was somebody solid and reliable. She simply had to rely on him. And quite apart from the work he was doing for her, she was already beginning to enjoy his company.

'I'd best be off,' she said reluctantly.

'Can I give you a lift?'

'Well, if it's not out of your way. I've got to pick up a friend in Henshaw Road and then we're off to see someone in hospital.'

He took her arm casually as they left the pub to steer her down the Lane and round the corner to where his Granada was parked, flicked the remote control to open the doors, and opened the passenger door for her, ready to offer a hand under her elbow if she needed it.

'What are *you* doing this evening?' she ventured as they drove off.

'Dunno. I might make a couple of calls, and then I've got a late night stint.'

'What'll your wife think of that?'

'Questions, eh? You ought to be doing my job.'

Rose backed off, embarrassed by her own clumsiness. 'I like the job I've got, thanks.'

'And what would that be?'

'We run a cleaning company.' As they stopped close to Carol's house behind a car she didn't recognise, she said, 'Anyway, I couldn't be a private dick, 'cos I've got a police record.'

She was halfway out of the car when he said, 'So have I.'

'Jesus, you mean I've hired a bloody criminal?'

'That's right. Guaranteed to find your kid, though.'

She walked up the path to Carol's front door, wondering what sort of mess he'd got himself into with the law. Next time maybe she'd find out. She reached for the knocker, but the door gave way under her hand.

'Carol, it's only me.'

She went cheerfully on into the living room to find Curly in the armchair and Carol on her knees beside him, rubbing away hysterically with a damp cloth which was only making things worse.

Curly's eyes stared lifelessly ahead. His throat had been

cut right across, and blood was seeping steadily down his chest and arm. 'It's all over me chair,' Carol was sobbing as every wipe of the cloth only made the stain spread wider and wider.

7

The day had been mild, with only the faintest breeze blowing off the sea. Sarah's birthday had started wonderfully, being swept up in her father's arms the moment she got off the coach in Blackpool. They ate '99' ice creams with nuts and a chocolate flake on top, and then they went down to the beach to paddle.

Joyce drew in a deep breath and touched Steve's hand. The kids were so obviously overjoyed to see him that she couldn't hold anything against him any more. They'd had so many squabbles after Gina's murder, spitting accusations at each other. But that was over now. There had to be a time when all was forgiven. The kids were the future, for both of them.

'How are you, love?'

'All the better for seeing you lot.' He was as happy as his daughter today, and Joyce could see why Gina had fallen for him and been silly enough to get pregnant by him. But he had stood by her, hadn't he? At least she had always granted that in his favour. 'The boss has given me the day off, so . . . well, Blackpool's all ours.'

Joyce sat on the sand watching them splashing about in the water: Steve with his trousers rolled up to his knees, holding on to little Michelle and dipping her feet into the shallows, until she was giggling and squealing for more. Joyce half closed her eyes and wondered how they were managing back at the Leisure Centre; then made herself not think about it. No point in spoiling the first holiday she'd had for ages.

'Hey!' Steve was shouting. 'Don't go to sleep, Joyce. Come on in.'

'No, it'll be too cold.'

'Get yer shoes off!'

'Come on, Nanna,' Joanne joined in.

Joyce couldn't resist. She kicked off her shoes and plodded over the warm sand. But she had been right about the water. 'It's freezing.'

'Rubbish. We don't think so, do we, Michelle?' He swung the baby's legs, trying to splash Joyce. 'Your nanna's a softie, isn't she?'

'Give up! I'll be wet through.'

Joyce retreated, and settled down again by their little heap of belongings. After a moment Steve came to join her, drying Michelle's feet and ankles, and kissing her toes until she was giggling again.

Joyce watched Sarah thoughtfully paddling through the shallows, looking down gravely as if hoping to see fish, or precious stones, or something – or maybe just her own toes.

'She gets more like our Gina every day.'

'She does.' Steve was staring far out to sea. 'Last time we came to Blackpool, she was seven months pregnant with her. We had a great time. I was working at the mill then, so we had some money.'

'We spent a week here when Gina was fourteen,' Joyce remembered. 'I'd just started seeing Bob. She bloody hated him, because every time she asked for owt he said she was spoilt. Poor kid, it was her holiday.'

Steve reached out and laid his hand on her arm. 'Come on, we're supposed to be having fun.'

'I like talking about her. I need to talk about her.'

He shielded his eyes against the glare, then turned away from it towards her. 'Yes. So do I. Only—'

'If I so much as mention her name,' Joyce burst out, 'everybody looks away like I should be over it by now, like she's dead and I should be getting on with my life.'

'I know, it's the same for me. Listen, do you want to get some fish and chips and take 'em back to my digs?'

'Won't they mind about that?'

'Landlady's away. There's only Lisa on, and I promised I'd let her see the kids.'

'Who's Lisa?'

'Oh, just a girl who works there.'

It sounded casual enough, but Joyce felt the faintest twinge of suspicion. If he belonged to anyone, Steve still belonged to Gina's memory.

'If you're sure it won't land you in trouble?' she said.

They went into the guest-house, and although Steve had told them to be quiet, the sound of the children's voices brought Lisa out immediately. Joyce felt slightly more alarmed. She was a very self-possessed girl in her late twenties, with dark brown hair drawn tightly back from a high forehead. She was wearing a plain white blouse and plain black skirt almost like a uniform; it showed off her figure to fine advantage.

She swooped on Michelle, lifted her up in her arms, and chattered eagerly over the baby's shoulder to the other two. Would they like her to organise tea to go with Sarah's birthday cake? And why didn't they all stay the night? She could arrange the bunk beds in the attic for the kids, and then they could all relax. 'What Mrs Simpson doesn't know won't hurt her. I'll change the beds and she'll be no wiser.' She smiled at Steve and he grinned back. Joyce felt that quite a few things had been arranged between Lisa and Steve before the rest of them arrived.

But Sarah's happiness drove everything else out of Joyce's head. Steve's room was cramped but quite magical with the lights off, the six candles burning, and just the last glow of daylight coming in through the window. She dug into her bag. 'You've just got one more present to open.'

Sarah took the small wrapped parcel and began picking at the coloured paper. 'Is this from Mummy?'

'That's right. Just to let you know she's thinking of you.'

Steve looked doubtfully at her; but this was what Joyce had been building up to, and she meant to go through with. They weren't going to forget Gina: she wouldn't let them.

Even Joanna was eyeing her grandmother uncertainly as Sarah finished unwrapping the present. 'How did she get it down from heaven?'

'She sent it with a fairy.'

Sarah let out a cry of delight. 'This was the one I wanted, in the shop.'

She opened the musical jewellery box, and a fairy began pirouetting to a tune. Steve smiled at Joyce, and everything was all right, couldn't be better.

Joyce said, 'Look, if we're staying the night, I'd better ring Rose and tell her I'll be back late tomorrow. Someone else will have to stand in for my shift.'

'Phone's in the hall. If you haven't got any change, ask Lisa. She's always subbing me.'

'Is she, indeed?'

There was no reply from Rose's number. Then Carol's phone rang for ages before she replied, breathless as if she had been running a long way.

'Oh, it's you, Joyce, can I ring you back?'

'I'm still in Blackpool. Look, I wanted to tell Rose I'll be back tomorrow, but she'll need to get someone to cover for me.'

She had been expecting a lot of reproachful moaning, but Carol was saying wildly, 'Yes, fine, I'll tell her.'

'Is everything all right?'

'Sure, great.'

'You sound a bit strange—'

'Great, fantastic. Enjoy yourself. Must be off. See you tomorrow, Joyce.'

And the phone went down. It was all a bit abrupt. Was Carol back on her old game, and impatient at being interrupted in a session with a punter or with that weirdo, Curly?

George Ferguson walked more confidently into the Leisure Centre than he would have done a week or two ago. It wasn't like going to the Town Hall and being caught off balance by those bloody women. This time the way had been nicely smoothed out for him in advance; that was, if Brenda had done her job properly.

It was dark outside, but lights were still on along the corridor to the manager's office. He walked along it beside Glenys Minkin, looking down through the glass panels at the swimming pool.

'You must be really pleased with how this place has taken off,' he said respectfully.

'I am, thank you. And thanks for coming in at such short notice.'

'No problem. I've been meaning to look round this place. Now I get the personal conducted tour, eh?'

She didn't make any warm response. He felt she still didn't really have a lot of time for him. But who else could she turn to after what she had just heard?

'I'd like to pick your brains,' she said, 'about somebody who used to work for you.'

He nodded knowingly, and lowered his voice to a suitably solemn level. 'Brenda Taylor?'

'Oh, you know, then?'

'I'm afraid I can guess. She's got a bit of a mouth on her, all right, but she's a good honest sort.'

He waited, leaving it to Mrs Minkin to make the running now. She said, 'She's been telling me . . . well, I thought they might be unfounded rumours, but . . .' George wasn't going to blunder into an interruption. Let her come out with it. 'It does seem that some of our cleaners have been . . . have had a rather undesirable previous occupation.'

'I'd heard that quite a while ago,' said George. 'But if they were turning over a new leaf and trying to earn a respectable living, I didn't think it fair for anyone to ruin their chances with idle gossip.'

'Exactly what I felt. But if it turned out they couldn't bring themselves to give up their old ways, and fancied trying to . . . er . . . combine the two, then that would be quite a different matter.'

'Indeed it would,' said George piously.

Mrs Minkin led the way into her office, unhappy but resolute. Brenda, it appeared, had told her she was worried about the way the rosters were organised. There were times when Carol Johnson would do the sauna and steam room, and leave Brenda to do the changing rooms and toilets. She had never actually seen either her or Rose Garrity soliciting on the premises; but then, she was only on the early shift. She was just going by what others had said. Those women had kept most of the evening shifts for themselves, except Joyce Webster, but then she wasn't a prostitute and never had been, so it didn't matter to her. 'Brenda wouldn't mention any names, because she didn't want to get anybody into trouble.'

'No, that's Brenda all over,' said George Ferguson warmly.

'But she assured me that some of the others had seen things. About Carol Johnson having been with a man in the sauna, and then they saw him giving her money. I suppose,' sighed Mrs Minkin, 'having half-naked businessmen in the pool and the showers and the sauna was all a bit too tempting: easy money for them, knowing all the ropes.'

'Rather like having a robber cashing up in a bank.'

She did not raise a smile. 'I just wanted your confirmation about Mrs Taylor. She seemed genuinely sure the others were telling the truth.'

'Just like Brenda herself. All the time she worked with me she was as straight as a die.' George shook his head in deep regret. 'These sort of goings-on must have shocked her. No wonder she's so upset. But I can assure you she wouldn't ever tell anyone something she wasn't pretty sure about.'

Joyce sat on Steve's bed with her shoes off and her back propped against the wall. She tipped back her beer can and waved it in a toast to Steve, who was sitting upright in a small armchair. 'D'you know – ' she could hear her voice slurring, and didn't give a damn '– it's ages since I've been drunk. I can't even remember, it's that long ago.'

'I got drunk last week. I was feeling sorry for myself, 'cos I was drinking on my own. I got legless.'

'You shouldn't be drinking on your own. I'm surprised you don't have 'em all chasing you.'

'All who? There isn't anybody.'

'Well, that girl downstairs for one. She fancies you, it's written right across her face.'

'She doesn't. She's got a boyfriend.'

As if that made any difference, thought Joyce. She knew that look. She remembered what it was like to want someone. Not that she could complain. She had had her fair share of blokes wanting her. When she worked on the buses there had been all the drivers queuing up to take her out. It was heaven in those days: best clippy on the job, with her little green uniform and her ticket machine, shouting out 'Hold tight, move right down now' and getting plenty of lip from some of those late-night drunks. But she could handle them all. And earn a fortune, pay her mother for her board, and still have money left for going out and having her hair done every week.

Without thinking she unclipped her hair and let it fall down. She could still be proud of it: still long and silky, and not too much grey in it in spite of everything.

She sprawled back on the bed, rambling aloud. 'My

mam used to take my skirts up for me, 'cos they were a bit old-fashioned and I used to say go on, make it a bit shorter. 'Cos I had good legs, y'see.' She pushed herself up on one elbow to have a look. They were still not bad. And Steve was looking at them, and didn't appear to think they were bad, either. 'Y'know, it's been a fantastic day. I'll remember it all my life. Just getting away from everything, all my worries gone – I feel like a different person, honest. I've loved every minute of it.'

'So have I.' He was handing her another can; but when she groped for it he didn't let go until their fingers met.

'Thanks.'

'My pleasure.'

Their hands were still together, and their faces were close. It seemed the most natural thing in the world to kiss him. Because it had, just as she'd said, been a wonderful day. Only she didn't want it to end, and their kiss lingered, and she felt the beer can roll away but made no attempt to catch it. Their mouths parted for a moment as Steve edged his way on to the narrow bed, and then met again while their bodies struggled for a new closeness in a long, shuddering embrace.

Rose had fetched a sheet from upstairs, trembling all the way down every step. She crossed the room to where Curly sat, and draped it over his head. Carol was incapable of lending a hand. She had nearly gone to pieces during Joyce's phone call, and now sat clutching the cloth she had been using to dab hopelessly at the flow of blood.

'Wash yer bloody hands, for God's sake,' Rose snapped. 'And then you'd better ring the police.'

Carol dipped her hands in the bucket of soapy water and disinfectant she had set beside the chair. 'I can't do that. They'll think I've done it.'

It had never occurred to Rose that Carol *hadn't* done it. Who else would want to kill the sad bastard? He was here in Carol's house, sitting in her armchair, with his throat slit. She came out with it: 'Who else would want to do it, anyway?'

'I wouldn't kill him. Why would I want to do that?'

'Why would you want to pour boiling water over him?'

'Because I was walking for him, and . . . oh, shit, no. He'd been asking me to do it again. Only I wasn't having any. Rose, tell me I haven't done it. Please? They'll take Emma off me, I'll never see her . . .'

'Keep calm.' Easy enough to say. 'Don't panic. Let's think about this.'

They heard the front door open, and Emma calling: 'Mam! Julie's here.' The two of them came shuffling into the hall. Carol sprang out of her trance and hurried out to meet them.

'What time do you want me to babysit?' asked Julie.

'About now.' Carol looked round for her purse, found a note, and thrust it into Julie's hand. 'Why don't you both go to the pictures? And then you could go for a pizza afterwards.' She realised that Emma was edging past her towards the living-room door. 'Where are you going?'

'To see Uncle Granville.'

'He's not here.' Carol grabbed her daughter's arm. 'He's gone.'

'His car's still outside.'

'It broke down. Go on, then. Off you go. And take your time.' When she was back in the room with Rose, she said desperately, 'His bloody car's still outside.'

Rose considered that this was just as well. Curly was going to have to be dumped a million miles away from this house. She set about things methodically, trying at the same time to jolt Carol out of shock by giving her orders: out to the kitchen to get some black bin liners and Sellotape, and helping to drag the corpse out into the hall. They would have to keep checking the street for people coming home or going out.

'Look at my bleeding carpet,' Carol moaned.

'I wouldn't worry.' Rose tore one of the bags from its perforated roll. 'There'll be no carpet where you're going if we don't get shut of this body. Get them gloves off,'

'Y'what?'

'Take his bleeding gloves off.'

Carol cringed. 'I can't do it. He's dead. I can't touch him. Besides, I . . . I know where they've been. I can't do it, so don't ask me.'

Rose tugged Curly's marigold gloves off, chucked them on the floor, and began going through his pockets, looking for his car keys. She tossed his wallet towards Carol, who found a photo of herself and Emma. 'He must have nicked it from my album.'

'Get that bag over his head.'

It was well past nine o'clock before there seemed to have been a good long lull outside. The street was deserted, all the neighbours' curtains were closed; but they had no time to waste if they were to get Curly disposed of and be back here before Julie brought Emma home.

'Right, grab his legs,' Rose ordered. When Carol still dithered, she did her best to yell in a hoarse whisper: 'Grab his frigging legs!'

Between them they lugged the misshapen hulk in the black bags towards the car and dumped it beside the boot. Rose fumbled with the keys until she found the right one, and the lid swung smoothly up. Before she could breathe a sigh of relief, the alarm went off: a harsh siren, and hazard lights flashing madly. Rose pressed a button on the key-ring, then another; and all at once there was silence. They froze for a good half-minute, waiting for any curtains to be plucked aside and faces to peer out into the street. When nothing happened, they got their arms under Curly's bagged body and heaved it into the boot.

As they approached the front of the car, Rose said: 'Who's driving?'

'Don't look at me. I've no frigging idea.'

'Well, I can't. You've sat next to him often enough, you must remember what he did.'

'Oh, Jesus.' Carol slid into the driving seat. After some prodding and fumbling with her eyes almost shut, trying to remember where Curly had shoved the ignition key in, how he turned it, and what sort of noise came next, she got the engine to roar into life. She remembered the way he had reached down for the handbrake, and how his foot had gone down over towards the right; and on the third go she got the car to lurch forward. But it went on lurching in a series of kangaroo jumps, with the engine racing madly.

'You're doing it wrong,' said Rose.

'I'm doing the best I can.'

'You're supposed to move that stick again.'

'Where to?'

'I don't know.' But she reached forward and crunched the stick into a fresh gear. 'What's that pedal down there for?'

'Don't ask me. All I know is that this one makes it go, so I'm sticking to it.'

'Well, which one's the brake?'

'No idea.'

'It must be that one in the middle. Try pressing that one.'

They ground round a corner, clipping the pavement, and a whole row of shop lights spread out at the foot of a low hill ahead. Carol whimpered and took her foot off the pedal so that the car coasted to a halt with its front wheel up on the kerb. 'Look, I'm frigging fed up with this. You do it.' She got out and walked round the back of the car to open the door for Rose. 'Go on, see if you can do any better.'

'Look, Carol, I was just . . .'

Rose had a creepy feeling that the pavement under her feet was moving slowly backwards. Then she saw that the car was beginning to drift slowly downhill. Carol had forgotten to put the handbrake on.

'Bleeding hell!' Carol saw it, too, and ran back round the car to get to the driver's door. But it was gathering speed too fast. The two of them ran after it, grabbing uselessly at the sides of the boot, and then dodging out of the way as it bounced off a parked car with a clang that echoed right down the slope. The impact hardly slowed it at all. It went careering on, across the road at the bottom, miraculously free from traffic for a brief moment, and crashed into a shop window filled with bright saris. Two mannequin models went flying like bodies in a fatal accident, and under the street lights a great swirl of silk saris looked like the fluttering of exotically coloured birds' wings, settling at last over Curly's car and its contents.

8

The sound of screeching seagulls whirling above an incoming fishing boat woke Joyce to a cool grey dawn. She wriggled awkwardly on to her side and saw Steve, turned away from her, sound asleep. There was a stale taste in her mouth and a throbbing in her head. She had had far too much to drink last night; and that wasn't all that had happened. She couldn't believe she had made such a mistake.

The alarm clock showed nearly six o'clock. Time to get a move on if they wanted to catch that coach. And right now, in spite of that awful feeling that she could only move slowly and dizzily, Joyce very much wanted to catch that coach and be out of here. She eased herself off the bed, gathered her scattered clothes up quietly, and padded out of the room.

It was cold under the attic roof, and she shivered as she bundled the girls into their clothes, ignoring Joanne's appeals as to why they couldn't stay another day. When there was a tap at the door she knew who it would be, and fussed even more over sorting out Joanne's and Sarah's socks.

Steve said, 'Good morning. Everybody ready?'

'Daddy, you've shaved your moustache off.'

It was true. Joyce took a hasty glance. It made him look younger, though why he should want to look younger she couldn't imagine.

Fleetingly his eyes met hers before he leaned over the girls. 'Come on, come on. I'll drop you off at the coach station.'

Joyce sat silently beside him as they drove away. In the

back seat, Sarah and Joanne squeezed Michelle in between them. The tinkling of the music box rose faintly through the rattling of Steve's ancient car. Apart from an occasional glance over her shoulder at the kids, Joyce stared straight ahead. She wondered if Steve felt as guilty as she did.

He didn't say a word until he was helping Joanne and Sarah on to the coach, and Joyce paused on the step with Michelle.

'I'll ring tonight.' He added hastily, 'To say goodnight to the kids.'

'Yes. Right.'

As inconspicuously as possible he slid something into her hand. 'You left these.'

They were her earrings. She remembered taking them off, and not caring where they fell. 'Thanks. Look,' she whispered, 'I'm sorry about—'

'It's not your fault. It's me.'

They would have to forget it ever happened. 'I'll speak to you tonight.'

'Yes.' Steve kissed Michelle, hesitated as if wondering whether to give Joyce a peck, but decided against it. 'Look after yourself.'

She climbed on to the coach. Joanne was blowing kisses to her father through the window, and he began blowing them back. Joyce looked out at him just once as the engine started up and the coach swung slowly out of the station.

A harsh whirring noise jolted Rose from sleep. She turned over in protest, and nearly fell off the edge of the bed. Only it wasn't her bed, but Carol's sofa. She swung her feet to the floor and blinked across the room. Carol, still in last night's rumpled clothes, was directing the blast of a hair dryer at the chair in which Curly had been murdered.

'Turn it off,' Rose begged.

'I'm trying to dry the—'

'Turn the bloody thing off.'

Carol thumbed the switch and stood by the chair, incapable of movement. With the hair dryer silent, they could hear a police siren in the distance, coming closer. Another one was added to it. How many were there going to be?

Carol steadied herself against the chair, then realised what she was touching, and jerked away. 'Oh God, I feel sick. They're gonna be knocking at me door.'

'Carol!'

'As soon as they see him, they'll know it was me. They'll think: she threw boiling water over him, now she's finished it off proper this time. Only they won't just be sending me to the loony bin—'

'Carol!' Rose grabbed hold of her and shook her violently. 'Will yer shut the fuck up! Have a tablet, for Christ's sake. You're making me nervous.'

Somebody had to take charge, and Carol was in no fit state. Rose saw that it was up to her once more. Somebody had to get to the Leisure Centre to stand in for Joyce until she got back. Carol would have to act normal, or the nearest she could get to it, and take Emma to school just as she usually did. And if the coppers showed up, she had to keep it simple and innocent. Curly had come round to the house, and then he had left. As simple as that.

'But check round, make sure we've got rid of everything.' Rose went out to the hall and fastened her coat. 'Now, don't go freaking out on me.'

'Don't go.'

'Don't be daft. I've got to. *Somebody's* got to.'

Before Carol could wail any more protests, Rose was on her way down the street and across town to the Leisure Centre. She would have to be ready with apologies for other women's absence if anybody came round on an inspection, and with plausible stories to tide them over until everything got back to a normal routine – if it ever did.

A photographer and a woman reporter were waiting in

the doorway of the Centre. They brightened up as Rose approached.

'Hi, I'm Leah Atkinson from the *Daily News*. Do you mind me asking, do you work for Scrubbit International?'

'Yeh.'

'Have you seen this morning's paper?' The woman held out a newspaper folded to display its front page headline:

LEISURE CENTRE IN BROTHEL SCANDAL

'Terrible, isn't it?' The reporter was grinning a deliberately provocative grin, thrusting the paper into Rose's hand. 'I think it's really unfair. Would you like to reply to the article?'

'Reply to it?' Rose screwed the paper up and dropped it at Leah Atkinson's feet. 'I wouldn't wipe me bum with it.'

She marched furiously indoors and along the centre corridor towards the gymnasium. Before she reached it, three people came out and began walking towards her. Her heart lurched. Glenys Minkin was flanked on one side by George Ferguson, on the other by that slimy little git, Councillor Baker.

'So you've got two basic areas,' Ferguson was holding forth with all his old bombast: 'one wet, one dry. The pool and changing rooms need interval maintenance, and the dry area just the regular twice a day.'

The sight of those two cronies back together again, planning God only knew what, and apparently back in Minkin's good graces, was too much for Rose. 'Well, look at this – hear no evil, see no evil, speak no evil.'

'Rose,' said Mrs Minkin, 'I've been trying to get in touch—'

'To tell me shitface here's taking over the contract?'

Ferguson smirked. 'Do you think you could be civil for half a minute?'

'Do you think you could curl up and die?'

'You do see what they're like.' Ferguson shrugged regretfully for Mrs Minkin's benefit. 'You can't even talk to them.'

She said, 'Rose, have you seen the paper this morning?'

'Yes. And whose doing d'you think that is? Someone not a million miles away.'

'You'd better be careful what you say, madam,' growled Ferguson. 'I've got witnesses here. I could have you for slander.'

'Oh, I'm terrified. Shaking in me boots. You don't stop, do you? Like a little kid, and someone else is playing with your toy, so you go stamping your feet . . .' Mrs Minkin had seized Rose's arm and was trying to drag her away, but Rose raged on, 'Screaming "I want me toy back . . ." You make me sick.' She almost shouted it into the woman's face: 'I'll kill him, honest to God, I'll swing for that man.'

Ferguson's outrage was all a pretence. He was enjoying himself enormously. 'They're paranoid, the whole lot of them. And she's the worst.'

'Rose, will you shut up and just listen, for God's sake.' As Ferguson and Baker moved a few feet away, their heads together, congratulating themselves, Mrs Minkin said in a fierce undertone, 'You've been using the Leisure Centre for prostitution, haven't you?'

'Bollocks. Who said that?'

'One of your employees.'

'Who?'

'Nobody was forcing her to say it. She came to me of her own free will.'

'Oh, yeah, sure. And you believed her?'

'Why would she lie to me? What for? I'll be honest with you, I'm extremely angry.' Mrs Minkin kept her voice down, but it came out in savage thrusts. 'I stuck my neck out for you lot, and you've dropped me right in it. The Council invested twelve million pounds in this building – twelve million, Rose, that's a lot of money – and they entrusted the running of it to me. That was no soft choice, I'll tell you. I fought bloody hard, tooth and nail, to get this place; but if I've still got a job at the end of today I'll think myself lucky.'

Rose half wanted to tell her that they knew Minkin had backed them, that they had worked their guts out to justify that, and couldn't believe it could all go so wrong. But it had gone too far now. Everything had been smashed. She couldn't hold back her fury. 'Stick yer bleeding contract up yer arse.' And she marched away up the corridor.

She thought of calling in on Carol again to see if there had been any developments, but she was still too tense. She would only start sounding off again, while Carol would still be twitching over Curly and what was going to happen to her.

The phone was ringing as she got home. It was Anita, clamouring from her hospital bed for news. Yes, she had seen the paper, that's why she was ringing, and what the hell was going on out there?

'We've been given the boot,' said Rose bluntly. 'That's right. We've lost the contract, and there's a lot of other stuff going on as well.'

'Does Joyce know?'

'She's not back yet.'

'Bloody hell, when does she get back? Look, you do know who's responsible for this, don't you?'

'Of course I know.'

'The bastard. When are you coming to visit me?' Anita's self-pity welled up once more. 'You will come, won't you? And will you bring me some clean clothes? I've only got what I had on when they brought me in.'

To shut her up, Rose promised to go in during the afternoon. Right now she wanted a shower, to wash away some of last night's awful memories, and the memory of Ferguson and the whole bloody cock-up of all their plans.

Halfway upstairs she sniffed at a faint, strange chemical

smell. It had to be coming from Tracy's bedroom. Had to be crack.

She didn't want to tangle with any more trouble today. But this was a bloody sight too much. She pushed Tracy's door open and glared in. The curtains had still not been drawn back, but morning light filtered in round the edges, falling on what might have been a beautiful picture: a white sheet lying loosely across the young, white bodies of Tracy and Colette, their arms wrapped around each other, with Colette's long dark hair splayed over the pillow and her face close to Tracy's as if about to kiss her. Only it wasn't beautiful. On the table near the bed lay a homemade water-bottle pipe, a half-open penknife, plastic lighters, and an overflowing ashtray. The smell was overpowering.

Rose dragged the sheet off the two of them.

Tracy still had a sheen of youth on her, but already it was going off, blotched with scaly patches. And when she squealed and opened her eyes, they were bleary and mascara-smeared.

'What d'yer think yer doing?' She tried to hold on to the edge of the sheet as Rose tugged it away. 'Get out of my room!'

Rose clamped a hand on Colette's pale arm. 'Not till I've got this piece of scum out of the house.'

'Get off her. Leave her alone, don't touch her.'

'Right.' Nausea came up bitter in Rose's throat. 'If that's how it is, then I'll go.'

Surfacing, Colette muttered, 'Yeh, and good riddance, that's what I say.'

As they floundered into wakefulness, the way their two bodies intertwined, the flesh moist and sticky wherever it touched and then sliding away, struck envy and horror into Rose's mind. She couldn't bear another moment of it. She left them and went back to her own room to drag that battered old case of hers off the wardrobe. It was getting to be a habit.

But this time she really had to ditch Tracy – and the rest of them as well.

Behind her the door opened and Tracy stood there, clutching the sheet about her. 'So you find it disgusting, do you?'

'I think *she's* disgusting. I think what you're doing to yourself is disgusting. One minute you're popping pills, next minute you're snorting stuff up your nose. God knows what you've been doing now – this place stinks to high heaven.' Rose snapped her case shut. 'Have you taken a long hard look at yourself in a mirror lately? Eh?'

'No. Have *you*? 'Cos you're no oil painting, either. Anyway, I'm glad you're going. Colette can move in, and she can afford to pay half the bills. That suits both of us fine.'

'I'll be back for the rest of my stuff later.'

But as Rose left with her case bulging and creaking at the seams, one last forlorn cry followed her to the door. 'You said you'd never leave me.'

She had enough things to feel guilty about and worried about. Tracy was sliding down to the bottom of the list.

On the way she bought a newspaper to replace the one she had thrown at the feet of that crappy little reporter. Sooner or later she would have to sit down and read the whole story through in detail. She still had it folded under the handle of her case when she caught up with Carol, on her way back from taking Emma to school.

Carol stared at the case. 'Where the frig are you off to?'

'Your place. I've had it with Tracy, she's off her head.'

'I'm going off mine an' all.' Carol looked at her wristwatch. 'Shouldn't you be doing that shift you went off to?'

'There's no shifts any more.' Rose tugged the newspaper out. 'Read that.'

Carol glanced down the page, slowing her pace as they walked on. When they were fifty or sixty yards from her house, she looked up, and both of them saw something they had hoped never to see again: Detective Chief Inspector Newall's car, waiting at the kerb.

'Fucking Nora,' Carol breathed. 'I'll have to leg it.'

'No, you don't. Carol, what did I tell you? You've got to hold your nerve, girl. You walk up to your door like it never happened.'

'I can't. They'll hear me heart thumping.'

'You can do it. For Emma's sake,' Rose urged. 'If you run, you're guilty, right?'

'And if I don't, I'm dead.'

'All you have to remember is that you didn't do it.'

'But I don't remember anything.'

'You didn't do it,' Rose repeated. 'Someone must have got into your house and slit his throat.'

'What for?'

'I don't know.'

'They didn't take anything. The hi-fi and the video were all still there. They didn't trash my house, they just killed the poor bastard. Who'd do that?'

Rose began to wonder just what Carol thought she was saying. 'Are you telling me *you* did – is that what you're saying?'

'I'm saying I don't know. All I remember is seeing his car parked outside, sending Emma round to Julie's, then finding him in there lying dead. He'd got a key, he'd let himself in, and I come back and . . . I can't remember what happened in between.'

'Well, you'd better start thinking fast.' Because, thought Rose desperately, if Carol really had done it, then she herself had helped get rid of the body, and that dropped her right in the shit.

Carol braced herself. 'You'd better not come in. I'll . . . see how it goes. Look, if I'm not back, pick Emma up from school, will you?'

Rose held well back as Carol walked ahead with as much courage as she could muster towards her front door. She was fishing about in her bag looking for the key, and conjured up a look of surprise as the police-car door opened and DCI Newall blocked her path.

'Carol.'

'Hi, What are you doing here? Not been moved off the patch yet?'

'Not yet.'

'Don't tell me I'm in trouble?'

'I'd like you to come with me to the station.'

'I've got a load of washing to do.'

'The washing'll have to wait. Your sugar daddy's been murdered, and your fingerprints are all over his car.'

She had been in the interview room for over an hour, and still Newall was keeping on at her. Hammering away, yet at the same time looking her over the way he'd looked her over many a time before: trying to break her down but in his mind still raping her, remembering the way he'd driven into her, and maybe still not sure which was the more enjoyable – the fucking or the frightening.

'What do you want me to say?' Carol asked wearily.

'The truth.'

'I've told you the frigging truth. He came to my house, he left. End of story.'

'What time did he leave?'

'I can't remember. I don't look at the clock every two minutes.'

'Approximately.'

Carol sighed and pretended to reflect. 'Emma was still up, so it can't have been late. He said he had somewhere to go, and took off.'

'He's been calling on you regularly, has he?'

For a moment Carol began to think she might be able to take charge of the situation. Newall's flicker of jealousy was too blatant to be missed. Tantalisingly, she said, 'Yes, he's a friend. A good friend.'

'Even though you poured boiling hot water over his prick?'

'Yes, even though.'

'So how often did you see him? Once, twice a week – more?'

'What's this got to do with him being murdered?'

'I'm trying to establish what kind of a relationship you had with him.'

She was feeling more and more in control. 'Why don't you just ask me?'

'All right. What kind of relationship did you have?'

'None of your bloody business.' But it was no time for scoring points. Tell him and be done with it. 'I walked for him,' she said, 'and he gave me money. Sometimes – ' she could see he was hating this, and she enjoyed him hating it ' – I didn't walk, and he still gave me money.'

Newall was thrown. The woman detective sergeant sitting in on the interview must have spotted this, and swiftly took up the questioning. 'When you say walked, what exactly do you mean?'

'You know, you put one foot in front of the other.'

Newall recovered himself with an effort. 'He had a stocking fetish, right? You walked and he wanked, that's right, isn't it?'

'Something like that.'

'What about the other punters?'

'He wasn't a punter.'

'Sorry . . . *friend*. How many other *friends* did you have?'

'Loads. Rose, Anita, Joyce—'

'This isn't a game, Carol.'

'Well, stop playing it, then.' Carol was sure she had won now. It would soon be over and she could go home. 'I work at the Leisure Centre, cleaning, and that's the only other money I get. So I'm hardly likely to slit his throat, am I?'

She heard the woman detective's sharp intake of breath.

And Newall was sitting back, insufferably pleased. 'How,' he asked very quietly, 'did you know his throat had been cut?' She knew, horribly, that she had shopped herself. 'Nobody's said anything about how he died.' He looked back over his shoulder. 'Sergeant Hoyle, get forensic around to the house. I want the whole lot going over with a fine tooth-comb. And get the duty solicitor on the job. I think we're ready for a statement.'

9

Joyce stared at the newspaper headline, still incapable of taking it in. She had gone away for just that one day, and while her back was turned they had lost the contract, everyone seemed to have fallen out with everyone else, and Rose was here in a fine old state, begging to move in.

'I rang last night, and Carol said everything was great.'

Rose, sipping a mug of tea, seemed to flinch. 'Yes, well, it isn't.'

'Why the hell didn't she tell me that then?'

'Because we didn't bloody well know till this morning. And you weren't back—'

'Jesus, I should be able to have one day off.' It was only half an hour since she had taken her coat off. Now she was putting it on again. 'I'm going down to talk to that woman.'

'I've said everything there is to say.'

'Well, I'll have to say it again.'

There was no way Mrs Minkin was going to hand that contract over to George Ferguson. He had taken Joyce's daughter, he wasn't going to take Joyce's livelihood as well. She'd swing for him before she'd let that happen.

Rose gulped down her tea. 'You want me to come with you?'

'No, it's best if I'm by meself. And I think it's better if you try Carol again, with me having the kids and all that. You'd have to sleep on the settee, and it's not that comfy.'

Rose looked round for her case. 'It's nice to know you can rely on your mates.'

After last night, Joyce had all the guilt she could carry. She wasn't going to let herself add this to it. 'Come on, Joanne, Sarah – get your coats back on. I'm taking you to school.'

'You said we could have the day off,' Joanne protested.

Joyce plumped Michelle into the pushchair and forced them all out into the street. Ignoring all complaints, she pushed the older girls in through the school gates and went on her way, bumping the pushchair over the kerbs and at last up the side ramp into the Leisure Centre. Glenys Minkin was on the phone as she arrived, talking cheerfully to someone; but the cheerfulness evaporated as she put the receiver down.

'What's all this about us getting the sack?'

'I've already explained in full to Miss Garrity.'

'You'd better explain to me as well. We either do the job right or we don't. Only the other day you were saying how marvellous we were and what a fantastic job we were doing.'

'That's right,' said Mrs Minkin frostily. 'But that was before I found out certain members of the company were using the Leisure Centre as a glorified brothel.'

'And why would they do that? Why would they risk everything we've been fighting for?'

'I don't know. I suggest you ask them.'

'I don't need to ask them, because I know it's not true. It's a bloody set-up, this is. If you tell me who told you I'll get to the bottom of it.'

Minkin looked uncomfortable. 'Look, let's just leave it, Mrs Webster.' Once she had called them Rose and Joyce; now it was Miss Garrity and Mrs Webster. 'It just didn't work out.'

'No, I'm not just leaving it. I've done nothing wrong. I bust a gut over this contract, I've put my heart and soul into it. It means too bloody much to me. I can't just leave it.'

'I'm sorry, you've got no choice in the matter. You don't have to worry about those other women you took on: I've made sure their jobs are secure, so—'

'But we lose *ours*, do we?'

'I could have a word with Mr Ferguson, see if he—'

'Over my dead body,' shouted Joyce. 'I'll not work for that bastard again.'

'Well, that's the best I can offer.'

'A poor bloody best is all I can say. And it's not going to end here, I'll tell you that for nowt.' Joyce gripped the bar of the pushchair until her knuckles went white. 'It's not going to end here!'

Colette was unpacking. She had dumped a small case on what had been Rose's sofa, and parked a heavily laden shopping trolley against one arm. Dragging bits out and inspecting them, she tossed a red leather skirt at Tracy.

'Here, see if that fits yer. Cost me a bloody fortune and I've only worn it twice. Try it on.' When Tracy looked at it doubtfully, Colette said: 'Listen, are yer sure this is all right? If you don't want me here, you only have to say so.'

'I've said you can stay.'

'I know you're cut up about her leaving, but you'll get over it. We're good together, you and me. We have a laugh, don't we? You couldn't get a laugh out of old hatchet face.'

Tracy fidgeted. She didn't want Rose talked about like that. She hated Rose now – hated her guts, of course she did – but still nobody else had any right to talk about her like that.

Colette saw she had overstepped the mark. Warily she said, 'Do you like me?'

'I slept with you last night, didn't I?'

'Yeh, but maybe that was only because we'd had a smoke.' She risked an arch smile. 'We can have another smoke.'

Tracy perked up. That was just what she was dying for. 'Have you got some?'

'Not on me.'

Tracy handed over her mobile. 'Ring him, then.'

'Not now. Later. You have to be careful, you can get

hooked on that stuff. We'll get some later.' Colette began to haul some bits of woodwork out of the trolley.

Tracy knew what it all added up to, and didn't like it. Crazy to feel a bit disgusted. If that was what some punters wanted, it was okay to let them have it. But she couldn't see herself going in for it. Colette was proud of knowing this carpenter who had made the stocks, and planned to have him make her a rack as well for the cellar. How anyone could want to be fastened in the stocks and then have muck thrown at them, Tracy couldn't imagine. But she knew Colette's motto: flog the tossers and take their brass.

Suddenly she remembered. 'Didn't you shove that Lionel of yours downstairs? Won't he be getting impatient?'

'If he starts complaining, I'll make his life a bloody misery.' Colette laughed harshly. 'Or maybe bloody marvellous.'

Right on cue, Lionel appeared at the head of the cellar steps in his charwoman's gear, but this time complete with pearls flopping all over his padded bosom. 'I've finished scrubbing the wall and floor, mistress. And I've laid your whips out. Is there anything else I can do?'

'Yes, there is, you snivelling piece of toad shite. Get these bloody stocks downstairs. And don't take bloody chunks out of the wall while you're doing it.' As she made ready to follow him, Colette beamed back at Tracy. 'It's gonna make a frigging brilliant dungeon down there.'

Tracy waited until the two voices had gone right down into the cellar, then reached for the mobile phone. If Colette was in no hurry to contact her supplier, Tracy was.

Five minutes later she was on her way, leaving Colette to scream abuse at the grovelling Lionel.

Rabbit was crouched in the darkest corner of The Hustlers' Arms bar, like a wary animal sniffing the air, ready to scuttle for cover if danger threatened. When Tracy came in he sized her up warily, wrinkled his nose as if to make sure he could identify her; then managed a sharp, toothy grin. He was staring hard at her legs as she came to his table.

'So Colette gave you my number, did she?'

'I stole it.' She was in flirtatious mood now that the stuff was so nearly in her grasp. 'I think she wanted to keep it for herself.'

He eyed her with growing interest. 'Nah, yer've got to share these things with yer mates.'

'That's right. I had something she wanted, and she had something I wanted.'

'We've all got wants,' he grinned. 'Shall we go back to yours?'

Tracy hadn't been expecting that sort of reaction, so fast and pushy. 'I've come here for me stuff.'

'Sure, sure. Maybe you've got somewhere comfortable we could take it?'

Tracy thought of Colette, and how livid she was likely to be if she found Tracy had gone direct to her supplier and was already bringing him back with her. 'I'm not going back home straight away,' she hedged. 'I've gotta go to hospital to see a mate.'

'Have a drink first?'

'They won't know what a Chablis is in here,' said Tracy loftily. 'Just get me a dry white wine, will you, but make sure it's chilled.' When he brought the drink to the table, she said, 'Are you gonna give it me, then?'

'How are yer paying?' His beady little eyes twinkled at her.

'I've got money.'

'What if I don't want money?'

She could tell he was desperate, fancying her like mad. It gave her a feeling of power. 'You can put it down on the slate, and I'll pay up at the end of the week.'

'What if I can't wait that long?' He was groping under the table for her knee. She had a good mind to shove it in where it would hurt, but she wanted the crack more than that. 'You'll get it Friday,' she said. 'Same day as Colette pays up. Now give it me.'

He leaned across he table. 'Give us a little taster, eh?' He kissed her on the mouth. Tracy tried to push him away, then felt something drop on to her tongue. He was laughing wetly through the kiss. When she had pulled back, she reached for her glass and drank, to conceal fishing the clingfilmed package out of her mouth.

Rose was dragging her suit-case along with its edge trailing on the pavement. It was like a ton weight, and any minute now might split open; but if it went all over the bloody shop, she was beyond caring.

A light bronze Granada pulled in close to the kerb, tooting its horn. Not so long ago she would have turned in hope of getting custom from a punter. Now she scowled as the driver wound his window down.

'Going on your holidays?' said Brian.

She had never been so glad to see anybody in her life. When he waved towards the passenger door and began to open it, she stumbled round and lifted the case over on to the back seat. As she settled in beside him, he handed her a slip of paper.

'What's this?'

'The name and address of where your daughter is.'

She read it; read it again; and then couldn't read it a third time because of the tears blurring her vision. Somewhere in Manchester. Primrose Park Crescent, Manchester. All this time she had feared that Hannah had been taken far away – to Australia, anywhere – but here she was: Hannah Levison was her name now, and she was only a coach ride away.

'You need a drink,' said Brian. When they were settled in a corner of The Hustlers' Arms, and Rose was thankfully pouring lager down her throat, he said: 'Right, then. When are you going to visit her?'

Rose was too dazed to think straight. 'I'll have to think about it.'

'Not for another twenty-three years, I hope?'

'I've got to plan it properly. I mean, I've got to think how I should . . . well, play it.'

'There's no rules. Play it by ear.'

It sounded simple. But now that the chance of a meeting was so close, Rose was already wondering what would happen if she went to pieces when she saw her daughter. During those weeks spent in London, she had thought maybe that was where Hannah had finished up, and she had stared at every girl with dark hair who looked about Hannah's age now. She had wanted to stop so many of them, saying, 'Excuse me, did you used to be Hannah Garrity?' And then what? 'I think I might be your mam.' And all the time she had been in Manchester.

'Might get my hair cut,' she reflected. 'Buy myself a new—'

She stopped, hearing a familiar voice raised in a show-off protest. 'This is bloody awful.'

The little rodent beside Tracy, with his hand under the table, obviously didn't want to be distracted. 'What's the matter?'

'This wine. Taste it. It's bloody horrible.'

He sipped it. 'All tastes the same to me.'

Tracy had become aware of Rose's gaze, and was playing up for all she was worth. 'That's because you've got no taste.'

'Your hair's all right as it is,' Brian was saying, when he saw that her attention had strayed. 'What's the matter?'

'Nothing, just somebody I know, that's all.'

He coaxed her back to the main point. 'You have to be careful. If you're seen watching the house too much, they'll think you're casing the joint and you'll have the police on your back. You need to think it through.'

'Maybe I should ring . . .' But Rose couldn't take her eyes off Tracy and that little bit of vermin, Rabbit. He was fairly new on the patch, but before quitting the Lane she had heard plenty about him. Tracy's earlier pimp, Dez, had been slimy enough. This one promised to be worse. 'What the bloody hell's she doing with *him*?'

Brian was amused and curious. 'Who is he?'

'A bloody two-bit Joey crack-head, that's what.'

Rose could feel Tracy's spitefulness a mile away. She was playing up, raising her voice so that it rasped across the room. Rabbit went on pawing her knee, and Tracy wanted Rose to see it.

Rose could restrain herself no longer. She marched across the room and stood above Tracy. 'What are you doing with *him*?'

'None of your business.'

'You know what he is, don't you?'

'Shut yer mouth.' Rabbit looked nervously around. 'Come on, let's get out of here.' He began to get up.

'Leave her alone,' snarled Rose. 'She's only a bloody kid. Tracy, he's a crack-head.'

Rabbit grabbed her shoulder, to push her out of the way or throw her on to the bench. 'I'll tear your fucking head off if you don't shut up.'

'All he wants is to get you hooked,' Rose shouted over his shoulder as he tried to manhandle her away from Tracy.

Brian came stalking towards them. He lifted Rabbit bodily and slammed him against the wall; but Rabbit was a vicious little fighter when he was scared – all claws and knees and head-butting, learnt the hard way against bigger competition. They crashed to and fro for no more than a minute, overturning one table and smashing three glasses, before Brian hurled Rabbit into a corner, knocking all the breath out of him.

Tracy drew her lips back from her teeth and sneered at Rose. 'Satisfied now?'

'You stupid little bitch, you'll end up dead in some gutter.'

'Not that you'd care.'

Brian came between them. 'Let's get out of here, Rose.

Come on, leave it.' When they were outside the pub, he said, 'Who the hell was she?'

Rose was furious. His hand was still on her arm. She shook it off. 'Don't you ever do that again.'

'What? I thought you were in a bit of a—'

'I fight my own battles. When I want help I ask for it, right?'

'Right.' He pulled a bill out of his pocket and thrust it at her. 'Here you are, then. Job's finished, you can send a cheque to the address at the top of the page.'

Her anger ebbed away as she watched him stride down the Lane towards his car. It had all happened so quickly, and been so bloody stupid. She wanted to call him back. But she knew she couldn't.

A mother and little boy were walking up the Lane; and suddenly she remembered Emma, and Carol asking her, just in case . . . She reached the school gates to find Emma on her own, beginning to sob faintly. She raised her arms in relief to Rose. 'I thought me mam'd forgot me.'

'She might forget some things, love, but she'd never forget you. Come on, let's get you home.'

Emma was cheerful again within a few seconds. But Rose wasn't so happy. Carol hadn't shown up. So something had to be seriously wrong. What the hell was going on in that police station?

DCI Newall was confident that all the pieces of the puzzle were fitting neatly by now. Not that it was much of a puzzle, really. Carol Johnson had once hated Granville Durkin enough to injure him by pouring boiling water over his balls and prick; but once he started offering money again, she was like all the rest of them – greedy, ready to do anything until she was driven mad again, and this time had finished the poor bugger off. How Durkin had come to be in his wrecked car in a smashed-up shop front he hadn't fathomed yet, but it shouldn't take long. He almost certainly hadn't driven there himself to wait for someone to come along, cut his throat, and then heave him into the boot.

Yet at the same time Newall wanted there to be a get-out explanation along those lines: somebody else committing the murder, well away from Carol's house. Just by being here, just by looking at him, Carol got under his skin. He would have been better off if his transfer had come through months ago, and Carol was out of his life, out of his memory.

Damn her. She wouldn't ever leave his memory.

It had been just after half-past two when he and WDS Hoyle began another session facing Carol in the interview room, and Hoyle had switched on the tape recorder. Carol still refused a duty solicitor, stubbornly saying she hadn't done anything and so didn't need a solicitor. Her dark face looked darker than ever with resentment. And fear. Oh, she was dead scared of something.

Newall let her stew for a few moments while he made a show of reading through Hoyle's notes. 'Right. Now, when we were talking before, you said "I'm hardly likely to slit his throat, am I?"'

'Well, you do say that, don't you? Slit someone's throat, it's something you say.'

'Is it?' Newall turned blandly to Hoyle. 'Do you say that sort of thing, sergeant?'

She took the cue. 'Not unless I knew he'd *had* his throat cut, sir.'

'That's right.' Newall leaned across the table towards Carol. 'You could have said you were hardly likely to stab him in the back, or pump a couple of bullets into his chest, or—'

'Well, I didn't. It were just bad luck that I picked the right one.'

'And bad luck that your fingerprints were all over his car, even on the steering wheel?'

'He were teaching me to drive.'

'Have you got a provisional licence?'

'Somewhere.'

He could tell she was lying. 'In your bag? In your house? Where do you keep it?'

'He keeps it. Curly . . . he keeps it at his factory.'

'Really.' Newall went on looking at her while he spoke to Hoyle. 'Ring Jameson, get him to—'

'Or it might be at his house.'

Hoyle hesitated at the door. 'Ring the licence office at Swansea,' Newall added. 'Get them to run a check.'

When she had left the room, Newall turned the machine off. He almost wanted to protect Carol, find a way of telling her what to say and what not to say, to keep her out of stumbling into one trap after another. Better still, to have her throw herself on his mercy. But she was looking at him with the sort of hatred that could have driven her to maim and then kill Durkin. He could stand being hated by a lot of people, but not by Carol. She still wanted him as much as he wanted her, he was sure of that; but hated him and hated herself for it.

He said, 'Look, Carol. Don't fuck me about. We've got the forensic boys round at the house, and they can tell who's been in there, if they had dog shite on their shoe, and if it had Pedigree Chum for breakfast. So.' He pounded the table. 'Did you kill him?'

'No, I didn't.'

DS Hoyle's head came back round the door. Forensic had brought some things in, and DC Powell was on the line and wanted a word – urgently. Newall nodded that she should stay in the room with the suspect, and went out. If someone didn't soon come up with enough material to charge Carol, they would have to let her go. He had a cowardly flicker of hope that things might work out that way, without him having to do anything further. But when he came back into the room he was in vengeful mood. No point in thinking of protecting Carol; and the greedy bitch didn't bloody well deserve it anyway.

He chucked a roll of black bin liners on the table, and a roll of Sellotape. He saw her start as she recognised them.

'So. He's found not far from your house, in his car, which

has your fingerprints all over it. Wrapped in black bin liners, Sellotaped together, and dumped in the boot.' He added a key ring to the collection. 'And he's got your front-door key on his key-ring. And forensic,' he threatened, 'have only just started. They've found traces of blood in your living room and hallway, and we're running matches on them right now. But that could take a couple of days, so I think we're going to have to keep you here until we—'

'I didn't kill him.'

'Really?'

He and Hoyle sat very still. Old professional instinct told them she was ready to crack.

At last she said, helplessly, 'I found him dead. He were sat in my armchair with blood all down his jacket.'

'You *found* him?'

'Yes. I'd been out. I'd been to see Anita in hospital, and when I got back I walked into my room and there he was – sat there like a leftover from a Hammer House of Horrors. I didn't know what to do.'

'Why didn't you ring the police?' asked Hoyle.

''Cos I knew I'd get blamed, 'cos of what I did before. I thought if I could just get rid of his body, if I could just move him somewhere else, out of my house, then I'd stand a chance. It were a stupid thing to do.'

They would check for signs of a forcible entry. But since Durkin had had his own key anyway and could already have let himself in . . .

Newall had to watch it: he knew he was already finding excuses for half-believing Carol's story, when it was ten to one that all this was another of those wild lies off the top of her head.

'Right,' he said as coldly as possible. 'So you lifted the body into the car, all by yourself?'

'That's right.'

'You must be a lot stronger than you look. It takes some

doing, lifting a corpse. Do you know that a human body doubles its weight when it's dead?'

'Really? You should be on Mastermind.'

She was covering for someone. No way could she have managed that on her own. He wondered who else was in on it, and what it was worth to them. Maybe the whole killing had been planned by the two of them, and carried out by someone with tougher nerves than Carol. But what was the payoff?

Thanks to Powell's phone call he had another one up his sleeve. This ought to be the clincher. 'You killed him,' he said, 'for the money.'

'What money? He gives me money, what do I need to kill him for?'

'I tell you what for.' He drew it out sadistically. 'For the ninety-eight thousand pounds that he's left you in his will. For his two-hundred-and-forty-thousand-pound house, and for his three-and-a-half-million-pound frozen chicken business. You've got the lot.'

Unexpectedly she looked relieved. She even forced a laugh. 'Oh, I get it, it's a trick.'

'Spare me the wide-eyed innocent routine. You got the poor bastard to change his will, then bumped him off, didn't you?'

'Sorry, but it won't wash.'

'Only,' Newall hammered on, 'you fouled up, somewhere down the line. What went wrong? Where did you slip up?'

Her tired, dark-rimmed eyes began widening. If it was an act, it was a brilliant one. 'Are you saying it's the truth?'

'You know bloody well it is. Every penny, all yours. And it's time we did have the truth. I'm sick of your fairy stories. When did he tell you he'd changed his will? Last week, the week before? How long have you been planning it?'

Her eyes were brimming with tears. It stopped him in his tracks. Her whole expression was not what he had expected.

'Get her a drink of water, will you, sergeant?' When Hoyle wavered, not sure she should be leaving the room, he barked: 'Now!'

'No,' Carol was murmuring to herself, 'no . . . no.'

'Turning on the tears isn't going to help you,' said Newall.

Her limpness turned to instant rage. She launched herself from her chair, lashing out and hitting him, across the face and the side of the head. He tried to grab her arms, but her fury was giving her a terrifying strength.

'You fucking stupid moron. I'm not crying to get me anywhere.' Another wild swing, a fist making his left ear sing. If he'd wanted evidence that she could be a killer, he was getting plenty. 'It's him,' she was sobbing. 'What he's done, what he did. I'm crying because he . . . because he were such a stupid soft bastard. And what I had . . . what I bloody had and . . . and . . .'

At last he pinioned her arms, and his face was close to hers. He couldn't hold back. He kissed her. She started fighting even more ferociously, trying to wrench herself free. She managed to spit in his face just as Hoyle came in with a polystyrene cup of water. Carol took it with a shaking hand. Hoyle moved close beside Newall.

'We've got the extension, sir.'

'Good.' He turned his face away, wiping the spit off with his handkerchief. 'Take her down.'

Carol looked up. 'Where yer taking me?'

He took her left arm. Hoyle neatly took the cup away and held her right arm.

'Come on, Carol.'

'Where to? I'm not going in no cell.'

'Don't make this difficult for us,' said Hoyle.

'I'm not going.' She threshed in a panic. 'You're not locking me up. Get off me. Get off . . .'

A uniformed police officer opened the door, took Newall's place, and between them he and Hoyle forced Carol kicking and screaming along the corridor until a door clanged open and then shut again.

10

Anita had stared at the headline and tried to persuade herself the treatment they were giving her in hospital had disturbed her vision. It couldn't be true. She asked for a phone, and they took an age to bring it. And then she couldn't raise anybody. Where the hell had they all got to; what the hell were they up to? She kicked her feet against the sheet and blanket to free herself, but they had been tucked in too tightly. Then a nurse brought her some painkillers: she had asked for them often enough, but when the girl got round to bringing them, Anita wondered if there was something special in them to sap her strength and stop her escaping.

Then came a man who introduced himself as Detective Constable Jameson, with a uniformed woman officer beside him. She settled herself back with an injured smile of reproach, waiting for them to go through the questions about her accident again and tell her if they were making any progress. She couldn't tell them who she suspected – who she *knew* – had done it. That was something she would work on herself; but if they found their own way there, that would be fine by her. She wasn't prepared for questions about someone called Granville Durkin. It was all vague, making no sense. She must be even deeper under sedation than they had led her to believe. Who the hell was Granville Durkin?

Jameson must have recognised her puzzlement. 'Better known as Curly.'

'Oh, him.'

'You know him?'

'Well –' with all the trouble going on around them, she didn't know how far to risk dropping Carol in whatever it was that this latest bit added up to '– he's a friend of a . . . an acquaintance . . . sort of.'

'He's been murdered,' said Jameson.

Christ, it was all getting worse than she could have imagined. 'Murdered? Who by?'

'He would appear to have been murdered in the house of a Carol Johnson.'

'You're having me on.'

'I believe you have a key to her house?'

'Me? What? Look, I'm lying here . . . you couldn't think it was anything to do with me?'

'You do stay there with Carol Johnson,' Jameson pursued, 'and you do have a key?'

Of course it couldn't be anything to do with her. If ever anyone could be said to have a perfect alibi, it had to be her. But what the hell had Carol been up to, and what ought she to know and not know?

When the detective and the policewoman had left, she asked for the phone again; but could still raise nobody.

Her next visitor was Tracy, with a bunch of flowers.

'About bloody time,' said Anita.

Tracy didn't take kindly to this. 'What's the matter with yer?'

Anita struggled up and eased herself back against her pillows. At last she had an audience.

'What's up with me? I'll tell you what. I've been concussed for thirteen hours, I've got internal bruising, suspected cracked ribs, and apart from Carol coming to visit me for half an hour, there's not one of you been near the place.'

'Well, I'm here now,' said Tracy peevishly. 'So don't go blaming me.'

'I'm not blaming you, just telling you. And I can tell you something else: I've had the police here.'

'Asking about who hit you?'

'A hell of a lot more interested in him who's dead.'

'Eh?'

'Didn't you know? Curly. She's finished him off proper this time. They've got her locked up.'

Tracy sat down. 'Who'd have done that?'

'I'm telling you, aren't I? You ask me, Carol was walking for him again, and it went to her head and . . . anyway, it'll be in the papers tomorrow. Bad enough with what's in 'em today.' She thrust the creased front page at Tracy. 'I just hope nobody thinks I've been doing punters in the sauna.'

Tracy skimmed the page and shook her head. 'It's bloody lies, is that.'

''Course it's bloody lies. But we've lost the contract.'

'Who's done this?' Tracy's pale, seedy little face looked more concerned about this than the fate of Curly. 'Who told the paper this crap?'

Anita had known from the moment she first saw the news story who it had to be. 'Frigging Ferguson, that's who.' Add that to everything else he'd done. 'But this time he'll get his comeuppance. I'll bloody well see to that. This time I'll make bloody sure . . .' She calmed it as she saw Nurse Stanley approaching, and said sweetly, 'Could you put these in water?'

'They're lovely.'

'This is my friend, Tracy, she brought them for me.'

When the nurse had gone in search of a vase, Tracy said, agitated, 'You shouldn't go telling 'em my name. They might be still looking for me – might remember me from before.'

This was something else Anita couldn't get to grips with. 'Before when?'

'When Dez hit me on the back of the head. I were in Ward eight down bottom end of that corridor.'

With so many of her own troubles to face, Anita had forgotten all about that little toerag who had gone for Tracy and landed her in hospital, and himself in prison. That made two of them: Dez wanting to teach Tracy a lesson, and George Ferguson thinking he could teach *her* a lesson.

'That's how I came in here,' she said aloud. 'Same idea. He drove his car straight into me. It's a wonder I'm not dead.'

'You're sure it was—'

'I haven't told anybody. But I'm going to get my own back. For that and the rest of it. Just as soon as I get out of here.'

When Tracy had gone, Anita turned over uncomfortably in bed. She was fed up with this place. There was too much going on outside, and she wanted to be there to find out just what it was all about. No way of finding out a bloody thing in here. She leaned over to drag the white hospital bag and her washbag out of her locker, struggled free from the torture of that sheet, and headed down the corridor.

Nurse Stanley was on her way back with the vase filled with flowers. 'You all right, Anita?'

'Fine. Just going to spend a penny.'

Way back, Tracy had made her own way out of here. Now Anita had the same idea in mind. There were so many things to be sorted out. Not least of them, George Ferguson.

She had changed into the crumpled, bloodied clothes they had taken off her and put in the hospital plastic bag as she approached the Klensit car park. It was dark, but not too dark for her to make out the familiar outline and red gleam of George's Jaguar. A sharp pain tugged at her side: not enough to stop her in her tracks. She hadn't planned anything particular. Her feet had just brought her here. Now she wished she had armed herself with something before she reached the car park. She looked along the wall. There was a cracked concrete slab propped against one upright, but it was far too heavy for her to shift. She looked at the Jaguar, longing to kick it until it shattered: but she'd do her toes more harm than the car. As her eyes grew used to the shadows, she saw the end of an exhaust which somebody had dumped in a skip against the wall. It would do.

Anita picked it up, braced herself, and began slamming it

down on the Jaguar's bonnet and then all along the sides. After five minutes she was panting happily, but the pain in her side had got worse. She leaned against the Jag, trying to hold on to herself and not pass out.

George Ferguson reached for the phone. He had worked late, planning every last little detail, and as far as he could see it was waterproof. First there were a few frighteners to be put on Brenda, which would be good fun anyway; and then he would organise the money, Alfie's payoff, and the build-up of his new scheme. He'd done this sort of thing before. Nobody could beat him at it.

When Brenda answered, he said in his most friendly, concerned tone, 'Oh, Brenda, George Ferguson here. About that job, I'm sorry, but it didn't quite work out.'

He heard her sharp intake of breath at the other end, and waited for her to fumble out an answer. It came as a strangled whisper. 'What d'you mean, it didn't work out? You can't do that. I went to Minkin for you, I shopped my mates, I said things 'cos you told me to—'

'No, Brenda, I didn't tell you to say anything.' He kept it smooth and reasonable. 'You told me about the whoring that was going on at the Leisure Centre. I didn't know anything about that.'

'But it was you who made me—'

'Now, listen. I'm taking over the contract, and as far as I'm concerned you can continue working there in some sort of capacity. I'll pay you cash in hand, three quid an hour, but on a . . . well, shall we say an informal basis? And *if* . . .' He let it hang in the air until she was ready to reach for it.

'If what?'

'We do have to understand each other, Brenda. For technical reasons, I'll want you to sign a few cheques and papers for me from time to time. Just a formality.'

'What sort of papers?'

'Leave that to me. Just a formality,' Ferguson repeated. 'Is that all right with you?'

He knew he had won when she said timidly, 'Will I still get me income support . . .?'

He sat back, poured himself a whisky from the bottle in his bottom drawer, and reached for the phone for the next stage.

'Robert, how you doing? George here. Yes, George Ferguson, Klensit.' He knew what was coming next, and interrupted before the man could get too far into his complaint. 'Yes, I know I haven't. I've been having a few problems. But there'll be a cheque in the post first thing tomorrow for last year's accounts. But that's not what I'm ringing about. Things have taken a turn for the better, and I want to buy a company. Limited, off the shelf, a.s.a.p. And I want it in the name of Brenda Taylor. Got that? Right – get back to me just as fast as you can.'

It was all shaping up nicely. He locked up the office, whistling as he went along the corridor towards the stairs. On the corner of the flight his mobile phone began ringing in his pocket. It would hardly be Robert – not that quick off the mark.

He wasn't sure he recognised the voice. And why the hell should anyone want to tell him things about Scrubbit he didn't know? There was nothing about Scrubbit he didn't know. Or maybe . . . well, there might still be something useful; something he could use against them. He said: 'Well, you've got me guessing now. So do come and tell me. Where are you right now?' He felt a moment of unease when he realised how close the caller was. 'All right, I'll be down in two minutes.'

He switched off the stair lights as he reached the bottom, and went out of the back door on to the car park. The security lights showed four cars left, and out of the corner of his eye Ferguson thought he saw a shadow move between them.

'Hello?' He was answered only by the squawl of a cat

darting out from behind the skip. 'Are you there? Come on, I'm waiting. If you've got anything to say, let's have it.'

When there was no answer, he shrugged. Bloody silly to have expected anything better. He went round the bonnet of a Ford Transit towards his Jaguar, and there was a sudden flurry of movement. Light glinted off a raised knife. George Ferguson held up one arm, felt it being knocked aside, and then felt the agony of the blade ripping into his throat. He gurgled a scream that died into a choked bubbling, and collapsed into the broken glass from his Jaguar's headlights, clawing at the gash across his throat, pleading for help until the words no longer had the strength to force themselves through the blood oozing out between his fingers and down his jacket.

11

In the Klensit car park a chalked outline was all that remained of George Ferguson's corpse, close to his Jaguar and sprinkled with slivers of glass from smashed headlights. Newall paced round the dented wing and bonnet, trying to think up any possible link between the damage and the body that had lain here. None of the fragments of glass had been large enough to slit Ferguson's throat quite so thoroughly. And it was hard to think of that podgy shyster giving heroic battle to someone vandalising his car, much as he might have cherished it.

Two uniformed constables were combing every inch of the concrete floor, while a forensic officer dusted one side of the car and then leaned over the contents of the nearby skip.

Newall slid back into his car, reaching for the phone to call the station. Only one thing was certain about last night's killing: it couldn't have been Carol Johnson's work. As DS Hoyle climbed in beside him, he was saying, 'Bail her.'

He could sense Hoyle's disapproval. 'It could be a copycat, sir,' she ventured.

'Copycat of what? Nobody knows how Durkin was murdered.'

'Things get out. People talk. Somebody could have wanted Ferguson dead, and deliberately killed him in the same way, thinking we'd link both murders.'

Newall thought of the man's throat, and was positive that an attack like that couldn't have been any careful, contrived copycat. It had been sudden and savage – a wild slash with a knife by somebody who was very, very sick in the head, killing in some spontaneous rage. And it couldn't have been Carol Johnson. They'd got the wrong person locked up.

Of course there were things there that had to be followed up. Carol had admitted trying to conceal Durkin's body, and she must have some idea of who had done it, or why would she have tried to cover up? Of course she was frightened of getting the blame for Durkin's death because of what she'd done to the man before – Newall believed that all right – but a second brutal murder in the same pattern must let her off any suspicion of actual killing. She might not realise how lucky she had been to be banged up at the time of this second death.

They reached the station to find that she had already gone. He hadn't expected them to have bailed her quite so quickly. Couldn't have been much else going on in the station this morning.

'Ranting on,' the desk sergeant reported with a straight face but a tinge of amusement in his voice, 'about how she was going to get a solicitor and – er – get you *done*, sir.' Hoyle also allowed herself the suspicion of a grin.

Newall went out and drove off. He wanted a word with Carol. Several words, in fact.

She had not got far. He caught up with her as she walked down the Lane, slapping her feet down as if to drive her heels through somebody's skull. Newall drew up alongside her, winding down the window.

'Get in.'

She went on walking. 'Piss off.'

He eased the car into matching her pace. 'I want to talk to you.'

'You can want what you like.'

'I know you're angry with me, but—'

'Angry?' She was spitting the words out in front of her. 'Why should I be angry with a pillock that's got no brain?'

'Listen, I could have kept you banged up for another week: accessory to murder, concealing evidence—'

'So why didn't you?' She quickened her pace. Newall kept cruising beside her. 'I'll tell you why you didn't: because you know I didn't do it, that's why, you bastard. You left me rotting in that stinking cell just for the hell of it, you didn't even come and see me.'

Newall felt a tingle of pleasure. In spite of that hostile tone of voice, she had been longing to see him, had she?

A girl came along the pavement with her head down, looking shagged out. Must be on her way home after a night's work.

Carol waved. 'Busy night, Tula?' She turned back to Newall. 'They'll have you for kerb crawling if you carry on like this.' She sounded a bit more relaxed and jokey.

He judged it was time to spring it on her. 'George Ferguson was murdered last night.'

Carol stopped in her tracks. Newall could see she was adding up all that this meant. Now she could guess why she had been released at such short notice.

'Well,' she said at last, 'it couldn't have happened to a better person. God knows where you're gonna start with that one, 'cos *everybody* wanted that bastard dead.'

He leaned over to open the door. She hesitated, but this time decided to get in. They were just turning the corner towards her house when a woman crossed the street and glared in. Newall realised that it was the most cantankerous of Carol's neighbours, and that he was being mistaken for one of Carol's punters.

They stopped outside the house. He kept the engine running and said earnestly, 'Look, get your locks changed. If what you've told us is true, then whoever cut Granville Durkin's throat must have walked into your house. And you still aren't going to say who it is?'

'I don't bloody know. How many more times?'

'You must have some idea. Or why would you—'

'No bloody idea. No bloody idea. Do I have to set it to music to make you listen?'

'Carol, he didn't break in, he just walked in through the door. So get those locks changed.'

'As if you're bothered.'

'I wouldn't be telling you if I wasn't bothered.'

Close to his gear-stick her knee was sleek, golden-brown. He was tempted to put his hand on it, and he was damn sure she knew it. Even without that he could feel the old tension building up between them. She wasn't looking at him, but she was all strung-up and waiting for something – a word, a movement, something.

'What are you sitting there for?' She was still staring straight ahead. 'Turn yer car off.'

'I'm not coming in.'

That had shaken her. 'Well, there's a first. So you don't want your freebie, then?'

'No.'

'I see. Getting it somewhere else, then?'

'No, I just want to keep sane this time, that's all.'

'So I send you mad, do I?' She was really beginning to enjoy herself, waiting for him to crack, staring at him now until he made his move.

He said, 'Do you *want* me to come in?'

He could tell that that was exactly what she wanted. But she wasn't going to admit it. She wanted him to be the one making the running. And he was damned if he was going to.

'No.' She kept it going. 'Do I hell.'

'So what's the point?'

'It never bothered you before.' She got her key out of her bag and reached for the door handle. 'What did you pick me up for?'

'What did you get in the car for?'

She was out on the pavement. 'Are you coming in or not?'

He went on telling himself he wasn't, until the sight of

her back as she went towards her front door got to him even more deeply than the mockery of her voice and the undertones of what she had been saying. He switched off the engine. By the time she had got her key in the lock, he was right behind her.

Carol went in without bothering to look back and acknowledge him. He followed, closing the door and fixing the chain and the bolt. Carol stood in the hallway, waiting. When he got his hands on her arms to pull her close, her head went back in a show of resistance. They had played all these moves before. Just a few more, a few seconds, and there would be a choice. Newall's right hand went behind her head, trying to predict whether she would lash out at him or let herself be dragged right up to him.

She wasn't resisting.

Then a voice came from the head of the stairs. 'I don't suppose you've got any painkillers?'

Carol gasped. Newall let go of her, said, 'Jesus Christ,' and stared up at the vision of a tousled Anita Braithwaite in her dressing-gown and a neck brace.

'Only I'm in bloody agony,' she cried.

'I thought you were in hospital,' said Carol accusingly.

'I'd heard *you* were banged up.'

Newall was furious. One way of venting that fury was to hit Anita with the news without trying to soften the blow. 'Your old friend George Ferguson is dead.'

'What?' She came to the foot of the stairs. 'When? What happened?'

'His throat was cut,' said Newall remorselessly, 'and he was dumped on the ground by his Jag.'

Anita swayed. Carol put an arm round her and led her towards the kitchen. Newall felt deflated, cheated by Carol yet again. He had wanted to get into her. Now all he wanted was to get out of here as soon as possible. At the same time there was something about Anita Braithwaite being here, out of hospital, that worried half-formed speculations at the back of his mind. He followed the two women into the kitchen and stood back as Carol found a packet of painkillers at the back of a cupboard, pushing them across the table towards Anita.

'I can't believe he's dead.' Anita was beginning to sob. 'I know he was a bastard, but he didn't deserve to die.' She swallowed a pill. 'I feel terrible.'

'You should have stayed in hospital,' said Carol. 'You shouldn't have come home.'

'What time *did* you get here?' asked Newall.

'Last night. Late. After I'd discharged myself from that deadly place.' Her sobs changed into a whimper. 'And you say they found him on the ground by his Jag?'

'That's right. They'd smashed that up as well.'

'Come on, 'Nita.' Carol was trying to coax Anita to go into the living room. 'He got what he deserved. Why don't you have a lay down on the settee, and I'll put the telly on.'

'He loved that car.' Anita seemed to be in a trance.

'So bleeding what?'

'So he tried to mow me down in it.'

Newall came wide awake. 'What was that?'

'It was him all right. On the Lane. That's why I . . . I smashed it up.'

'*You* smashed it up?'

She was weeping out of control, not caring what she said or what anyone thought about her. 'He'd been asking for it. Me there in that frigging hospital, with this bloody thing round my neck because of him trying to shut me up, and him all set to get away with his dirty deals all over again . . .'

Newall could no more believe Anita Braithwaite capable of calculated murder than Carol. But somehow they were all in the same frame. He was going to have to ask some questions – and preferably down at the station.

For the first time Tracy was beginning to worry about the lifters which had kept her going over the last few months. Lovely, swimming dreams she was used to. Distorted faces out of the past were a different thing altogether. She tried to brush them away like cobwebs, but they came back to cling stickily round her forehead and her eyes. There was the ghost of her father's face in the wardrobe mirror, leering at her and inviting her to come back and take up where they had left off. And Carol Johnson's Curly, murmuring in her ears and then fading away when she thumped the wardrobe well and truly shut. What right had he to be here in her room, haunting her? What were any of them doing, shoving their way in here?

She covered her ears as she left the room and went downstairs to see how Colette was getting on in the cellar. She still wasn't all that happy about what was being planned down there; but a lot less happy being on her own.

Rose wouldn't have liked what had happened to the cellar. But then, Rose wasn't here any more and not likely to come back. Hard work over a day and a half had transformed the place. Walls and ceiling were deep, dark purple. Three large mirrors had been angled at crucial points. Colette's whips were hung from black hooks, and there were strips of black leather and blindfolds on a cupboard painted crimson.

Bill, the carpenter, was a large man with a drooping grey moustache and rheumy eyes. His hands looked strong and competent, but at the moment he was out of his depth. 'We're talking complicated here.' He was studying with mounting mistrust the two strips he had attached to the wall, each with a manacle at shoulder height.

'No,' Colette insisted, 'they're dead straightforward. You just need a bit of wood with some knobs on the end I can tie their hands to, and a handle that makes it stretch.'

'No, love.' He was quite unconcerned with the ultimate reason for this gadgetry, and worried only about the technicalities. 'We're talking mechanical, we're talking ratchets and pulleys here. It's not my area, love. You need an engineer for that. I'm more of a wood man, meself.'

Colette's mobile phone began ringing. She waved to Bill

to stay, but as she spoke he was already kicking shavings into a corner and gathering up his tool-bag.

'Colette speaking.' Tracy admired Colette's cool voice. She kept practising an imitation of it – an enticing tone that could get freezing and offputting whenever you decided a thing was no go. 'Twenty-four, long dark hair,' Colette was reciting. 'Thirty-four double D cup, five foot ten. With a very short temper. You could get hurt. Yes, I do mean hurt. What kind were you thinking of? Eh? *Crucifixions . . .?* Just a minute.' She put her hand over the mouthpiece and called, 'Bill!'

He stopped halfway up the cellar steps. 'Mm?'

'What about a cross? Full-size crucifix, sort of thing. What would that cost?'

When he had said he'd come back to her on that and left, Colette did her phone deal and began sweeping up the remainders of the shavings. 'A hundred quid, I reckon, for being nailed up. And all it's gonna take is a couple more pieces of wood.' She looked up happily at the low ceiling, in her mind estimating the clearance. 'I could advertise speciality crucifixions.' She shook her head over the neat pile of shavings. 'I should have left this for Lionel. Didn't think.' She kicked them all over the floor again. 'He'll love sweeping that lot up.'

Tracy was staring at the manacles and the whips.

'You know,' she said awkwardly, 'when you hit 'em . . .'

'Yeh?'

'Does it really hurt?' Tracy fingered the thong of a whip. 'I mean, do you do it properly?'

''Course I do. The more it hurts, the more they like it. Some of 'em, sometimes, they're red raw, and I'm knackered by the time they're done.'

'Do you like doing it?'

Colette looked defensive. 'Well, it's better than having a dick stuck in yer. And if I'm really pissed off at summat I can always take it out on the punter, d'yer know what I mean?'

Tracy put her wrist into one of the handcuffs, let it take some of her weight, and then clicked it shut. 'Here – *you* put my other hand in.'

'Get lost. What for?'

Tracy had a shivering feeling that worked its way down from a dull ache in her stomach to an ache between her legs, like a pulsating electric current. 'I want you to do it to me.' The rhythm was becoming insistent. 'I want to know what it feels like, that's all.'

'It bloody hurts, that's what it feels like.'

'I want you to hurt me.'

The impatience to be punished frothed up in her mouth, and trickled down from her lips on to her chin.

'You're mad.' Colette was looking really uneasy. 'What's up wi' yer?'

Tracy was obsessed with the need, she was ready to scream for it, beg for it. 'I want you to stop my brain from thinking. I want you to make me feel better.'

'Oh, yeh? And make me feel like shite. No way I'm doing it, so you can forget it.'

'But it's what I want,' Tracy begged.

'Well, tough tittie, get some other pillock to do it.'

'I want *you* to do it. Don't you understand?'

Colette came impatiently up to her, fitting the key into the manacle to release it. Tracy smelt her sweat, and the perfume she used round her throat, and longed to have that lean right arm raised, swinging at her, lashing her. 'Help me, Colette.' She drove her lips into Colette's neck, kissing her, gently biting. 'Do it. Please do it.'

Colette was twisting away from Tracy's mouth, then sagging greedily back against it. 'No, Tracy.' She still had the strength to resist that notion, anyway. 'I can't bloody do it.'

'Why not? You said you liked doing it.'

'Yeh, to them sick bastards. To people I don't like.'

'Well, pretend you don't like *me*. Pretend I'm one of your punters. Just cut off.'

'You don't understand, do you? It'd hurt me to hurt you.'

'But I want to be hurt.' Tracy settled her teeth very gently into Colette's flesh. 'That'd make both of us, doing it together. Hurting. If you love me, you'll do it.' She felt the throb of Colette's bloodstream through her teeth and lips. 'Do you love me?'

'You know I love you.'

'Then do it. For me.'

Colette drew on every bit of strength she had. 'I can't. I couldn't do it to you. I have to find the hate to do it, and I could never find the hate. Not with you.' She wrenched herself away, leaving Tracy abandoned, cold in every limb and with a chill going right down into the depths of her stomach, killing what had been there a few minutes ago.

'You will, though.' Tracy smarted with the ache of rejection. 'I'll make sure of that. You will . . . you will!'

She clattered back up the stairs from the cellar and out into the street. She had gone only a few steps towards the corner of the Lane when a Rolls Royce drew up almost silently beside her. Smiley's pinched little face with its gash of a grin peered out at her.

'Now then, Tracy, we've been trying to ring you. You've had yer mobile turned off.'

'I'm not working today.'

'Great. Then you'll have bags of time for a chat with Alfie.'

'And what does he want this time?' She was in no mood for Alfie, always talking big and acting the hot shot, but with a prick about as exciting as a soggy fish finger.

'He's got a little job for yer.' Smiley got out and opened the back door of the car for her, with a thin little smirk of phoney politeness. 'Go on, get in.'

Tracy wanted nothing better than to brush past the little creep and go on her way. But she glanced back towards the house, and saw Colette watching her through the window. That settled it. She made a big show of climbing defiantly into the back of the Rolls, and let herself be driven off.

It was just the way she had guessed it would be. All right, so there was no hassle about money. And Alfie had everything laid on in his penthouse bedroom – lights, music, mauve sheets, the lot – but however good the background might be, the action was pathetic. He puffed, struggled, trying desperately to climax.

'You're taking your time,' grumbled Tracy at last.

'I don't know what's the matter with me today.'

Or any other day, she thought, but kept it to herself. 'You'll have a heart attack if you don't watch it,' she warned as he sank back on to his expensive pillow with a rasping hiccup.

'It's all this stress that's doing it,' he tried to excuse himself. 'I'm in the middle of a big business deal, you see.' His damp hand on her hip pulled her towards him. 'Give me a bit of a cuddle, eh? See what you can do.' His hand slid away towards hers, and tugged it under the bedclothes. 'How would you fancy a little holiday in Belgium, all expenses paid?'

'With you?' Automatically she started on her hand job.

'No. With whoever you like. With your friend. I need someone to pick up a package for me. I need someone . . .' He was beginning to react to the tug and twist of her fingers. 'Someone I can trust. Ah . . . not so rough.'

'And what do I get out of it?'

'I'll see you right, don't worry about that. There'll be a couple of grams on account. I know what you like, right? And you know what I like, eh?' He grabbed her hair and forced her head under the cover. 'Oh, yes, that's it.'

Anita Braithwaite sat across the table in the interview room where Carol Johnson had sat only the day before. She was dabbing a film of perspiration off her brow with a tissue which DS Hoyle had provided. Newall was quite happy to make her sweat. He wasn't going to be pissed about by another of this gang of troublemaking bitches.

'Why didn't you tell the police it was George Ferguson who knocked you down?' he demanded. 'According to DC Barstow, who interviewed you at the hospital, you said—' he looked down at the notepad on the table '—"I was thinking about the party I was going to, I didn't see the car coming. I stepped out into the road and the next thing I remember was waking up here".'

'I didn't tell them,' said Anita shakily, 'because I didn't want to get him into trouble.'

'Well, that's bloody amazing. The man deliberately mows you down, and you say you're worried about getting him into trouble.'

'That's right.' She ran a finger inside the neck brace. 'Look, I'm going to have to lie down. I feel awful.'

Newall had no intention of letting up. 'I think you're a saint. Don't you agree, DS Hoyle? I do think it's pretty incredible. In fact, I think you're lying.'

'I am not!'

'I think you didn't want to involve the police because all the time you were laid in that hospital bed you were planning your own revenge on George Ferguson.'

'Well, as soon as I found out he'd shopped us to Minkin and the newspapers . . . all right, I did. I did start thinking.'

Newall was thrown by this new aspect. 'Sorry – what was that?'

'He told the papers about Carol and Rose being hustlers, and we lost the cleaning contract. So I thought that's it, he's an out-and-out bastard, I'm going to get my own back.'

'I see. So it was revenge for what he'd done to your friends as well?'

'That's right,' said Anita self-righteously. 'What he'd done to Scrubbit, what he'd done to all of us.'

'So tell us: how did you do it?'

'It was easy. I just got this bit of metal and bashed his headlights like . . .' She raised her arm and then squealed with pain. 'I don't think it did me neck much good, though.'

When she had been given permission to leave, but had been warned that further enquiries would be made, Newall and Hoyle went along to the incident room. 'Get round to the Leisure Centre,' he ordered. 'Oh, and I want a list of all the Scrubbit women.'

One detective had brought in a batch of photographs of the staring faces and gashed throats of Granville Durkin and George Ferguson. Set side by side, the comparison flattered neither of them. Another man produced a sheaf of notes gleaned from a company search to Hoyle. By the end of the morning Newall had the supplementary list of Scrubbit operatives as well. There was not much he didn't already know; but it still didn't tell him where the most likely killer was.

Rose Garrity, for starters. Ex-prostitute, several offences for soliciting, and one for theft of a rented TV set. Carol Johnson had claimed that Garrity was looking after her child the night Ferguson was murdered. But they could all be in it together, covering for each other. Reluctantly he added Carol's name to his list, though she couldn't have done the Ferguson murder, unless she was Houdini.

Then there was Anita Braithwaite, who signed herself out of hospital – or actually didn't even stop to sign anything – and who admitted to smashing Ferguson's car. But she was still in hospital when Granville Durkin was murdered. You could say she was a link between the two men, since she had known both of them. But then, so had Carol. And they had already seen that Anita Braithwaite would have had problems lifting her arm above her shoulder. It was doubtful that she could have hit Ferguson over the back of the head, let alone cut his throat. There was Mrs Ferguson, of course, the sleeping partner of the company; but Hoyle's information was that she was out of the country at the moment. Of the directors of the firm, that left Joyce Webster.

Joyce Webster, mother of Gina Dixon, murdered last year when she went on the game to pay off an outstanding loan she'd had from Ferguson's company. And according to Hoyle, the Leisure Centre manager had said she was the hardest working. She and Garrity were the backbone of the company, and she took the loss of the contract very hard. Apparently there were some threats made that she was going to take things further.

It made sense. Much more sense than trying to drag Carol into it, Newall assured himself. It must have really pissed the Webster woman off, losing everything she'd worked for, to the likes of Ferguson. But enough to kill him?

She would have to be next on the list to be hauled in.

12

From early morning Rose had been racked by spasms of impatience and worry until she heard that Carol was actually being let out. She had agreed to take Emma to school; but there was no way she could get back from her trip to Manchester in time to collect her in the afternoon. And that trip to Manchester was the biggest event in her life right now: the thing that mattered most in all her life so far.

After the phone call, on the way to school she squeezed Emma's hand and said, 'Guess what?'

'Me mum's coming home,' said Emma at once. There could have been nothing else on her mind.

'Right. You're pleased about that, right?'

Emma nodded, gave a little skip, and then said, 'Auntie Rose, what's a prostitute?'

Rose gulped. 'What d'you want to know that for?'

''Cos Tina's mum said my mum's gone to prison 'cos she's a prostitute.'

Rose thought of Carol's sour-faced neighbour, and guessed the pleasure the woman would have got at seeing police cars swooping on the premises and guessing the worst. 'Tina's mum should keep her trap shut,' she said. 'Tina's mum knows nowt.'

She watched Emma run across the playground, and wondered which of the waiting cluster of girls was Tina, and how much more would be asked or hinted at during break.

She hurried off to the bus station, and just caught the express coach that would take her into the heart of

Manchester. Then she had to get out her map and ask for directions, and get a local bus the short distance to Primrose Park. It was well on into the morning by then, and she had no reason to suppose Hannah would be at home; but she was hungry for just a glimpse of her and where she lived.

Primrose Park was not much more than a narrow patch of grass and trees enclosed in ornamental railings, but it was very trim and private, and the Victorian crescent houses were just as smart and sure of themselves. Rose tried to imagine living in one of them, behind those leaded windows and the ruched curtains. She couldn't manage it; but she could imagine her daughter being in there, used to all of it and comfortable with it.

She found number 104 and stared at the front door for a good five minutes until she remembered Brian's warning. Too much staring and she might attract the notice of the police, or a neighbour as nosy as Carol's. She made herself walk right to the end of the terrace and then along the other side of the trees, all the time glancing over at number 104 in case she saw something.

Maybe Hannah wasn't in there at this time of day. Wherever she worked, she might use a snack bar every day instead of coming home. Or maybe she was away at some college or something.

Just after half-past one the front door opened and a girl came out. She was in her early twenties and looked very trendy, with short cropped hair, a leather jacket, jeans, and a bag slung across her left shoulder. Rose caught only a glimpse of her face, but it looked bright and self-confident: just like her walk as she strode off towards the bus stop. This had to be her Hannah. The dream was coming true more beautifully than she had dared to hope.

She hurried behind the girl, and was two seats behind her when the bus moved off. Between them was a woman with a small daughter, wiping chocolate off her mouth. Rose smiled, and the kid smiled back. It was all part of the wonderful day.

When Hannah got off, it was only a short walk down a street of shops before she turned in at the door of one of them.

It was a secondhand music shop, with three or four instruments in the window and rows of music along both sides. Rose tried to peer in, but everything beyond was in shadow. She couldn't just hang about on the pavement; and she wasn't going to turn and walk away. She took a deep breath and pushed the door open.

Hannah was at the back of the shop, talking to a young man who kept scratching his jaw and looking disbelieving. 'She fancies you, honest,' Hannah was saying. 'You're such a coward, Sean. Do you want me to ring her for you? Look, there's a few of us going to Dare Cafe tonight. Meeting in the usual place, and . . .' She became aware of Rose. 'I'm sorry, can I help you?'

'No, no, it's all right. Finish what you were saying.'

'We were just nattering.'

'It sounded interesting.'

'It's not, it's boring.' It was an easygoing, musical laugh. She prodded Sean in the forearm. 'Go on, ring her.' When he edged away, she spread her arms despairingly at Rose. 'Sorry, but he's driving me mad. My friend wants to go out with him, he wants to go out with her, but neither of them have the guts to ring each other. It's driving me bonkers. Sorry.'

'Will you stop saying "sorry".' Rose wanted to reach out and touch this sparky, bubbling girl; but instead found herself sounding like a bossy mother.

'Sorry.' Hannah laughed. 'Oh, dear. I won't say it again, I promise.' The lilt of her voice almost took Rose's breath away. Her foster parents must have sent her to a posh school, and probably talked that way themselves, too. 'Now, are you looking for something?'

'Er, well . . . yes, I'm looking for something.' Rose stared helplessly about her. 'A musical instrument for me daughter.'

'What does she play?'

Rose hadn't thought this far ahead. 'I don't know. Anything. I mean, she doesn't play anything yet, but she wants to. I thought I'd buy her something as a surprise.'

'That's nice. Is it her birthday?'

'Sort of.'

Sean was eyeing her with some doubt; but the girl was happy to keep on chatting. 'It's quite a big decision, you know. It might be better if you brought your daughter into the shop. I know it'd spoil the surprise, but it's really about what she has a feel for, musically.'

'You seem to know a lot about these things,' said Rose adoringly.

'I studied music for three years. I'm only working here – ' she made a face at Sean '– till I can get some regular engagements.'

'What do you play?'

'Electric guitar. I studied the cello for three years, but I packed it in. My father wasn't best pleased.'

The beauty of her daughter and her daughter's talents grew with every second. In a hushed voice Rose asked, 'Did you go to university and everything?'

Sean made a derisive noise in his throat and went through a door into the rear of the premises.

'Dublin,' said Hannah. She glanced at the door to make sure Sean was not on his way back. 'I suppose,' she said quietly, 'if she didn't like what you chose, we could always change it for you.'

'What?' Rose had been lost in a daydream of universities, an orchestra, a daughter becoming a famous soloist.

'The instrument. We could change it if—'

'Oh, yes. Yes, right. D'you know, my mother came from Dublin.'

'Did she. It's really beautiful. I'd love to go back sometime, but my boyfriend doesn't like it.'

Bit by bit the picture was being added to. A boyfriend, now. Rose wondered what he would be like. 'You mustn't let him tie you down,' she urged. 'You're only young, you've got all your life ahead of you.'

Hannah laughed. 'You sound like my mother.'

Rose had to laugh back. 'I suppose I'm a bit like you, trying to sort out people's lives for them.' She nodded towards the door at the back. 'That young man who works with you—'

'I work with him, rather. He's the manager here. I'm only part-time.'

'Oh. You seemed to know . . . well, so much more than him.'

'Only in some things. But I swear I'll get those two together this evening somehow.'

'I'll ask for an update when I come back tomorrow, then?'

'Yes. Are you going to bring your daughter with you?'

It was such a crazy question, but there was no way the girl could know how crazy. 'I might do,' said Rose. 'I don't know yet.'

'Because if you think she'd be interested in a cello, say, I've got my old one at home, and I've been thinking of selling it.' She lowered her voice. 'It's a lot better than that one in the window there. I'm not supposed to tell you this, but the neck on that one has just started to warp a bit.'

'I'd love to see your cello. You could play it for me.'

'If I can still remember how. But it's got a lovely sound, and it's perfect for someone who's learning. Look, I'll give you my address. I'll be in here tomorrow morning anyway, but if you don't turn up I won't be upset, okay?'

'Okay,' said Rose. Her heart pounded as she asked, 'By the way, what's your name?'

'Sarah.'

Rose could hardly have expected it would still be Hannah. But she felt a twinge of sadness. She would have to get used to thinking of her daughter in a different way, almost as a different person. She made herself say, 'Sarah, that's a nice name.'

'Sarah Levison, 104 Primrose Park Crescent.'

Rose took the scribbled note, not telling her how unnecessary it was: the address was written on her heart.

Vinnie Marshall had had only twenty minutes of real joy after his uncle's death. He had taken over the Durkin office, swivelled round a dozen times in the chair by the big desk, and decided that a lot of the junk on the shelves would have to go. The desk itself was a quarter of a century old. It was time to have a new one – sliding drawers, computer on a ledge at the side, a stack of trays for things awaiting his signature. A new carpet was essential. And he was none too keen on being overlooked every minute by June. She was getting a bit long in the tooth, as well. It shouldn't be too difficult to find someone younger and a bit livelier to replace her.

First thing would be to dictate a memo to let the staff know what was going on. And they should all be notified that he would be parking in his Uncle Granville's spot from now on.

He lit a cigar. Within a few seconds June was in, pretending to rearrange the pending tray, but anxious to come out with it: 'Mr Durkin didn't like people smoking in his office.'

'He's hardly going to smell it from the morgue, is he?'

Her lips tightened. And that was when she went to the filing cabinet in the corner, tugged open the lower drawer, and took out a folder embossed with the name of a law firm and some sort of crown and leaf design. She opened it on the desk in front of him. 'I think you ought to read that.'

He read it; and the dream collapsed.

His uncle, his bloody double-crossing pervert of an uncle, had already done what he'd been mumbling about. He hadn't wasted any time: his will had been altered, just the way he had hinted.

A dozen times that day and again the next morning Vinnie tried phoning Carol Johnson at the number in his uncle's address book. There was no reply. Did she have somewhere else to live, or did she work long hours somewhere?

He couldn't sit still. The refusal of anyone to answer the phone was driving him mad. Best to march up to her house and have it all out face to face. He had been round there that once before, and knew his way well enough. Maybe she didn't want to answer the phone because she was too busy planning what to do with all the money that filthy old wanker had left her.

Nor did she or anyone else answer the door. The house was shut and silent. He went back to start phoning again. It was not until his fifth attempt that someone lifted the receiver.

He said, 'I want to speak to Carol Johnson.'

'You're talking to her.' She sounded nervy and suspicious at once.

'My name's Vincent Marshall.' He kept his voice as low and menacing as possible. 'I believe you were a friend of my Uncle Granville.'

'What's it got to do with you?'

'I think you'll find it's got a lot to do with me. I think we need to talk.'

'What about?' She sounded even more edgy. 'I've got nowt to say.'

'No, but I have.' He had meant to keep it level and reasonable for as long as possible, but he couldn't hold it in. 'I saw you with my uncle. I saw what you were doing to get round him. And I want you to know you're not getting a penny of his money. Not one. Look, I can either come round to your house or you can come here to the office.'

'I'm not doing neither, so you can piss off.'

She slammed the phone down just as Claudia lounged past June and posed herself in the office doorway, in the sort of attitude she must have seen in one of the glossy magazines she was always leaving in Vinnie's car. She wouldn't be too pleased if she knew he was broke – all his plans and boasts beyond reach.

Into the phone he said brightly, 'Yes, that's fine. I'll come to you then. Bye.' He winked at Claudia. 'Just a customer.'

'Really? What are you sweating for, then?'

Sooner or later he was going to have to tell her. But right now there was something else that needed doing.

'I'd better chase this character up,' he said. 'Look, I'll drop you at our usual place and pick you up right after. Shouldn't take more than twenty minutes or so.' He made it as brusque and businesslike as he could, to silence any arguments she might be dreaming up.

Mr Ernest Chubb had little comfort to offer. He was a drab little man with rimless spectacles and a lifeless voice which told of years of practice reciting long legal paragraphs and soberly telling people the worst. As executor of Mr Granville Durkin's will he could assure Mr Marshall that he and his client had talked the matter over at some length, and the terms of the will were exactly what Mr Marshall's uncle had wanted. He began intoning one particular paragraph with all the rhythm and solemnity of a psalm. 'Twenty thousand pounds to be left to Miss Emma Johnson and the residue of my estate to her mother Miss Carol Johnson and failing that to my nephew Vincent Marshall.' Mr Chubb peered over the top of his glasses. As if to turn the knife in the wound he said very clearly and carefully: 'The net estate is valued at two and a half million.'

'What does "failing that" mean?'

'Say she were to die or something – but that's hardly likely, her being a young woman. It's just a formality really.'

Vinnie's brain was racing. 'What if they found out she was the one who murdered him?'

'Then obviously she would not inherit.' Mr Chubb looked mildly reproachful. 'There really has been no suspicion of that, so far as I am aware.' He began tidying up the deeds and sliding them neatly back into their folder. 'Realistically, if you think your uncle's will is unreasonable, you can appeal under the 1975 Family Inheritance Act and take it to court.

But I wouldn't hold out much hope. It's not as though you were a child of the deceased.'

Vinnie went out, his mind seething with possibilities and hatred. Carol Johnson wasn't going to get away with this. And that Miss Emma Johnson – the one June had said, only a few days ago, his uncle doted on . . . What the hell would a brat like that do with twenty thousand?

There was no way either of them was going to get a penny.

Joyce had just finished putting clingfilm over her dad's dinner and was reaching for her coat when there was a tap at the door. In her high chair, Michelle let out a squeak; and then another one as her father came in. He kissed Joyce awkwardly. 'Job's finished, so Harry said I could go early. I didn't know if you'd be at the Leisure Centre.'

There was no time to tell him all their problems right now. Joyce was buttoning up her coat when she saw the girl edging into the room behind Steve.

Quickly he said, 'You remember Lisa from my digs in Blackpool?'

'Hello,' said Lisa.

They were both of them nervous. Steve was rabbiting on, 'I gave her and her little boy a lift over here. She was supposed to be staying with her mate in Keighley, but—'

'I think she must have gone away, because there was nobody there.'

Joyce began to suspect a good reason for Steve hoping that she would have been at the Leisure Centre, out of the way.

'We were wondering,' he said, 'well, *I* was wondering if she could stay at yours just till her friend comes back.'

Under my own roof, thought Joyce. Probably been at it ever since she left that Blackpool guest-house, and now wanted to do it right here under her own roof.

'No, she bloody can't. What d'you think this is? Don't you

think I've got enough on my hands with the kids and my dad to see to? I think it's about time somebody did summat for me for a change.'

'She did plenty for us in Blackpool.'

Lisa was moving back out of the room. 'It's all right, Steve.'

'Yes.' Joyce looked Steve straight in the eye. 'I just wish she hadn't bothered.'

'What's that supposed to mean?'

'Nothing.'

'Yes, well, you're not the only one that wishes they could turn the clock back, Joyce.'

There was a loud knocking at the front door. Lisa was already there, about to open it.

'Joyce Webster?'

'No, I'm . . . er . . .'

Joyce went out into the hall, to be confronted by a burly man with a carefully serious face and a voice booming with authority.

'Detective Constable Barstow,' he said. 'We're investigating the murder of George Ferguson. We wondered if you'd mind coming down to the police station to answer a couple of questions.'

Steve was at her shoulder. 'What's all this about?'

Joyce, stunned, thought of slamming the door in the detective's face. What the hell did she have to answer for? But if she didn't go along with them, they'd surely find a way of coming for her again. She didn't want a scene; not right here, on her own doorstep.

High time for Steve to do his bit for his family. She said, 'You'd better take that dinner to me dad's, and pick up the kids from school.'

'But I—'

'Sorry if it spoils your plans for the day.'

She went out to the waiting police car.

DCI Newall was impatient. She got the impression that

he'd been asking a lot of people the same questions, and was getting hoarse, and still getting no suitable answers.

'Sorry to drag you down here, Mrs Webster.' He wasn't the least bit sorry. 'But perhaps you'll be good enough to tell me where you were at the time of George Ferguson's death.'

'I don't know what time he died, because I wasn't there.'

'To save us all a lot of trouble, perhaps you can tell us where you *were* on Thursday evening between eight and nine-thirty?'

'Thursday? I was at the Leisure Centre, having words with Mrs Minkin. She'll tell you that.'

'Having words?' he echoed.

'About a misunderstanding.'

'And what time would you have left that meeting?' When Joyce did not reply, he went on, 'And would your way home by any chance have passed the Klensit cleaning company offices – George Ferguson's office?'

'It's my usual route. I didn't even notice where I was going, it was so much – well, as I say, routine.'

'A bit more than routine that night? After what George Ferguson had just done to you and your company? And your family?'

'All right,' blazed Joyce. 'Dead right, so I wanted him dead. And if I'd had the guts to kill him I'd be the first to own up. But I've got three grandkids to look after, I can't afford twenty years in jail.'

'Well, I suggest you think very carefully about your movements between the times I've mentioned.'

'Why pick on me? I didn't kill him.'

'You blamed the man for your daughter's death, didn't you?' Newall was very quiet, and all the more deadly because of it. 'When did Gina die, last year?'

'You know bloody well when she died.'

'And how many times do you think about her?'

'Every day.'

'Every day. Every time you look at her children, every time you see a photograph?'

It was no use telling a man like this that you didn't need a photograph to bring Gina back. Gina was inside, she would never go away, and Joyce didn't want her to. She was here with her all the time. A copper like Newall would never come within a million miles of understanding that, feeling it, always *feeling* her near.

He was trying a sympathetic tack now, but might as well have been reading a death sentence. 'George Ferguson robbed you of your daughter. He ripped her life from you, and all you were left with was a great gaping hole, and nothing or no one could fill it. So you threw yourself into that cleaning company, you worked like nobody had ever worked before. You were the best. But then, as if the man hasn't taken enough from you, he tries to wheedle his way into your company and you fought back with everything you'd got, till one day you turn up to work and you're told he's won. He's taken your contract, just like he took Gina's life. And something inside you snapped, and who'd blame you? The man's evil, the man's a bastard, the man deserved to die, didn't he? Didn't he, Joyce?'

Tears were streaming down her face. 'Yes. Oh, yes. But I didn't kill him.' It was no good; she had to tell him the truth; had to give up all her secrets to this stony-faced swine who wouldn't quit badgering her until he got what he wanted. She gave in. 'I dropped the kids off for an hour at Brenda's. Then I went to Gina's grave.'

He sat back, shaken. 'At nine o'clock at night? In the dark?'

'I had to. I had to tell her something. Had to make my peace with her.'

'And did anybody see you there? Did you talk to anyone?'

'No. I was by myself. There might have been people there, I don't know.'

'Well, that's very helpful,' said Newall sarcastically.

DS Hoyle shifted uneasily on her chair, a couple of feet back from the DCI. 'Why did you have to go to the grave?' It was the first time she had joined in the questioning, and she sounded unexpectedly gentle. 'What did you have to tell her that was so important?'

Joyce hedged. 'That I loved her. You see, I never told her that; I can't remember ever saying it.'

Newall's temper snapped. 'So you decided to go that night in the pitch black to the cemetery to tell her you loved her—'

'And other things.'

'What other things? Why didn't you wait till morning? Why didn't you wait till the kids were at school? Why drag them round to somebody else's house and leave them there when they should have been in bed? I'll tell you why, Joyce. Because you decided you'd had enough. You'd decided that—'

'I'd betrayed her.' She might as well get it over with. 'I didn't mean to, it just happened. I was happy for the first time since she'd gone. I was meself again. I was Joyce. One minute I was laughing, and the next I was kissing him – kissing her husband, my son-in-law. I don't know how it happened. It just did. And I needed to tell Gina. I needed her to forgive me.'

She let the tears run freely. Newall looked at Hoyle; and the young woman got up and came to put an arm round Joyce's shoulders.

There were no further questions. She was still mopping her eyes when they went out to the outer office, where the desk sergeant was trying to calm Steve down.

'You've had her in there long enough. I want to see her. I've got to talk to her.'

'Look, sir, if you want to wait, that's fine. I'll let them know you're here.'

'I don't understand why she's in there. For Christ's sake,

what's she done?' He looked round to see the two women approaching. 'Joyce, are you all right?'

'Where're the kids? You haven't left them with *her*, have you?'

'Next-door neighbour's looking after them.'

'Take me home, will you?'

Steve said, 'You'd better know right away. Your dad's been taken into hospital.'

13

Carol was plaiting Emma's hair. Rose, just back from Manchester off the afternoon train, watched with a wistful smile. She hadn't ever had the chance of looking after her daughter at that age; but at least there was a chance of making up for lost time now. Carol had been listening to the story while she got Emma ready to go out to a party, but it had been interrupted by Anita shambling into the kitchen and demanding everybody else's attention. She hadn't slept a wink last night, and it had been a dreadful day. Tugging the cork out of a bottle of sherry, she popped two painkillers in her mouth and poured a large glassful of the sherry to wash them down.

Carol eyed the bottle accusingly. 'I thought you had no money? You owe me two weeks' rent.'

'It were only two ninety-nine,' Anita whined. 'I found some change in my jacket lining. I don't think you realise what it's like to have pain all over your body.'

Rose came out of her snug daydream. 'You're not supposed to have booze when you're taking pills. It'll knock you out.'

'That's what I'm hoping. I keep seeing George's face. That's why I didn't sleep a wink last night.'

'Now that he's dead,' said Rose thoughtfully, 'maybe we should go see Minkin again.'

'Nowt's changed. She'll already be getting somebody else in to do the job.' Carol stood back and decided Emma looked presentable enough. She picked up the school bag. 'There y'are. Now, you've got your swimming costume, and Melanie's present's in there. I'll come for you about eight o'clock, right?'

'Melanie's mum said she'd drop me off.'

'You're sure?'

A horn beeped outside. Emma grabbed her things. At the door she looked back at her mother. 'You'll be here when I get back, won't you?'

''Course I will. Go on, enjoy yourself. Don't forget to put your armbands on, and don't go in the deep end.'

When Emma was well on her way, Rose persuaded Anita that a long soak in a hot bath would do her good. At least it got her out of the way, and spared them the continuous drone of her voice. Carol waited until she heard the bath water stop running, and reached for Anita's sherry bottle. Anita owed her a few glasses.

The evening was wearing on when it struck them that Anita hadn't come down to resume her tales of woe; and they hadn't heard the bath water running away. Rose went up, and was back in ten minutes.

'Silly cow were asleep in the bath. I've put her in your bed. I'll sleep in the boxroom tonight.'

'It's a bloody good job I haven't got a feller in it.'

Carol took another swig of the sherry. It struck her that she hadn't had a shag in nearly eight months. She had gone from shagging twenty men a night to living like a nun. Maybe if she tried to go back to the old routine she'd find she couldn't even pull a trick any more.

'Don't you ever miss being on the Lane?' she asked.

'Oh, ay. Like I miss having a hole in me head.'

'We were good, though, weren't we? I mean, we knew what we were doing.'

Rose pursed her lips in wry recollection. 'Remember Johnny One-leg?'

'Liked you to stick a finger up his bum.'

'Stopped him from falling over.' Rose's mirth faded. 'But we can learn to do summat else.'

There were only those two things Carol could feel she had been good at: hustling and cleaning. Now she couldn't do either. Last night, in that cell, she had been visited by Newall. He just walked in, strip bollock naked, and stood there with a hard-on the size of Blackpool Tower. She had just got off her bed, climbed on him, wrapped her legs round him, and thought she had gone to heaven. Then there was a hell of a bang, the door of the cell opened, and a sow of a policewoman stood there with breakfast on a tray. It had all been a dream.

She was shaken by another banging on the door. Only this time it was real. Somebody had pressed his face against the glass panel and was thumping the woodwork. Carol headed for the hall, then stopped herself in the living-room doorway.

He must have caught the shadow of movement. 'I want to speak to Carol Johnson.'

She recognised the voice from that phone call. 'Well, you can't. She's out.'

'Open this bloody door, or I'll kick it in.'

Rose squeezed past and silently waved Carol back into the room. She went to the front door, made sure the chain was on, and opened it a crack. 'Have you got a screw loose, or something? She's not here. My boyfriend's upstairs trying to sleep. If you wake him he'll kick your head in. So piss off.' She slammed the door and bolted it.

'You'll be sorry, I'm telling you. You'll be bloody sorry.'

Vinnie was turning away, tight-lipped and still not sure whether he ought not to have a go at that door and smash his way in, when an old banger drew up by the opposite kerb. Kids' voices rose high above the stuttering of the engine, suddenly louder as the far passenger door opened to let one of them out.

''Bye, Emma.'

'Ta-ra.'

The car coughed and racketed away, leaving the little girl looking gravely to the right and the left. Obviously she had had her green cross code drummed into her. Just as she was about to set off across the road towards her own house, Vinnie stepped out to meet her.

'Hiya. You must be Emma.' Her father, he thought, must have been black.

The excitement left over from the party faded. 'Are you a copper? Have you come to get my mum again?'

It was a gift. He seized it. 'It's all right. Nothing to worry about. She's at the police station, she's sent me to pick you up.'

He had been driving for five minutes before Emma began to fret. 'My mum says I shouldn't get in cars with strange men.'

'Does she, now? But you want to see her again, don't you?' He turned the Porsche into a quiet side street and punched a number on his carphone.

'Yes? Hello?'

'There's your mum,' said Vinnie. 'Just say something to her.'

'Mum, it's me.'

'Where've you got to? Mrs Clark said she'd dropped you, and—'

'I'm with this man . . .'

Vinnie took the receiver out of its holder and clicked it on to hand-held. Very slowly and deliberately he said, 'Be at the canal, down by the lock, next to Radium Street, in half an hour. On your own. No funny business, if you want to see your daughter again. On your own, get it? And then we can talk business.'

'You touch her,' the woman was screaming, 'and you're dead, d'you hear? Dead.'

Emma was crying as he hung up.

*   *   *

Newall slowed as they neared the slope down to the canal. In the seat beside him Carol had been raving hysterically. In the back, Rose Garrity was almost as steamed up.

'He must be the one who did it,' Carol babbled. 'He must have followed Curly to my place and killed him 'cos he'd found out about the will.'

'And if he killed Curly,' said Rose, 'he must have killed Ferguson to frame you.'

'To make it look like I did it.'

'That's right. And if he killed Curly and Ferguson, he must have his eye on you next.'

'Shut up,' Newall said. He leaned towards his radio control. 'Just the two of you, right? Silent approach, no lights. Park just past the bridge and gaze into each other's eyes if you have to.' He turned to Carol. 'Did he say he was armed – a knife, a gun, anything?'

'Oh, God. Emma . . .' Carol looked back over her shoulder. 'Pray.'

'Y'what?'

'For our Emma. Go on, you're a Catholic, you must know—'

'I can't,' Rose protested. 'I haven't done it for—'

'Please.'

'Hail Mary full of Grace, the Lord is with thee. Er . . . blessed art thou amongst women, and—'

'Listen.' Newall drew up behind a car parked without lights under the shadow of the bridge and craned his neck back towards Rose as well. 'Make sure she stays in the car, will you?'

'I'm coming with you.' Carol tried to open her door.

'No, you're not. You're too involved, you'll blow it.'

Rose came round to the front, settling herself beside Carol and keeping a hand ready to grab her if she made a dash for it.

Newall moved along to the dark shape of the other car and beckoned DS Hoyle to get out. When she was on the pavement he took her arm and they began walking down to the canal and along towards the lock. He was impatient to have it finished: to get his hands on Vincent Marshall and shake him till every bone rattled. But he had to force himself to keep their pace slow and dreamy. He made a pretence of nuzzling Hoyle's neck, and heard her stifle a protest – or maybe it was a laugh. They swayed to and fro; stopped once, even though it seemed to last an hour; then sauntered on closer to the lock and the dark mouth of a small tunnel under the arches.

Hoyle made a little moaning sound. It was an authentic lover's sigh; but she was drawing his attention to two figures not far from the tunnel. A man was walking hand in hand with a small child.

Even now Newall and Hoyle kept their slow, dreamy pace, speeding it up only just enough to be sure of gaining on the two.

Marshall glanced back. Newall and Hoyle veered in closer to the steep bank and the brick column of an arch. Then Newall could restrain himself no longer. There were only a few yards to cover.

'Go for it!'

He launched himself at Marshall while Hoyle grabbed Emma, teetering for a moment on the towpath above the water. Marshall swung a vicious punch into Newall's stomach, ducked, and began to run towards the tunnel. He was nearly there when DC Barstow dropped from the bank above, hurling him against the brickwork and getting a hand up his back.

'All right, sir. Got him.'

'Good. Get him down to the station.' He nodded to Hoyle, no longer sentimental. 'Go with them. Book him for the abduction of the kid, and suspicion of the Durkin murder.'

She was reluctant to let go of Emma. 'But someone ought to—'

'I'll see to it.' Newall took Emma's hand. Delivering her personally to her mother was a moment he very much fancied.

Abruptly Carol erupted from the tunnel mouth, with Rose in hot pursuit. Stupid bitch – she would never do anything the way he wanted it, could have mucked up the whole situation.

'Emma!'

The little girl dragged herself out of Newall's grasp and hurled herself at her mother.

'He didn't touch you, did he?' Carol was sobbing. 'He didn't hurt you?'

'No.'

Carol raised her eyes to the yellow glow of the night sky. 'Oh, Jesus, thank you.'

'I did have something to do with it as well, you know,' said Newall dourly.

He drove her and Rose and Emma back to the house, waited to see if Carol was going to offer tearful thanks and suggest getting together tomorrow or the next day, or anything; and then went on to the station to deal with Vinnie Marshall. He was in the mood for a showdown with that seedy layabout.

'We've spoken to your uncle's secretary. She tells us that you and your uncle had a violent row the morning Granville Durkin was killed, and later that day she said you came back to the factory specifically to ask about the woman he was seeing. So what did you do, Vincent? Drive to her house, find the two of them together? And continue the row you'd been having that morning?'

'No, you've got it all wrong. It wasn't—'

'And then when your uncle told you he'd changed his will, you took a knife and cut his throat.'

'No. That's crazy.'

'And Carol Johnson saw it, didn't she? But you threatened to kill her kid if she went to the police. Or did you make a deal with her? Promise to split the money if she kept her trap shut?

What went wrong, Vincent – wouldn't she play along, did she step out of line? Who put the body in the car – both of you? And whose idea was it to kill George Ferguson as well?'

Sweat was dribbling into Marshall's left eye. He dabbed at it, shaking his head helplessly. 'I don't know what the hell you're talking about. All right, I did go to the house. I was going to talk to her, but I saw my uncle's car there, and . . . well, I wanted to see what she was like, so . . .' He was looking embarrassed. More embarrassed than frightened.

'So?' Newall prompted.

'Well . . . I got an angle on the window. Looked in. And I saw her wearing these black stockings, walking up and down while he was having a wank.'

'And you just stood there and watched.'

'Yeh,' Vinnie muttered.

'And you were angry. This slut was going to get everything, all the things you'd been waiting for.' Newall felt sick at the thought of Carol parading up and down. Of course he had known about it, she had made no secret of it. But still it turned his stomach, and the thought of this little sod peeping and being turned on by it . . .

Vinnie Marshall said, 'Look, Carol Johnson killed my uncle. I tell you, that's why she wouldn't open the door to me, wouldn't talk to me. She found out about the money and she wanted him dead.'

Newall offered a fifteen-minute break. Marshall looked relieved. But it wasn't for his benefit. Newall wanted Carol in here, to set the two of them contradicting each other, cheating and lying and yet out of all that throwing up the truth. The moment she arrived he wheeled her into the interview room.

She didn't hesitate. Before Newall or Barstow could catch her she had thrown herself at Marshall, spitting venom, jabbing wildly at his face. 'You touch my daughter again and I'll kill yer. Get that, you dirty little—'

'Get her off me! For Christ's sake—'

'You frigging bastard, I'll claw your bleeding eyes out.'

By sheer brute force Barstow got Carol away and into a corner.

Vinnie stared, awestruck. 'Who the hell is *she*? Bitch from hell, what's she doing here?'

'This is Carol Johnson,' said Newall. 'As if you didn't know.'

Vinnie's stare became even more incredulous. 'No, it isn't. The woman I saw in that room was white.'

14

The door opened and Hannah was there, smiling. No, not Hannah; Rose would have to get used to thinking of her as Sarah; until maybe when they were closer and the truth was out, Sarah might even like to go back to being Hannah.

'Come in.'

Rose tried not to look too obviously impressed by the floral designs on the flocked wallpaper, and the small crystal chandeliers on the stairs and the first-floor landing. She followed Sarah along the rich pile of the landing carpet, past a large painting of a country scene that was probably by somebody famous, though she hadn't a clue who it might be.

'You haven't brought your daughter, then?'

'Er, no. I haven't got round to telling her yet. I mean, I haven't made my mind up.'

'Yes, it's a big decision to make.' Sarah was so friendly and understanding, so well brought up, it made Rose's heart miss a beat. 'The cello might not be her instrument, and it's a lot of money to spend.' She pushed the bedroom door open. 'Sorry about the mess.'

To Rose it didn't look a mess. A blouse flung casually across the back of a chair looked expensive. There might be a scattering of magazines not tidied up for some days; but they were posh magazines.

And the books on the shelves were leaning all over the place, but they looked like pricey books, and there were hundreds of them.

'Have you read all them?'

'Some of them.' Sarah moved a chair aside and opened the cello case propped against the wall. 'Here we are. Would you like me to play it for you?'

Rose had been longing for this. She moved out of the way as Sarah settled herself on the chair and set the instrument's spike into an Indian rug at her feet. Unsure whether to remain standing or to perch on the edge of the bed, Rose decided she would be less in the way if she sat in the window alcove.

Sarah began to play. It was clear at once that she loved the music and was happy for any excuse to sink herself in it, letting herself be carried along by it. She had a beautiful, smooth right arm; and it moved smoothly and confidently to guide the bow across the strings. The melody that throbbed into the room was slow, sighing and sad, yet at the same time so lovely in its swoops and yearning that you wanted it never to stop.

When the last note vibrated away, tears were trickling down Rose's cheeks.

Sarah, wiping her own eyes, smiled. 'You're as bad as me.'

'That was the loveliest thing I've ever heard. Did you just make it up?'

'I'm not that clever. It's called *The Swan*, from Saint-Saens' *Carnival of the Animals*. It makes me cry every time.'

'Can I just have a hold of it?'

It was really Sarah she wanted to hold. There was a moment when they brushed together as Sarah got out of the chair to make room for her, and put an arm right round her to adjust the angle of the cello.

'Just hold the bow lightly at the heel. That's it.'

'Your mother must be very proud of you,' said Rose; and silently added: *Oh, if you only knew how much*.

'It's my dad who really talked me into playing the cello. He's the musical one: he plays the violin. My brother Robbie takes after mum, they're both into the sciences.'

'It's funny you taking after your dad – ' it came out without her planning ' – when he's not . . . well, not your blood.'

Sarah was taken aback. 'Sorry?'

Rose had got this far. She simply had to go on. 'I'm sure when we met yesterday, you said something about being adopted.'

'No, why would I say that?'

'Because . . . well, maybe they just haven't told you.'

'Told me what?' Sarah was beginning to look cross. 'I'm not adopted. I had an older sister who was, but she ran away from home when she was twelve. They brought her back, but she ran away again. I think she ended up in a children's home in Sheffield.'

Rose felt dizzy. She let Sarah take the cello away from her, and whispered, 'What was her name?'

'Hannah.'

The beautiful girl was drifting away into a haze, slipping away from Rose's grasp like the cello's dying melody. A few more minutes and Sarah and the instrument and this lovely room wouldn't exist at all. 'No,' said Rose. 'Oh, no. Please God, no.'

'Are you all right? Can I get you something?'

Rose struggled to sort out the words in the right order. 'My daughter. I'm Hannah's mother. They took her off me when she were two months old. I haven't seen her since. I thought you were her, that's why I followed you yesterday. I wanted her to be you. I'd have given anything for her to be you.'

Tears blurred into Sarah's eyes. 'Oh, Lor'. I'm sorry. I'm so sorry. Do you want to speak to my mother? She'll be home soon.'

It was the last thing Rose could face right now. All she had wanted was to see her daughter, to hold her . . .

'I'm sorry,' said Sarah again. She had been saying that a lot when they first met, and Rose had told her off like a mother telling off her own daughter.

Only now they were neither mother nor daughter.

* * *

Tracy had left Alfie's in a better mood than when she had got there. All that boring bloody fumbling and cack-handed shagging had been worth it in the end. She had come away not just with some nice juicy promises but with a rock the rest of them would be ready to fight for – or drop their knickers as many times as anyone asked.

She swaggered into The Hustlers' Arms. Tula might have been waiting there specially to cut her down to size. 'Hey, I've just heard your ponce is getting out next week.'

Tula was about Tracy's size, but dark and with a mole on her left cheek. Some men were turned on by it. Others tried not to look at it. She was about the age Tracy had been when she started on the Lane; and just as cocky.

'I haven't got a ponce,' said Tracy. 'Who told you that?'

'Her who hangs out down bottom end. She said his name's Dez, and he's gonna mark yer.'

Once the thought of Dez on the loose would have terrified Tracy. Now he just didn't seem to matter. One move from Dez, and she'd call on Alfie. No bloody good in bed, but deadly out on the streets.

Tula looked disappointed that her threat hadn't scored. Switching to the friendly approach, she asked, 'Have yer got any wash?'

'Three grams.'

'You're joking. Who off?'

'This bloke I do,' said Tracy airily. 'He's that loaded, he wipes his bum with tenners. I'm off to Belgium soon to pick up some golf balls for him.'

'Tell him I'll pick up his balls any time he likes.'

Across the bar she saw Rabbit looking at her. And scowling at Tula. He came round, wasting no time. 'Piss off, you.'

'Just a minute,' said Tracy. 'I was talking to her.'

'She's off her brain, don't tell her nothing.'

Tula looked as if she might let fly with a comeback; but she wasn't up to it. Not yet. She slunk away.

'You're paranoid,' said Tracy.

'I'm telling you, I've seen her out there grovelling in the gutter, looking for a lost bit.'

Tracy couldn't resist it. She opened her hand to show him Alfie's advance payment. Rabbit was gobsmacked. 'Jesus! Is that a rock or a bollock?'

She had got over the loathing she had once felt for the little squirt. Little he might be in some ways, but not as little as Alfie in other ways. Rabbit wasn't called Rabbit just because of that twitchy little nose of his.

'How about you finish your drink,' she suggested, 'and we'll go back to mine and have a bit of both?'

As they left the pub, she saw Tula leaning into the open window of a car. Maybe chatting up a punter. But for some reason Tula glanced back, grinned spitefully, and then looked away. What was really cheering was the sight of Colette coming up the Lane. All the better because Colette was certainly not pleased to see her with Rabbit, least of all when Tracy made a big show of putting her arm round him.

Colette stopped in front of them. Ignoring Tracy, she snapped at Rabbit, 'Are yer live?'

'No – but *she* is,' he sniggered, pinching Tracy's arm. 'Chill out, love. If you want some stuff, ring Dean.'

Colette's eyes made it clear enough that she did want some. Reluctantly she turned her attention to Tracy. 'Are you coming back for a pipe?'

'No. I'm going back to his.'

She felt Rabbit twitch. He hadn't expected this. As they lurched past Colette, still arm in arm, he said, 'What's going on with that one? You look like a couple of cats ready to go at one another.'

'She's going to hate me,' said Tracy. 'I'll see to that.'

It had been sheer impulse that had led her to change her mind about going back to the house. There would be no peace there if Colette decided to pester them for crack or deliberately break up their afternoon. Let her guess, let her imagine what she liked and get her knickers in a twist over it. But when they approached Rabbit's place Tracy wasn't sure she'd made the right decision. He had never brought her here before; and it was one hell of a shock.

From the outside the building looked like a doss-house. One broken window had been covered with hardboard, and the door was covered with graffiti. When Rabbit shoved the door open, it screeched on its hinges, and a smell came out that was made up of a dozen different things – none of them fragrant. Opening straight off the bare hall was a room without a door and without a scrap of furniture. There were five or six people sprawled about the floor, smoking various pipes. An empty butane gas cylinder was propped against one wall, a young black man with his eyes shut against another. A girl who Tracy had seen a few times on the Lane was scraping the inside of a used Vittel bottle with a knife to recycle the residue and have another hit.

'It's a dump,' said Tracy, dismayed.

A voice from under the boarded-up window grumbled: 'I thought yer were the pigs. Why don't you shout that you're comin' in?'

''Cos it's my house, Danny, that's why,' Rabbit snarled back. 'It's not a crackhouse.'

He led Tracy along the hall and up bare, creaking stairs. His own room was not much better than the shambles down below, but at least it had a threadbare rug and a bed. A thin curtain in the last stages of falling to bits hung from a string above the window.

'It's a dump,' Tracy said again.

'Come on. We're all right up here.'

He was impatient to take the rock off her and put it in a chipped glass ashtray, cutting a piece off while Tracy opened her bag and took out the Vittel bottle and her lighter.

It took less than ten minutes for the shabby room to take on new colours. And Rabbit was part of a glowing dream, and she was borne up on clouds and went floating about the room.

There was a lot of music singing in her ears. Until it got a bit harsh, and she felt herself turning over uncomfortably on the hard bed. Somewhere far under the bed there was a crash like a door being forced open. And somebody was shouting, and there were a few screams, and feet pounding up the stairs.

'We're busted,' yelled a faraway voice. 'Shite, half the frigging force . . .'

Tracy sat up as the dream turned nasty. Instinctively she put her thumb in her mouth. The curtain was flapping in a breeze, and vaguely she knew that Rabbit must have climbed out and made his getaway – a getaway from the police officer who stood above her bed and told her it was time to move and accompany him to the station.

Even then she could not get herself to concentrate. She was still too woozy to understand exactly what they were saying to her about that crack they'd helped themselves to. And there were other things. Somebody seemed to have shopped her. She had a vague vision of Tula leaning into a car, and the man across the desk in the interview room could have been the same man. Or was that just another of those faces from her sickening dreams, going more and more sour? Unwin, he called himself. Not that she much cared. She wasn't going to be shacking up with him now or any other time.

'You're not leaving this station,' he was saying, 'until you tell us who gave you that much crack.'

'Santa Claus.'

'We've heard a rumour that it's on account. Somebody's got a job lined up for you.'

'Such as?'

'Look. Maybe it's not that.' Unwin switched tactics. 'Could be that you're dealing. Nobody has that much stuff unless they're dealing. You'll get five years for this, love.'

'Prove it. Show me one person I've done business with.'

'No problem. We can wheel in half a dozen.'

That was a load of bollocks. She knew it, and through the haze tried to hold on to it.

The man beside Unwin said, 'Hang on a minute. You're not stupid, are you, Tracy? D'you know what that stuff does to you? It's dead simple: it kills. It's killing the Lane and before long it'll kill you. How long have you been smoking? We can help you try and get off it. All we want to know is who gave it to you. We're not interested in busting you, love, all we want to know is who gave you the crack.'

'And you can walk away,' Unwin agreed. 'Are you gonna tell us?'

Of all the hateful faces swimming in and out of her mind, there was one Tracy wanted to fasten on. Love, and hate, and everything else that happened when you had a lifter – it all added up to one thing.

She wondered what the whip would feel like across her naked back.

She told them.

Half an hour later the second man, Stevenson, escorted her down to the corridor to another interview room.

Colette was standing there, refusing to sit down. A uniformed policewoman stood close to her left shoulder. Unwin was there, sitting down, looking hopefully from the newcomer to Tracy. He let them glare at each other for a good half-minute before he said to Tracy, 'Is this who sold you the crack?'

'Yes.'

Colette threw herself forward. 'You bitch.' But the policewoman had been ready for this, and got her in an armlock that wrenched her back against the wall.

'Mm,' said Unwin. He leafed through a batch of police records in front of him. 'Hannah Levison – that's right, isn't it?'

'Clever, aren't yer.'

'Soliciting,' recited Unwin. 'Child sex rings, actual bodily harm, shoplifting . . .'

'You've got that wrong. I'm sure I was *Anna* Levison when I got done for shoplifting. Aw, no, I remember now.' She was sneering at them while glaring at Tracy. 'That were the sauna bust, and after that I changed me name to Colette.' She tried to hold out her left arm with its homemade tattoo, but had it clutched by the policewoman as if she had been brandishing a lethal weapon. 'That's a C, look. And that's an H for me.'

'How old are you?'

'Twenty-four.' Colette tried a seductive smile. 'Look, I know I've done loads wrong, but I didn't sell Tracy the crack. You've got it wrong. She's just saying that to get me done.' She suddenly shrieked it in Tracy's face. '*Aren't* you, you bitch?'

Tracy said, '*Now* do you hate me enough?'

15

Tracy let herself thankfully back into the house. She was dying for a lifter, but didn't fancy risking any contacts right now. No telling who they might have set to watch her and check out on her story; or tap her phone. She rooted in a drawer to see if Colette had left anything, but there wasn't a sign.

From somewhere down below came a hoarse noise, like an airlock or something in the pipes. Tracy was all set to ignore it until the up and down moaning began to sound like a human voice, followed by some heavy thumps and then what she was sure was Anita, panting and puffing. Warily she went back downstairs, and approached the door at the head of the cellar steps. Stooping, she could see across the cellar floor. There was one hell of a mess on it. The cross which Bill had hastily set up under Colette's impatient orders had come adrift, bringing a large chunk of the wall plaster with it, and leaving a gaping hole in the brickwork where the horizontal beam had been. And tottering to his feet, groaning and covering Anita with a scattering of loose mortar as she unfastened him, was one of Colette's clients.

Anita looked up and saw Tracy. 'Don't just stand there. Give me a hand. When those coppers carted Colette away, she must have forgotten all about her customer here.'

As Tracy hurried down to take some of the man's weight, she giggled. It wasn't a tactful sort of noise to make. He cursed as they helped him towards the steps, still hunched up and clutching his aching knees. 'Broken me bloody nose.'

The adenoidal whine confirmed this. 'Where did she get to? Walking out on me and—'

'She's helping the police with their enquiries,' said Tracy happily.

'Helping them with . . . look, they're not coming here, are they?'

'Couldn't say.'

He looked around for his coat, which sprayed a grey dust as he picked it up. 'I'll sue her,' he babbled as he stumbled up the steps. 'Take her to court. Tell her that when you see her. Tell her . . .'

Tracy giggled again as the front door slammed, and made her own way back upstairs. Anita followed, asking what had happened and what they were going to do, and just what *was* going on with Colette. All Tracy could offer was that she didn't think Colette would be home for a while. With a bit of luck, she thought, they'd hold her until morning. And then, maybe, she'd turn her fury on the one who'd dropped her in the shit. Tracy's shoulders writhed in anticipation.

'I'm aiming to go to bed early,' she said over her shoulder to Anita. 'Got to be up early in the morning.'

It was still cold and dark when she set out, shivering; but she had decided it was more important to dress in a flimsy and tantalising outfit than to keep warm. When Dez stepped out of the gate of Wakefield prison, she was smiling her best hustler's smile.

She was the last person he had expected to see. When she reached him he grabbed her face between his hands as if he fancied squeezing it into a pulp. But Tracy kept smiling. 'I've missed you.'

He didn't know what to make of that. And she wasn't going to give him any hint of what her long-term plans were. He tried putting on his old swagger, and by the time they got back to her bedroom he had convinced himself he was still the big shot in any situation.

She stood calm and still as he began undressing her, his

hands shaking with eagerness. 'You know I didn't mean to hurt you, don't you, babe?'

' 'Course not. You were me boyfriend.'

He ran a hand over her breasts. The months in prison had built up a raging appetite. 'I only did it 'cos I loved yer, you know that, don't yer?' She nodded, remembering the savage blow on the back of her head – oh, somehow remembering more clearly now than anything she had felt at the time. 'I didn't mean to hit yer that hard,' he drooled on, dragging her closer and running his hands down her back to her bottom. 'I just wanted to show you what could happen if I wasn't there for you. All I wanted was to look after yer, and them slags off the Lane were trying to take you off me.'

'I know.' She made it an innocent little girl sound.

He shoved her towards the bed and climbed impatiently on her. Dez had never been much of a one to worry about loving technique. While he was roaring like a rutting animal she let herself lie back, feeling nothing, staring at the ceiling and thinking quite calm, sober thoughts. Let him enjoy himself and think everything was back where it always had been. Might as well enjoy the short time he had left.

When he had finished, the payoff was like the lead-in. No time for tenderness. Hardly even for thanks. He swung off the bed and started dragging his trousers on.

'Got to get back, sort all me stuff out. See yer later in the pub. What time d'yer finish?'

'Ring me.' She waved thin, waxy fingers towards the dressing table. 'Get one of my cards off there.'

He picked one up and smirked. 'Tracy's massage parlour, eh? Nice one.' He jarred his elbow on the partly open wardrobe door. 'What's in here?'

She sat up with a jolt. 'My clothes. Leave it.'

He looked calculatingly along the rail. 'You've been doing all right, then? Must be worth a frigging fortune.'

'I don't come cheap any more. They pay good money for me.'

This was the kind of talk to grab his attention. 'How much?'

'As much as I can get. Start at fifty; sometimes I can get a ton.'

'Tell you what – I'll bring a little lifter in tonight?'

She wanted it to be clear that she wasn't that dependent on him any more. 'I can find my own little lifters, thanks.'

'Really? What you on then, babe?'

'I like a lick of pipe now and then.'

'Crack?' Dez was comically disapproving. 'I wouldn't touch that shit. Who d'you get it off?'

'That'd be telling.'

There was a tap at the door. Without waiting for an answer, Anita put her head round the door. 'Tracy, I was wondering if . . . if you needed me to . . .' Her voice trailed away. 'Sorry, didn't realise you were working.'

'You remember Dez, don't you?'

Anita was not sure how to play this. 'Yes. Er, you were her ponce, weren't you?'

'What you on, love? I'm not a ponce. I used to look after Tracy, that's all. Didn't I, baby?'

''Course you did,' said Tracy levelly.

'I see,' said Anita. 'Er, sorry. Er . . . I was just wondering if you still want me to answer the phone for you?'

'We'll talk about that,' said Tracy, 'later.'

Keep them both guessing: it would do them good.

They had been talking all through the night, sitting on opposite sides of the bed, with old Mr Webster lying silent and unmoving between them. There was a faint buzzing, almost out of hearing range, from the machines attached to the old man. But every time there was an unusual sound, something different in the room or somewhere outside, Joyce started, not knowing what any of them meant.

There was nothing to be said to her father, who was beyond hearing; and nothing to be said about him, or done for him.

But there were still things to be said about themselves, and she wanted them spoken and then done with. She still felt raw, as if she had opened a wound. At Gina's grave she had asked her forgiveness, and had now been trying to explain it to Steve. But all he could do was trot out a load of mushy bromides.

'It was a spur of the moment thing. That's why she'll forgive you. Both of us. It was a way of being close to her.'

This was more than Joyce could take. 'Don't talk shit. When you were between my legs you weren't thinking of Gina. Jesus, at least let's be honest about it. I wasn't thinking this is Gina's husband, this is my son-in-law. I wanted you right then. The only person I was thinking of was myself. Like you.'

'All right, Joyce. What d'you want? D'you want me to feel bad? I feel bad. Do you want to punish me? All right, I'm punished.'

The fading wreck of the old man on the bed stirred, moaned; and opened his eyes without seeing anything.

'It's all right, Dad,' said Joyce hurriedly. 'You've taken poorly again, you're in the hospital.' She didn't know whether this had reached him, but at least he closed his eyes again and drifted off. In a whisper she said across the bed at Steve, 'I don't want you screwing that woman.'

'What woman?' He knew damn well who she was talking about. 'Look, I'm not screwing Lisa. I was just giving her a lift, that's all. Anyway, she's gone back.' When Joyce refused to comment, he said bitterly, 'Look, Joyce. Gina didn't want me any more.'

Joyce tried to reach out for her daughter, but there was nobody there, not even a ghost. There were only the children. She said, 'You'd better get back and get the kids ready for school.'

Fifteen minutes after Steve had left, her father struggled up in bed and smiled at her. The nurse fetched him a drink, and it was only then that Joyce realised she was dying for a pee. She went off to the toilet, and took her time over soaking her hands in lovely warm water and splashing it over her face. When she got back, the curtains had been drawn round the bed. Inside, the nurses were bending over the prone figure.

'What yer doing to him?'

'I'm afraid your father's passed away, Mrs Webster.'

'He can't have. He were sat up when I left him. You saw him yourself, he even had a drink. He was getting better.'

'They often do,' said the nurse soothingly, 'just before they go. It's like they want to say a proper goodbye.'

'But I only just left him for a minute. I didn't want him to be on his own when he . . . when he went. I wanted to be with him.'

'Maybe he preferred to be on his own. Maybe he waited for you to nip out, so that he could.'

There were arrangements to be made, all kinds of things to be sorted out; but the hospital was used to this. She was taken into a quiet office and given a cup of tea and a biscuit, and a few things to sign: all very gentle and helpful, easing her through formalities as painlessly as if she'd had a jab of anaesthetic. Then perhaps she'd get in touch with an undertaker, and put him in touch with them?

Joyce was choking back tears and a salty thickening in her throat as she left. Yet below that was the knowledge that at last one burden had been taken off her shoulders.

She had to talk to someone. There was only Steve. By now he should be back home on his own, back an hour or more from delivering the kids to school.

Only he wasn't on his own. She heard voices as soon as she turned her key in his lock and stepped into the hall.

Lisa was saying, 'My friend'll be meeting me off the train tomorrow.'

'So you're leaving me?' Steve was hamming it up like a joke; but Joyce could hear genuine disappointment in it. The liar. After what he had said about Lisa having left already.

'You'll be glad to see the back of me.' And the girl was phoney, too.

'It's been nice having you here. The house is so empty without . . . well . . . Look, I'll drive you down to the station.'

Joyce confronted them, sitting nice and close together on the sofa, all cosy and domestic. 'You lying bastard.'

'Joyce, Lisa's just going. We've just been—'

'I can guess what you've just been—'

Lisa was on her feet. 'I'll make my own way to the station.'

'No, you won't.' Steve stood up beside her. 'I'll take you to the station like I said. When it suits the both of us, not when *she* tells you. She's only come round here to cause trouble.'

Joyce said, 'I came round to tell you my dad's died.'

Steve stared, then put out his hand to her. 'Joyce . . . I'm so sorry, love. Is there anything I can do?'

'Get rid of *her*, for a start.'

Lisa waved down Steve's clumsy attempt to argue again, kissed him lightly on the cheek as if to defy Joyce, and went upstairs. The thought of her up there, the thought of her in Steve's bedroom, in the kids' bedroom, was too much. Joyce turned and stumbled out the way she had come.

Steve came racing after her, and caught her arm.

'Joyce, there's the funeral arrangements. You'll need help. Let's talk about it—'

'Get rid of that bloody girl. She's not having those kids. I'll see you in court first.'

'There wasn't anything going on, Joyce,' protested Steve. 'She slept in Michelle's room.'

'D'you think I'm stupid or something? You've got it written all over your faces. But she's not going to get the kids. I'll not have my dad to care for now, so I'll be able to manage them on my own.'

'Joyce, just a minute—'

'They're not staying here. I'll take them to my place.'

'Joyce, why are you doing this? Just because Lisa stayed over that extra night—'

'Did you used to lie to Gina an' all?'

'I only lied to you because I knew anything else I said, you'd take the wrong way. I don't know what's the matter with you. You're acting as if we were married or something.'

'I'll tell you what's the matter.'

'Go on, then. Tell me. For Christ's sake, I want to know.'

She hadn't meant to go this far. 'I just want . . .'

'Yeh? Say it!'

'Us to be together.'

'What d'you mean, *us*? What're you talking about?'

Joyce tried to back-pedal. 'As a family. I mean . . . I'm losing everyone . . . I need . . .'

She wasn't sure just how much she really meant all this; and Steve couldn't grasp it anyway. 'Look,' he was fumbling, 'you need time to get over your dad, that's what you need. I know he was knocking on, but I don't think you're ever ready for these things.' His hand was firmly on her arm. 'You can leave everything to me. I'll sort things out and ring you tomorrow. I'll do all the arranging. Won't that help? Joyce . . .?'

She ought to be grateful for it; but it wasn't, deep down, what she had really been talking about.

Rose had walked the streets for hours, unwilling to get on the coach with her return ticket and slink back home. When night fell she was still tramping aimlessly, telling herself it was too late to go back to Bradford now, though she hadn't enough spare cash to be sure of finding a bed-and-breakfast place, no matter how cheap. In the end she curled up on a park bench. That made her just one among dozens. In every dusty or damp bit of park in Manchester, in every shopping precinct with a few seats, people were huddled into old overcoats and layers of cardboard or newspaper.

In the morning she knew what she had to do before giving up altogether. She trudged back to Primrose Park Crescent and rang the doorbell at number 104.

Even at this time of the morning the woman who answered the door was very trim, her hair pulled neatly back, and smelling of expensive soap. She had clearly been half-expecting Rose to show up.

'You must be Hannah's mother.'

Rose hadn't planned what she was going to say. It just came out in a rush, 'And you must be the woman who gave her away.'

'You'd better come in.'

The furniture in the sitting room was just what Rose would have expected. The carpet, the rugs, the sideboard, the tea tray with its floral china – everything just what she would have wanted for her daughter. Only the girl sitting on the plump arm of the sofa wasn't her daughter, but Mrs Levison's daughter.

Sarah had brought the tray in, and poured tea for the three of them. It was all so polite. Rose seethed within. She needed their help, or at least their sympathy; but anger was overcoming every other emotion.

'I thought she'd be with someone who really cared about her.' She held her voice as steady as she could; but it wasn't going to last. 'That's what kept me going. I thought she'd be with someone who could give her everything I couldn't.'

'Do you think I didn't try?' said Mrs Levison quietly. 'She wasn't an easy child. She was jealous of Sarah – in fact she hated her. And then when Robbie was born she was even worse. She went completely wild, I couldn't do anything with her.'

'So you gave her up.'

'Not at first, no. I kept thinking things would be better. We took her to see child psychologists, doctors, we took her everywhere, trying to get to the bottom of it. I felt such a failure.'

Rose didn't believe a word of it. Once the woman had got children of her own, she didn't want this other one getting in the way. They had taken her in, they could just as easily chuck her out.

'So you dumped her,' she said. 'She didn't really matter, because she wasn't yours.'

'No, you're wrong. I never thought like that. I didn't kick her out. I loved her like my own.'

'Only she wasn't, was she? *Like* your own, but not your own.'

'But I was the one who got up six, seven times a night to feed her and rub teething gel on her gums. I nursed her through measles and chickenpox, sat hour after hour at the doctor's surgery because I was worried about her weight and her not thriving. I was the one who took her to school on her first day and was sick with fear because I knew . . . I *knew* she wasn't going to be able to make friends. And where were *you*?' demanded Mrs Levison.

'Mum, don't get upset.'

Sarah had reached out to put her hand on her mother's wrist. It was all so cosy, so easy for them. Rose was ready to hate the girl whom she had only yesterday loved as her daughter.

'Crying for my daughter,' she blazed, 'that's where. Walking the streets wondering where the hell she was. I didn't give her up: they dragged her off me. I screamed the bloody house down when they took her from me, and they gave her to you. They must have thought you'd look after her better with your big posh house and your musical instruments. They couldn't have got it more wrong, could they? 'Cos all you did was bang her into a home. Well, she'd have been better off with me. I might not have been the best mother in the world, but I could have given her love. Maybe that's all she needed. Did you ever think about that? Maybe that's all she wanted.' She was almost choking. 'D'you know what day it is today?'

'All right.' Sarah slid off the arm of the sofa. 'I think we've had about enough of this. I think you'd better go.'

'It's the day she was born,' Rose ploughed on. 'My daughter's twenty-four years old today.'

'Big deal!' Sarah's voice no longer had that musical lilt which Rose had fallen for so quickly. She was harsh and discordant. 'Do you want to see what your daughter did when I was nine years old?'

'Sarah, don't.' Her mother raised a feeble hand, but Sarah went furiously on:

'No, I think she should see what her precious daughter did.' She pushed her hair to one side above her neck and shoulder. Three livid scars marred the beauty of her milky skin. 'She said she was going to cut my hair for me. She tied me to the chair before I knew what she was up to, and cut it all off until my scalp was bleeding. But she wasn't content with that. She stabbed me seven times with the scissors. I had forty-eight stitches. *That's* why my mother let them take her away.'

Rose wanted to deny it, to argue, to tell them they were lying and ought to be ashamed of making up such hideous stories. But she had only to look at the faces of the two of them, mother and daughter, to know it was true.

Time to leave. Time to turn her back on hopeless dreams.

Her first call when she got back to Bradford was at the address on Brian's card. Somehow she had to get it all out of her system. Somebody had to be blamed and it couldn't be herself. She could no longer even blame the Levisons.

Brian was outside the block of flats with his head under the bonnet of his car.

Rose said, 'If you're gonna do a job, make sure you do it right.'

He straightened up, looking pleased to see her. 'It's difficult when you can't get hold of the spares.'

'I'm talking about finding people. You know, the job you're supposed to do – what you get paid for, being a private investigator. Only you're crap.'

Brian carefully wiped his hands on an oily rag. 'I gather she wasn't there?'

'You gather right. If you'd done your job properly you'd have found out that they put her in a children's home in Sheffield when she was twelve.'

'You've been to Sheffield?'

'I slept on a park bench in Manchester last night. I've just bloody well got back, and I'm knackered. I thought *you* could go to Sheffield, earn some of your money.'

'What money? I haven't seen a penny yet.'

'And you're not going to, neither.'

His patience was running out. 'Now, hang on a minute. What the hell's up with you? Why do you always give me grief every time I see you?'

'Because I thought I'd hired a private dick, not a dickhead, that's why.'

'Look, I thought I'd found her. When kids are adopted they usually stay with the parents. I knew the Levisons still lived there, it seemed a good bet. I suppose I could have checked it out a bit further, but that all takes time, and time's money in my business, and I knew you didn't have much.'

She half wanted to apologise, half wanted to go on yelling at him. Because somebody had to be responsible for this bloody misery. But it was no good. While he was still trying to find something else to say, she went off before making even more of a fool of herself by bursting into tears in front of him.

16

There were times when Carol felt things were going to do her head in again. Any minute now they'd be hauling her back into that psychiatric unit and making sloppy soothing noises over her again. Only it was other people needed their heads fixing, really. How the hell could anyone explain what Vinnie Marshall had seen – or claimed he'd seen? Some other woman here in her own house, walking for Curly? And some white girl at that, someone the shithead must have brought back here while she was out, because he couldn't do without it. All that talk about him and Carol just having a quiet supper together, and all the time he was fitting in a quick bit of the old wanking while she was off the premises.

And yet he *had* left her the money he had promised: more than she'd ever dreamt of. Or had he? None of it had reached her so far, and she had a feeling in her bones that it never would.

None of it made any sense.

She took Emma to school and came back to find the electricity bill on the mat. That was something else to drive you out of your mind. And on top of it came a thumping at the door.

Vinnie Marshall wouldn't have been let out, would he – coming back to threaten?

'Who is it?'

'The big bad wolf.' It was Newall's voice.

She was glad he couldn't see her expression. She must have been smiling, glad to see him; but she wasn't going to let on.

'Red Riding Hood's not coming out to play.'

'Just as well, because I want to come in.'

She took the chain off, half expecting him to make a grab at her as he came in or start cursing her and saying there was new evidence about something or other, and she had lied to him again. That was his usual approach. Instead, he went on into the kitchen and moodily propped himself against the drainboard.

'Go on, then,' she prompted. 'What's happening? Still got that nephew of his banged up? Because I've been wondering—'

'I don't know,' he said bleakly. 'I'm off the case.'

'Y'what?'

'Suspended till further notice.'

'What for?'

'Possible abuse of authority, neglect of duty, acting in contravention of PACE, take your pick. Off the case and every other case pending official inquiry and disciplinary hearing.'

Carol was at a loss. 'Why, what have you done?'

'What d'you think I've bloody done? I let you off, for starters. By rights you should be banged up in Risley – accessory to murder, concealing evidence. And I didn't follow proper identification procedure. That bitch Hoyle's grassed me up. She's gunning for DI, and she wants me out.'

'And you let her win? You must want your head testing.'

'Oh, that's nice. That's frigging fantastic.' She had stung him out of his depression. 'I blow twenty-six years in the Force for you, and all I get is I want my head testing.'

'You didn't blow it for me,' she snapped back. 'I've done nothing wrong. I've murdered nobody.'

'You tried to cover up a—'

'Happen if you'd spent less time pulling us lot in and more time looking for the crazy bastard who's going round killing people, you wouldn't have gone and got yourself sacked.' The wretched anger in his face, the way it was all knotted up, brought her to a halt. She hated the idea of going soft on him, but found herself wanting to reach out and touch him. Hastily she said, 'What are you going to do? What are you going to live on?'

He shrugged wearily. 'They still pay me. For the time being.'

'Oh, well, what are you worrying about?'

'What am I worrying about? Jesus, I've got twenty-six years' good service in, I've been a copper since I was nineteen: for Christ's sake, it's my life. It's all I've got. And now they're going to put me through the mangle, and it'll go on for months, and all the time they'll be working on nice official reasons for getting me out. It's cost me everything.'

'What d'you mean, everything? You'll still get your money. You've just said so.'

He pushed himself away from the drainboard and stomped back into the hall. 'Jesus, you've got a one-track mind. Is money all you ever think about?'

'Yes.' She pursued him. 'When you haven't got any, that's all you do think about: morning, noon and night. D'you know how much I'm going to get from the SS? Sixty frigging quid. You want to try living on that. Here y'are, take a look at my electric bill.' She thrust it under his nose. 'Eighty-seven pounds.'

'What about all Durkin's money?'

'You reckon I'll ever see a penny of that?'

'More likely than me being reinstated, I'd say.'

As he tugged the door open, she called after him: 'Where are you going?'

'To rob a bleeding bank. Try and match you quid for quid.'

She wanted to make him come back, so they could start all over again and talk sensibly. Not that they'd ever done much of that. But in any case he wasn't even glancing back.

At the same time Rose was trudging along the pavement. From the sag of her shoulders and the way she looked straight past Carol as she came in, she showed every sign of casting another cloud of gloom over the morning.

'Not another one with a mawk on?' Carol challenged her. 'How'd it go? Did you get to talk to her?'

'It wasn't her' said Rose bitterly. 'They'd put her in a home when she were twelve, the bastards.'

'Oh, no. Where?'

'Somewhere in bleeding Sheffield. Look, I'm knackered, and I feel like shit. I'm off to bed.'

She didn't look as if she could make it up the stairs. She was only on the third tread when there was a heavy knocking at the front door. Carol jumped. That was a copper's knock if ever she'd heard one. For a moment she thought – hoped – that Newall might have come back. But when she opened the door, a woman she'd seen before and the man she knew as DC Barstow stood there.

The woman smiled as she showed her card, and emphasised her new rank, 'Acting Detective Inspector Hoyle.'

'You don't say? Acting, are we? Acting up? Who's been a good girl, then? You were sergeant last time I saw you. What happened: you didn't grass somebody up, did you?'

Hoyle ignored the comment and said frostily, 'I'd like to speak to Rose Garrity if I could.'

'Well, I'll have to see if she wants to. She's a bit choosy about who she talks to.'

'Is she in?'

Carol looked back over her shoulder, up the stairs. 'Rose, do you want to talk to a two-faced piece of toad shite?'

Rose came warily down the few steps and looked out at the two officers. 'What d'you want to talk to me about?'

'We'd just like to ask you a few questions regarding Granville Durkin. Would you mind coming down to the station with us?'

Through the fog of tiredness and utter despair, Rose could blearily see that this woman was enjoying her new role. She barked out what she thought were shrewd questions, and chivvied Rose along when she was slow in answering. Not that there was any way Rose could hurry things up. Half of her mind was still groping through helpless confusions to get a grasp on Hannah, and how she could have been so hideously disappointed, and whether to start again and have more hopes and more let-downs. The other half tried to understand the crazy suggestions Hoyle was slinging at her.

'No.' She made an effort to get to grips with it. 'I wasn't living there – at Carol's – when Curly was killed. I was living at seventeen Belsize Road. I stayed over that one night to look after Emma, 'cos you lot had got Carol in here.'

'But it's fair to say you spent a good bit of time in that house?'

'Of course I did. She's my mate.'

'Do you know what kind of relationship Carol Johnson had with Granville Durkin?'

'He gives her money. Look, I don't know what this has got to do with me.'

'In return for her dressing up in black stockings?'

'Sometimes, yeh. Sometimes not.'

'Do you know how much money he gave her?'

'I think she did all right out of him,' said Rose cautiously. 'He was a bit of a soft touch, if that's what you want to know.'

Hoyle nodded as if she had just stumbled on a great discovery. 'So all his money would have come in handy for Carol, with your company losing the cleaning contract.'

'That was before—'

'You were all getting desperate. Things were looking dicey. You knew that George Ferguson was about to blow the whistle on you being prostitutes.'

'Who told you that?'

Abruptly Hoyle said, 'Did you ever walk for Granville Durkin?'

'Me?' Things were getting fuzzy in Rose's mind. 'Walk for Curly?'

'Yes, why not? We've been informed a white girl was there, not Carol Johnson. You said he was a soft touch, and Carol had gone off the idea of walking for him. So why not put a pair of black stockings on, parade around for a couple of minutes, and earn yourself over a hundred quid? Makes sense to me.'

'To me an' all,' Rose agreed. 'But he were Carol's punter, not mine.' She began to get the drift of what they were getting at, and of course they were wasting their time. 'I was with someone when Curly got it,' she said. 'Brian Roberts. Do you want me to give you his address and telephone number?'

They were none too keen. It didn't fit in with the ideas they had already dreamed up. But Rose hauled herself up into wakefulness and had the strength to say they wouldn't get another word out of her until they had checked on her alibi. She could only hope Brian was in and she wouldn't have to hang around here too long.

He was not in.

Hoyle suggested that while they kept trying to phone, and while maybe a police car could go round to the house to leave a message through the letterbox, Miss Garrity might care to fill in a few more details. By this time Rose was quite determined not to say another word. A cup of tea and a fag made no difference.

It seemed a lifetime before Barstow came to report, reluctantly, that they had at last contacted Brian Roberts and that he confirmed Rose Garrity's story. And not only was he prepared to come to the station to put it on record, but was actually insisting on doing so, and should be already on his way.

'Must have a keen sense of justice,' said Hoyle sarcastically, eyeing Rose with distaste.

Her snide attitude didn't matter any more. Brian was coming to the rescue. Rose felt a pang of remorse about the way she had sounded off at him earlier on.

That didn't stop her saying, as they left the station and walked towards his car, 'You took your bloody time. Where were you?'

'Sheffield. You know, doing that job I'm crap at. And when I got back and those coppers started on at me, it'd have served you bloody right if I'd said I'd never clapped eyes on you.'

'Sheffield?' she said, not daring to hope.

'Seems like she legged it from the home when she was fifteen, her and a mate.'

'And nobody knows where . . .?'

'They ended up,' said Brian, all at once not daring to look at her, 'on Spencer Place in Leeds.'

Rose bent forward, winded, struggling for breath. No, she wasn't going to believe this one. Not her Hannah, no. The Lane was nowhere to be proud of, but the mere name of Spencer Place stank. Brian had got it all wrong again. He had got Hannah mixed up with someone else.

He was holding the door of the car open for her.

'Where are we going?'

'Leeds.'

'No, there'd be no point, there's no way . . .'

But she got in, and was silent for a long time as he wove his way through the traffic and out on to the eastbound dual carriageway.

At last he said, very coolly, 'You had this romantic picture in your head, didn't you? Buying yourself into a pretty fantasy. So she's not your perfect little daughter, all dressed up in ribbons and bows: she's a hustler, like her mother was.'

He sounded so calm and matter-of-fact, but it came as another sickening jolt to Rose. 'Who told you I was—'

'I didn't need telling.'

Mother of God, was it written across her face or something? Maybe Carol was right after all, and they weren't any good for anything else. *Born to Hustle* stamped on their foreheads and running through them like a stick of Blackpool rock.

'So I suppose,' she said dully, 'you think it's no wonder she's turned out the way she is? It must run in the blood.'

'Bollocks. Born survivors, maybe, but nobody's born to hustle.'

'Well, how come she's brought up in a posh house, had everything money can buy – books, music, the right schooling – but she ends up same as me? How d'you reckon with that?'

He pondered it. She thought how reassuring he could be when he looked so serious and genuinely concerned. Not that he had achieved much so far. As they approached the outskirts of Leeds he said, 'Maybe she went looking for *you*. Ever thought of that? D'you think she'd have been disappointed if she'd found you on the Lane, pulling a trick?'

'I think she'd have run a bloody mile.'

'Maybe not. You ask me, I'd say she wouldn't have cared if you'd got two heads, she'd have just wanted you to want her.'

The last couple of days and the misery of that sour-faced woman in the police station at last took their toll. Rose had managed not to cry outright so far. Now she slumped forward against her seat belt and let herself break down entirely.

'I did want her. I *do* want her.'

'Still? In spite of—'

'Yes. Oh, yes.'

Brian found his way into Chapeltown and parked on a patch of waste ground behind Spencer Place. He seemed to know the place pretty well. At least he had done his homework here for one reason or another. He did not hesitate when they turned the corner and found a young hustler leaning on a gate, but started asking her questions in an undertone, keeping Rose well behind him. Then he nodded, and in spite of the girl asking for something to make it worth while talking to him, took Rose's arm and hurried her down the street.

When he began telling her about himself, rattling it off at a great speed as he looked about him at the houses and the girls who drifted from one side of the street to the other, she had the feeling it was just as much to distract her as enlighten her.

'My mother left home when I was five,' he was saying. 'My dad brought me up, only he had a problem with the booze. And by the time I was nineteen, so did I.'

'Nineteen?' she echoed.

'When I was twenty-one, I got this notion . . . oh, it was bloody stupid. Thought I'd find my mother. It was a sort of birthday present to myself. So I set off looking for her.'

'That's how you got started in this business?'

'It's how I ended up in Armley nick,' he said morosely. 'It was easy enough finding her. My auntie Jean told me she was in Sowerby Bridge, and it's not that big a place, so I got myself well tanked up and knocked on the door. This bloke answered – he was about thirty, I hadn't a clue who he was. I said could I speak to Eileen Roberts, and he said no one by that name lived there, and then I heard my mum from inside the house asking who was at the door. Couldn't mistake her voice.' His grip on Rose's arm tightened. 'I don't remember much after that.'

'What did you do?'

'They said in court that I smashed his face in with my fists, knocked most of his teeth out, kicked him in the stomach and broke two of his ribs. But all I can remember is my mother saying she never wanted to see me again . . . and then she got in the back of the ambulance with him, and I got banged up for GBH.' Before Rose could begin thinking of anything she might possibly say, he let go of her arm and stopped in front of a hustler in her mid-twenties. She was wearing skin-tight lycra jeans above black stiletto shoes, and her hair was cropped into a shiny black helmet to make her look like a boy. Brian said, 'Are you Madeleine?'

'Who wants to know?'

'Sharon sent us along to see you. She said you might be able to help us.'

Madeleine looked suspiciously down the road. 'She did, did she? Yer not the Old Bill, are yer?'

'Do we look like coppers?'

'They come in all shapes and sizes these days, love.'

Rose decided to move in. She knew girls like these; felt at home with them. 'I've worked the front line myself,' she said. 'I did the Lane in Bradford for half my life.'

It made an impression. Madeleine studied her, and smiled a matey smile. 'What d'yer want, then?'

'I'm looking for my daughter. Her name's Hannah. Sharon said you've worked this patch for a bit.'

'Ten years. What did you say her name was?'

'Hannah Levison,' Brian supplied. 'She'd done a runner from a children's home in Sheffield.'

'And before that,' Rose rushed on, 'she lived in Manchester.'

Madeleine scratched her shoulder. She seemed to give it some genuine thought. 'Did she have black hair?'

'That's right.' Rose was daring to hope again.

Madeleine was interested, but not so interested that she could keep her eyes from straying, checking for punters or maybe her ponce, who would want to know why the hell she was wasting time with a couple of non-starters.

'She used to knock around with a blonde chick called Colette,' she recalled. 'They worked this patch for a couple of years. They did well, then one of them took some bad stuff – I think it were blondie, or it might have been the other way round.'

The idea that Hannah might not still be alive had never occurred to Rose before. And the nasty echo of a name like Colette . . .

No, scrub round it, it couldn't be right. No connection.

'Anyway,' Madeleine went on, 'it sent her off her head. And the other one got busted.'

A car with tinted windows drew up, blasting out loud rasta music. The man inside was scowling out at Madeleine. Rose didn't need telling that this was the girl's ponce, doing his rounds and checking up. Desperately she said, 'What happened to her?'

'Dunno. I never saw either of 'em again.'

Another trail gone cold. Another dead end.

17

A phone started ringing. Anita, massaging her neck where the collar had left it feeling stiff and itchy, was taken unawares. She had promised to answer Colette's and Tracy's calls and play the receptionist, but she could still never be sure whether it was the phone in the hall ringing or one of their mobiles chucked aside on a chair or under a sofa cushion while they were blissfully stoned.

She found a mobile on top of the television where Colette had left it when the police came to cart her off for questioning. The caller was well-spoken but diffident, keeping his voice down as if in an office where he dared not be overheard.

'May I speak to Colette?'

'She's . . . er . . . involved in an interview at the moment. May I take a message?'

'Could you tell her Lionel would like to make an appointment?'

'Lionel?' Anita was delighted. 'The solicitor Lionel?'

'Um, yes.' He sounded embarrassed.

'Oh, it's lovely to hear from you. This is Anita, you must remember me. I kicked your arse – not very hard, but it was my first time. And I've been practising.'

He sounded even more flustered. 'Yes, well, er . . . I'd be grateful if you'd ask Colette to ring me back this afternoon about two o'clock, so we could fix something for this evening. She knows my number.'

A wild idea blossomed in Anita's mind. If Colette still wasn't back, it would be such a shame to disappoint a customer, and Lionel *had* been such a gentleman, and she *had* rather enjoyed herself. 'Give it me again,' she suggested. 'Save her looking it up.' She jotted the number down. 'Oh, and by the way, all that information you gave me about that dodgy money came in very handy.'

'Of course. Now I remember you very well. You're the lady with the rather nice black spangly dress, right?'

'Right.'

Anita would have been only too glad to continue the conversation, but she heard the front door open and crash shut. Colette erupted into the room like an avenging angel, her hair wild and her expression even wilder.

'Where is she? Tracy – she's around?'

Anita gestured towards the cellar steps; slid the phone unobtrusively back on the television; and when she was sure Colette had reached the bottom of the steps, edged towards the open door.

She heard Tracy trying to sound very bright and offhand. 'They let you out, then?' When there was no reply, she chattered on, 'That bloke on the cross, that punter you left hanging, like. Forgot all about him, didn't you? Must have tried to fight his way off it, and it came to bits. Anita had to untie him. Says he's going to take you to court, he's broken his nose. It did look a bit skewiff to me.' Still no reply. 'Aren't you talking to me?' Tracy was getting plaintive. 'Look, I told the coppers it were you 'cos I knew you were clean. Yer didn't have any shit on yer, so in the end they'd have to let you go. Aren't yer gonna say owt, then?'

Colette spoke at last. Or, rather, screamed. 'You do anything like that ever again and I'll carve you apart. Understood? Just once again like that, and you're dead.'

Anita made herself scarce.

It was early evening when Carol rang the doorbell of the poky little flat. Opening the door, Newall was dressed more casually than she had ever seen him – shirt unbuttoned, greasy slacks – and was clutching a large tumbler of whisky in his hand.

'Started visiting the sick?' He stood aside to let her in. No grabbing this time. No sudden lunge at her, either in fury or in lust.

She looked round the cramped room with its chipped coffee table, two armchairs with faded covers, a sofa worn through at the arms, and a rental video. 'I'd've thought they'd have given you summat better than this.'

'It's standard police temporary property.' He eyed her without his usual self-confidence. 'How did you find me?'

'I've got a bloody sight better contacts on my old beat than any copper on his. We can smell any one of you out at any hour of the day.'

'All right. *Why* did you find me?'

'I've come to say I'm . . .' Carol became aware of the fact that there were two plates and an empty pizza carton on the coffee table. 'I'm not interrupting anything, am I?'

'No.'

He looked round for the bottle. Carol, still sizing the place up and feeling more and more sorry for him but more and more suspicious, spotted an overnight case in a corner of the room; for going away . . . or the property of somebody staying here?

'You're all packed?' she probed.

'Not yet.'

'Where you going this time?'

'Dunno. I suppose I can go where I like now.'

'Or stay if you like?'

'Not here. I'd have to find myself somewhere.' It was the first time she had realised how brown his eyes were: almost like a dog's soulful eyes . . . now a beaten, downtrodden dog. That made a change from the snapping, snarling beast she had encountered so many times. She wasn't sure she didn't prefer the savage animal.

She sauntered towards a closed door beside the gas fire. 'That the bedroom?'

'Yes.' As she put her hand on the knob, he said, 'I didn't say you could go in there.'

'I see, got somebody hidden?'

He was on his feet, but she was already marching into the bedroom, positive there would be some woman in his bed.

Light from a street lamp fell through the window on to the face of a boy about ten years old: even in this uncertain light, clearly a kid of mixed race. Whatever she might have expected, it wasn't this.

'Little boys?' she shuddered.

'He's my son.'

'Your son? Since when did you have a son?'

A drowsy voice from the bed croaked, 'Shut the door, Dad.'

'Sorry, Liam. Goodnight.' When they had backed out he poured her a drink and set the glass on the coffee table so that she would have to sit close to him. 'He travelled up from Birmingham this afternoon. I think it's tired him out. I'm taking him go-kart racing tomorrow.'

She couldn't get her brain round this one. She spluttered on her whisky, lost for words.

'Something wrong?' Newall was more like his old aggressive self. 'Because I'm not just the bastard screw any more? Because I happen to be a human being as well – a father, even? Can't you handle it?'

What she couldn't handle was the colour of Liam's skin. It was all dawning on her. 'His mother were black, right?' She almost shouted it at him: 'You like screwing black women, do you?'

'If I've got the choice, yes. Will you keep your voice down.'

'I suppose she were a hustler an' all?'

'She was a copper,' said Newall. 'We trained together. I

was married to her for nine years. Her name's Diana, and I adored the ground she walked on: her face, her character, her mind . . . *and* the colour of her skin.'

They sat for a long time without a word as Carol tried to digest all this. She wanted to ask more about Diana, and whether she was alive or dead. All at once there were so many things she wanted to find out. 'D'you know, I must have shagged you sixty times, but I know sod all about you. I don't even know your name.'

'David.'

'David?' He didn't look like a David. 'I think I'll stick to Newall.'

'Call me what you like, as long as it isn't Bastard Screw.'

'It suited you. Anyway, you liked being called Bastard Screw. Just like you loved me being a hustler. You loved the frigging battle, trying to keep me down. Bang 'em up behind bars or bang 'em up in bed. You think you've got the power, but one flash of leg and your brain drops between your bollocks.'

He stared into the golden liquid in his glass and swilled it moodily around. 'I wasn't looking for power.'

'Don't make me laugh. You're a copper, it's what you get off on.'

'Did maybe in the beginning.'

'And now?'

He downed the rest of his whisky in one long, slow draught before answering. Only it wasn't an answer but a question. 'So what did you come round for?'

She had fallen so easily into the old sparring and stabbing temper that she had almost forgotten the impulse that had brought her here.

'I wanted to say sorry about you losing your job,' she said haltingly. 'Seems like it was my fault.'

His mouth twisted. 'I think I was to blame somewhere down the line.'

'Well, I just wanted to say . . .' What the hell *did* she want to say? 'Look, if you want to come round sometime . . . I mean, before you leave, or if . . .'

'Got no one to look after Liam.'

It sounded like an excuse, like he was playing her at her own game.

Carol got up. 'Well, I'll see you, then.' She looked down on his bent head, with a streak of iron grey behind his ears. 'You know summat, you even look different.'

'Better or worse?'

'I haven't worked it out.

'Well, when you have, let me know, will you?'

Carol left without attempting any smart come-back, and made her way home.

Upstairs she heard a bumping and rustling sound. When she was halfway up the stairs she was greeted by a way-out vision at the top. Rose had helped herself to Carol's old hustling boots, and found an old hustling top and a coat from somewhere. She was fluffing her hair up, ready to come downstairs.

Carol stared. 'What are you tarted up like that for?'

''Cos I'm off out.'

'Hustling?' She couldn't believe it.

'Why not? I've only got a couple of years left. No point wasting them.'

Lionel approached across the thick maroon and purple carpet of the Norfolk Gardens Hotel bar with his briefcase, like any overworked businessman dropping in for a drink before making his way home. Anita knew that the briefcase would be holding women's clothes rather than business documents; but all the same, she still liked the classy look of him.

'Have you been here long?' he asked politely.

'About twenty minutes. I didn't want to be late. It's lovely to see you. I'm sorry Colette couldn't make it, but as I explained when I rang you, the alterations we're having made in the house—'

'Yes, yes.' He could quickly switch from politeness to impatience; and she realised he wanted his women to be bossy, not apologetic. 'Lovely to see you, too. Shall we go up?'

'I thought we might have a drink in here first.'

'There's a mini-bar in the room, and I'd like to get started.'

'Oh. I thought we might have a little chat.'

'A chat?' This wasn't at all what he wanted. 'What about?'

'Just to get to know each other.'

He didn't want that, either. 'I'm on a very tight schedule. I've got to pick my wife up from bridge at half-past nine.'

Well, if that was the way he wanted it, she supposed she'd have to go along with it. A pity, though, that he couldn't be just a little bit more of a gentleman. Anita giggled as she sat on the edge of the double bed, waiting for him to change his clothes. After all, it was him not wanting to be a gentleman that was paying for all this. She opened the mini-bar fridge and took out a miniature gin bottle. She wasn't all that keen on gin, but she had knocked it back and started on vodka by the time he had got his dress and pearls and pinny on.

'There's a lot of gunge in that fridge,' she said. 'And there's a leakage on the bottom shelf. Get it cleaned up.'

'Yes, mistress.'

He went down on hands and knees, and moved some tonic bottles and two miniatures of brandy off the shelf on to the top. Anita swung her right leg experimentally, and placed a neat kick on his bottom. He whimpered, and waited for another, harder one. The second time, she drove so hard between his buttocks that his head cracked against the edge of the fridge door.

'Don't make so much bloody noise.'

'Sorry, mistress.'

She threw one of the empty miniatures at the back of his neck. 'I don't like gin.'

'What's that, mistress?'

'Don't you ever listen to a word I say? I said I don't like gin. I don't much care for any of this stuff. I want some Malibu. I drink Malibu and Coke, not this rubbish.'

'You could ring room service, mistress.'

Anita picked out another vodka from the scattering of miniatures, and took it down in one searing gulp. 'Oh, I could, could I? Well, how about *you* ringing for room service?' Then, as he grovelled on the floor at her feet, an even happier notion occurred to her. He loved humiliation, didn't he? Right: she would put him well and truly through it. By the time she'd finished, he would really come to respect her. 'No, I've got a much better idea. How about you go down to the bar and buy me a bottle?'

Now he was really alarmed, not sure of enjoying it. 'I'm sorry, mistress,' he stalled. 'I'm not allowed out of the room.'

'Who says so?' She was beginning to revel in this. 'I'm your mistress, and I'm the one who says if you can or can't go out of the room. And I'm saying you can.' She pushed herself groggily off the bed and propped herself against the wardrobe door while she took some fivers out of his trouser pocket. 'Here – get down those stairs and bring me a large bottle of Malibu, a bucket of ice, and some lemon slices.'

For a moment she thought he would refuse. This wasn't what he had bargained for. And yet the sheer horror of it was turning him on. He would go through with it because he was so afraid of going through with it. Yet still he was hesitating.

Anita took his trousers right out of the wardrobe and draped them over her arm. While he still dithered, she went to the window and opened it, holding the trousers out into the night air. 'I'm going to count to a hundred, and if you're not back with that bottle of Malibu, I'm going to let these pants fly. Right, then. Here we go: one . . . two . . . three . . .'

He disappeared, clutching his own money that Anita had

so generously handed to him. She stooped to see what bottles were still left, and almost fell over with dizziness. As she opened what might have been a small whisky or a sherry, she tried to visualise him crossing the hotel bar while everybody stared at him. She half wished she had followed him down and stood watching. But if he had seen her there it might well have spoiled her hold over him.

When he came back into the room – wretched yet crazily happy about his degradation – Anita was back at the window, holding the trousers out.

'I'm back, mistress.' He clanked the ice bucket and held the bottle of Malibu abjectly out to her.

She was tempted to order him to go down on one knee and lick her shoes. But right now she had other ideas in mind. 'Ninety-nine,' she intoned joyfully. 'A hundred.'

And she dropped the trousers as he cried out in real horror that gave him no kick at all.

Anita beamed at him. She hadn't enjoyed herself so much for weeks – months, even. She was just discovering what a real talent she had for this sort of thing.

Rose huddled into her coat and set off inevitably towards the Lane. The walls and pavements were as drab as ever, and the drunk in the gutter might have been there for the last ten years. Yet she hadn't the energy to feel any real despair. She was drained. She couldn't be bothered. Let it happen, the way it had always happened and now would go on until she was too ragged to cope any more. Sod the lot of 'em, sod everything.

She steered away from the open door of The Hustlers' Arms. Time enough for a drink later, when she had made some money; lots of drinks, sitting on her usual stool and raising her voice at the stupid kids who thought they could ever take over from her.

Wrapping yourself in a coat was no way to pull the punters. Easing it back over her shoulders and undoing the three top buttons of her blouse, Rose looked around. It was all so familiar. Crazy to have thought she'd ever get away from it.

A car slowed, but when she hurried towards it the driver wound his window up again and drove off.

On the far side of the Lane she saw Tracy and couldn't make up her mind whether to wave to her or to cower shamefully away. The decision was made for her when she saw who Tracy was with. It was unbelievable. Taking up with Dez again, after what that little shit had done to her? Tracy must be beyond saving now. Which made two of them.

A car hooted its horn. Rose summoned up a smile and began crossing the street; then saw Brian beginning to get out. She turned hurriedly away, but he was coming after her.

'How much, love?'

'Piss off.'

'Come on, how much d'you charge?'

'Fifty quid,' she said furiously, sure he would refuse.

'Okay. Get in the car.' As she hesitated, he peeled off two twenty-pound notes and a tenner and handed them over. 'Money up front, right? We've done a deal.'

She got in the car, and now she really was capable of hating herself.

Brian didn't make it any better. 'So you packed in the Lane for your daughter, did you?'

'We can go round the back of the Careers Advice Centre, if you like,' she said sullenly, 'or in the mill yard. And I don't do blow jobs.'

He switched on the interior light and handed her a photograph. 'You'd better have a look at this. Don't say I haven't been doing my bit.'

The mug-shot obviously came from criminal files. The girl was glaring out with her lips drawn back in a contemptuous snarl which Rose recognised only too well.

'Why would I want to look at a picture of Madam Leather-Knickers?'

'Madam who?' Brian was startled. 'D'you know her, then?'

' 'Course I bloody know her.'

'Well, she's your daughter.'

'Oh, yes, sure. Come on, drive on, will you. This is all extra time.'

'I'm telling you. That's her. I've got a contact at the nick, and this is a print of Hannah Levison out of her criminal record. It all fits.'

It all fitted? Hannah Levison . . . Colette?

Rose shook her head. The nightmare was getting crazier. She had to make herself wake up and shove all this muck out of her mind. But she went on looking at the photograph, waiting for the truth to sink in.

18

Tracy would have thought nothing of Tula easing her legs out of a punter's car if she hadn't caught a glimpse of the driver's profile. And that was no punter. She had seen him in that same car in the police station yard. Until now it had never occurred to her that Tula, stupid young amateur, might have been the one to grass and lead them to Rabbit's place. But there had been that glimpse the other day of Tula nattering to someone in a car; and she hadn't been best pleased when Rabbit gave her the brush-off in the pub.

Tracy stood where she was until the car had driven off, and Tula had turned and seen her. She looked guilty as she caught Tracy's eye, and gasped out the first thing that came into her head. 'Got any stuff?'

'No, I bloody haven't. We got busted, in Rabbit's place.'

'No?' said Tula, all wide-eyed, shocked and innocent. 'You and Rabbit?'

Now Tracy was sure. The glee was too bloody obvious. And Tula was chattering too fast, too eagerly. 'Here, did yer tell that bloke yer off to Belgium for that I'm in on it? Any time I'm needed. It's as dead as a dodo out here.'

Another car slid up beside them, and this time it wasn't a punter or a policeman. Smiley held open the door of the Rolls and jerked a thumb at Tracy. 'Alfie wants a word.'

When they got there, Alfie was sitting in his huge jacuzzi, well on its way to being a small swimming pool, chomping away at a sandwich. The hair on his belly waved like seaweed in the water, interleaved with some shreds of bacon dropped from his sandwich.

'Tracy, me little cherub, what a surprise.'

'I bet.'

'Now, then, I hear you've been a naughty girl. A little birdie tells me you've been down the cop-shop chirping away.'

'What little birdie's that, then?'

'Why don't you take your clothes off and get in here with me?'

She looked at him twitching about, as flabby as ever. ' 'Cos I don't want to, that's why.' She didn't fancy ducking her head under water to get him going.

'What did you tell our friends in blue about that little donation I gave you?'

'Nothing. I told 'em I got the stuff off a mate.'

He reached out, got hold of her foot and wrenched her shoe off. 'You've got lovely feet, look at those toes, all nice and perfect.'

'Get off, I'm falling over.'

'Can yer imagine if they got broke, you'd never be able to wear those nice clickety shoes again.'

Tracy took a deep breath. 'I told 'em I got it from Colette. My mate. They believed me. She had to spend the night in the nick. Now will you let go? Yer hurting my foot.

'Sorry, petal.' Alfie stared up her skirt. 'Mm. Very appetising. You've got my favourite on. Come in the water, don't be a spoilsport.'

She walked down the three steps fully clothed.

'I hope your dress don't shrink.'

'You'll buy me another if it does.'

'Will I, now?' purred Alfie. 'Anyway, look – Belgium's off. They're gonna be watching yer. You've blown it, sweetheart.'

'Not me,' said Tracy. She felt the water churning about her, and Alfie's hand groping up; and thought of Tula, who'd be so pathetically keen to get in on this sort of thing. 'Listen. What if I know somebody else that'll do it? She's a mate. Not the one I grassed on, a different one. She could go instead of me, and you'd let me have a share of her cut?'

If it worked, she'd get that share. If it didn't and Tula walked right into trouble, that would still be well worth it.

'And before I go,' she said as Alfie pulled her down and clamped the damp folds of the dress closer to her, 'I can do with another lifter.'

'Smiley will see to it,' said Alfie, 'on your way out.'

Tracy's first thought when Smiley had delivered her at her door was to get rid of her clammy clothes and drag on a blouse and jeans. She thought of going down into the cellar to see how Colette was getting on with tidying up the bits of the wooden cross; but was still not sure how she'd be received. In a swirl of weird currents which meant she would soon have to reach for Alfie's latest little present, she was unprepared for the slow menace of the cellar door beginning to creak open.

It was her father, ready to come out and grin at her. Couldn't be, but she knew it had to be. Her father, reaching for her the way he had been reaching more and more greedily just lately. She kept seeing him just at this stage, halfway between one world and another, one chunk of memory and another. He was grinning that sly way he had, whispering to her not to mention to her mother all the fun they were going to have together . . .

Her thumb was in her mouth, and she was murmuring 'No, please no', when knuckles clenched round the edge of the cellar door. Only that couldn't be her father. He was still in the wardrobe, waiting for her.

The phantom of her father disappeared. He was replaced by Colette, dragging herself upright only by clinging to the door. Her fingers were smeared with blood, and the flimsy

top had been torn from her bloodied shoulders. The onl
sound she could make was a choking, sickening gurgl
Tracy cried, 'Jesus Christ, what you been up to?' and thru
herself up and across the room to catch Colette as she fe
forward.

As she helped her slowly up the stairs and laid he
carefully, wincing, on the bed, Colette was beginning t
gasp out shreds of the story. It had been that maniac Ka
– the one who had already beaten Tracy herself up an
ordered her to call him 'daddy'. If Colette had realised
she would never have let him in. There was no way c
controlling him. She had shown him into the dungeon an
said that she was usually the one who did the dom, bu
when he insisted she agreed to let herself be tied up o
condition that, whatever he did, when she cried 'daddy
he would stop. But after he had fastened her securely an
begun beating her with his belt, he couldn't stop laughing
and shouted her down every time she screamed 'daddy', an
called her a filthy little slut, and went on beating even mor
savagely. When she screamed louder, he stuck a length o
parcel tape across her mouth and went on lashing her bacl
and shoulders. In the end she had passed out; and whe
she came round, he had gone without even leaving th
money for her.

Tracy turned Colette over tenderly on the bed, and bega
pulling the shreds of material out of the bloody mess. Sh
fetched ointment from the bathroom and began massagin
as gently as she could; and even then Colette moaned an
winced at every movement.

'Take it easy,' Tracy crooned. 'I'm back. I've come hom
to make friends. I brought a rock for us to smoke.'

'I kept saying the password,' Colette wept. 'Kept sayin
"daddy", like we'd agreed, but he wouldn't stop.'

'You should have known better. I told you about him
that time in the hotel when you came looking for me
remember? Only wait a minute – it was you put him o

to me in the first place. Your own fault.' Cruelty worked both ways; lovely, either way. She eased Colette's left arm out from under her, and began to undo the black wrist-band.

'What yer doin'?' Colette drew her arm quickly back. 'I never take that off.'

'Why not? Come on, Colette, give me it.' Tracy wanted to keep it gentle; yet at the same time wanted to torment Colette and see what she was being so secretive about. 'Come on, love.'

Colette surrendered, burying her face in the pillow. Tracy unfastened the buckle and released the strap. In the wide mark left in the skin was a pattern of deep cuts, one of them beginning to fester, and the pale weals of some older ones. There was no doubt about it: they were self-inflicted.

Tracy stroked the wrist as if to rub the marks away. 'Why?'

''Cos it stops me thinking, that's why. I see blood and I know I'm alive.'

Tracy kissed the worst of the scars. 'You don't need to do that,' she murmured. 'I'll look after you, I'll never leave you again, I'm sorry.' She kissed the drying blood on Colette's back, and her lips worked their way up to her shoulder.

'You won't go back to yer ponce, will yer?' Colette pleaded. 'I couldn't stand it if yer did that.'

'No. Never. I've just been stringing him along, waiting till I can get my own back.' Tracy's mouth nuzzled Colette's neck. 'You can help me, if you like.'

'I'll do anything yer want. Anything.'

Tracy turned her over carefully, and this time Colette's moan was not one of pain. 'It's you and me together now.'

'Yes,' whispered Colette, staring up into her eyes. 'It's my birthday today. Or was it yesterday?'

They kissed, and let it last. When Tracy spoke, their lips were still brushing to and fro. 'I shouldn't have grassed on you like that. It was just crazy. I don't know what happens to me sometimes.' Her mouth moved down, and she felt Colette's nipples harden between her lips. 'I want to love you, but I keep thinking if I let myself go, you'll hurt me. Everybody I love hurts me.' She thought her father's shadow was falling across Colette's breasts, and hurried to get her own head in between that stalking shadow and Colette, seeking even further down.

'I won't.' Colette was trembling in ecstasy. 'I promise I'll never hurt yer.'

Yet Colette had been the one Tracy had wanted to hurt her. Maybe, later, the love and the hurt could be made to go together. Right now there was only one direction to go in. Tracy said 'Many happy returns', and then her mouth and tongue plunged towards the deepest intimacy of Colette's yielding body.

Ten minutes later they unwound from a waking dream, so different from Tracy's other foul dreams, to the sound of a phone which refused to stop ringing.

Tracy swore, and groped for her mobile.

Dez's voice rasped in her ear. 'I'm in the pub. Get your arse down here.'

Colette held out an arm. 'Come back. Whoever it is, let him wait.'

Tracy said, 'It's him. Dez. Now's as good a time as any. If you're with me.'

'I'd sooner be with you, like this.'

Tracy gave her a long, lingering kiss, and set off for The Hustlers' Arms.

Dez's welcome was typical. 'Where the frig have you been?'

'Doing a punter,' lied Tracy brightly. 'He took a long time.'

'I hope yer bloody charged him plenty.'

She looked at his dark, slimy face, and wondered how she could ever have thought him anything but crap. Without bothering to answer his obvious interest in the money, she said, 'I'll have a dry white wine.'

'Uh-huh. Had a busy day, then?' His eyes, she thought coldly, flickered like the figures on a supermarket till.

'Busy enough. My mate got beaten up by a punter, so I had to hang about and see to her.'

'Which mate's that?'

'Colette. You don't know her.' She dangled the bait. 'She's good. She's got punters coming out of her ears. But she does let herself in for trouble. I keep telling her: time she found someone to keep an eye on her.'

As Dez went to the bar, thinking about this, Rabbit appeared: like a rabbit out of a hat, Tracy thought, and laughed. Rabbit was always suspicious of people who laughed, but he wanted to sound her out and see how to get round her again. 'D'yer wanna drink?'

'Dez is getting me one.' And since he wanted to know where he stood, she snapped, 'Where did you piss off to, then?'

'I heard 'em coming up the stairs, but it was too late.' He slid his arm round her. 'I tried to tell yer, but yer were way out of it.'

'Funny how everyone got busted but you.'

Dez was beside them, putting the glasses down on the table and then shoving his face close to Rabbit's. 'What's this, then?'

'Piss off.' Rabbit twitched his eyebrows at Tracy. 'Where did yer find bollock-brain here? Come on, dump him. I've got some stuff.'

Dez pushed between them. 'Outside. Now.' There was a knife in his hand, prodding Rabbit towards the door. 'Touch my woman again, and I'll rip yer head off.'

'All right, man. All right. I heard yer.' Rabbit's courage had never been anything to shout about. 'I was just talking to her.'

'Well, don't. I decide who talks to her . . . who looks at

her, who shags her . . . *Me!*' On the step he kneed Rabbit, then punched him in the stomach. 'If I see yer even near her, yer dead. D'yer hear? Dead.'

The glint of his knife was tucked away as he swaggered back to Tracy. 'Smile, baby. C'mon, let's go see this mate yer've been talking about. Give her a helping hand, eh? Get her sorted.'

Tracy let him take her arm as they strolled away down the Lane. Dez was strutting in his old way, seeing himself back in business, already calculating his rakeoff from the new contact he was being promised. As she let herself in, Tracy called out quietly, 'Colette.' Then she led the way down the cellar steps and stood aside so that Dez could get a full picture of the dungeon.

The cross lay propped at an angle against the wall where Colette had heaved it aside. Dressed in a vest top deliberately showing her wounds, she was brushing some wood shavings up.

'This is Dez,' said Tracy solemnly. 'I was telling you about him.'

'Yeh.' Colette straightened up. 'Tracy said you might be able to help me.'

Dez preened himself and put on a knowing leer. 'Makes good sense not to operate on your own. Look where it gets you.' He was sizing up the equipment in the dungeon: the instruments and contraptions, the manacles, the cross leaning above the whole collection. 'Right, I know that time is money for you lot. Let's talk business.' He touched a whip hanging from the wall near him. 'So how much do you charge for a straight flogging?'

'If they're regulars, about forty. Depends on how long it takes.'

'So how many d'yer reckon to pull in a week?'

Tracy intervened. 'She makes a fortune, I can tell you that. How d'you think she affords all this stuff? Here, look at these.' She steered him towards the manacles hanging from the wooden strip on the wall. 'This is what they really go for. She does all sort of things when they're in these, don't you, Colette?'

Colette licked her lips and nodded.

'I bet you do.' Dez was surveying her admiringly.

'Put your hand in.' Tracy pressed gently under his left shoulder so that he would reach up towards the manacles 'Go on, you need to know how these things work if you're going to look after her.'

Dez was beginning to look uncomfortable.

'It's all right,' said Colette. 'I've got the key.'

Reluctantly Dez let Tracy slide his arm into the handcuff and lock it shut. She held on to him, kissed him on the mouth, and began unfastening his trousers. 'Got you where I want you now.' Her body against his was warming him up the way it had done when he got out of prison. 'Come on, now the other one.' He was only too happy now to let her raise his right hand towards the other manacle and let her secure it. 'Me and Colette are going to do all sorts of nice things to you.'

Staring into her face with randy impatience, he was eager for her to go on. But suddenly she backed away, and stood taking a long, thoughtful look at him.

Colette was shifting excitedly from one foot to the other. 'What we gonna do now, Tracy?'

Dez was part excited, part worried. Trapped in that position with his arms splayed out, his lust was the first thing to seep away. 'All right,' he said as decisively as he could. 'I get the picture. Now get me out of these.'

Tracy slowly, dreamily picked up her bag and took out her coke knife. Colette watched her hopefully; then took an uncertain step forward.

'Tracy!'

Tracy stretched up almost lovingly towards Dez, raised the knife, and in one slow but steady movement slashed his throat right across.

'Smile, baby!' she taunted.

Colette let out a howl. Blood began pumping out of Dez's neck. Tracy smiled, feeling better with every steady pulse of that blood down Dez's neck and chest. After a few moments she settled herself on the floor at his feet, with her thumb comfortingly in her mouth.

19

Rose sat hunched in her dressing-gown at Carol's kitchen table, still staring at the photograph of her daughter. Carol could tell from her reddened eyes that she had spent a sleepless night; and the day wasn't going to be any more cheerful if she didn't shake herself out of her trance – or have a friend do it for her.

'All that claptrap you gave me about never going back on the Lane,' jeered Carol. 'It was a pile of shite. First bit of bad news and you start hitching your skirt up again.'

'A bit of bad news? For Christ's sake, I found me own daughter had been hustling. How would you like it if it'd been your Emma?'

'I'd kill her.'

'I can't take it in. Colette! I always thought I'd know my kid the minute I saw her. I thought summat would twig in my brain.'

'It did. You hated her. Had it in for her the minute you clapped eyes on her.' Carol plucked a few bits of fluff off her skirt. 'D'you think this looks all right to go to the solicitors?'

Rose wasn't to be distracted. 'How could I not have known? She even looks like him.'

'I don't know why he couldn't just tell me over the phone that it was all a mistake, or someone's had a go at them, and I haven't got a bloody penny.'

There was a creaking on the stairs as Anita came down, rubbing sleep out of her eyes but looking oddly triumphant.

'Where did you get to last night?' Carol challenged her.

'I . . . er . . . I had to meet someone. I do have a life of my own, y'know. I mean, you don't tell me everything *you* do.'

'That's because you've got a mouth the size of the Mersey Tunnel,' said Rose.

Anita slapped four ten-pound notes on the table in front of Carol. 'Twenty-five pound rent money,' she said airily, 'and fifteen towards the electric.'

'Come up on the scratch cards, have you?'

Before Carol could reach for her coat and be on her way, there was a knocking at the door. She hesitated, wondering whether to escape out the back. But it wasn't a copper's knock; she would have recognised one of those.

Joyce stood on the doorstep. Rose let her in and followed her into the kitchen.

'I've got to talk to someone.'

Carol glanced at the kitchen clock. She couldn't just walk out when Joyce looked like that. But she mustn't let things drag on too long.

'It's me dad,' Joyce explained. 'I've nothing to bury him with. No insurance policy, no nowt. It took every penny I had to bury our Gina.'

'Have we got anything left in the Scrubbit account?'

'Three hundred.' Joyce had already worked this out. 'But we owe two-seventy to Handycloth.'

'Bugger Handycloth,' said Carol. 'Use it to bury your dad.'

'I can't do that. We'd be in debt then, and we wouldn't be able to start up again.'

'Well, we're not likely to, anyway, are we?'

Joyce slumped down on a hardbacked chair. 'I had Brenda round, grovelling. Seems like she was the one Ferguson got to, so he could drop us in it.'

'I bloody knew it.'

Rose glared at Anita as if it had been her fault. Anita suddenly showed an interest in the kitchen taps.

'She was quaking in her boots,' Joyce went on. 'Says Ferguson was setting a company up for her when he copped it. And now some other bloke who says he's owed a lot of money is round giving her a hard time. Maybe he's the one who killed Ferguson, and now Brenda thinks he's set to kill *her* if she doesn't play along with him. Only she hasn't a clue what it's all about.'

'Why would Ferguson set up a company for Brenda bleeding Taylor?'

Carol would have liked to know the answer to that one, too; but she had to get away right now. She fancied she'd soon be back, with more bad news to add to the morning collection.

Although she had arrived at exactly the time arranged, Mr Chubb didn't seem to be ready for her. Or maybe he treated everyone this way: riffling through papers, shoving them to one side and then diving into a drawer for some more, and wiping his eyes at two-minute intervals as if to remove tears of remorse for what he was about to say.

At last he began reading aloud in a steady monotone, so that words ran into one another without making any sense.

Carol brought him up short. 'Hang on a minute. You're going too fast, I can't get it. Are you saying I have or I haven't got anything? Anything at all?'

Mr Chubb looked hurt, wiped his eyes again, and with exaggerated slowness went on. 'I am saying that your daughter has inherited a legacy of twenty-thousand pounds, and I have a cheque here for her.'

'Frigging Nora.'

Mr Chubb winced, but kept to his solemn tone. 'And providing all the criteria are met, you inherit the rest of Mr Durkin's estate. There are four conditions in total . . .' Carol hardly dared to breathe as he paused for effect before reeling them off. 'One, that the chicken factory name and signage remain the same.'

'Yeh.' There didn't seem to be any catch in that.

'Two, that the business isn't sold or merged within a period of ten years.'

'Yeh?'

'And three . . .' Mr Chubb was clearing his throat and dabbing at his eyes at one and the same time. He seemed flummoxed for a moment. 'A rather unusual condition. Er . . . that under no circumstances is Miss Carol Johnson to employ her services as a common prostitute. I'm sorry, Miss . . . er . . . but your . . .' He was at a loss how to describe Curly. 'Mr Durkin was adamant that the latter condition was included. I am to oversee this particular requirement for a modest annual fee.'

And how was he going to do that? Carol had a vision of Mr Chubb spending every evening strolling up and down Lambton Lane to see if she popped out.

'And what about his nephew?' she asked.

'Ah, yes. The final condition of the will—' here comes the stinker, she thought '– is that Vincent Marshall be retained as company manager of Durkin's chicken factory. He will be paid an adequate salary and a small dividend each year based on a percentage of the profits, provided there is no serious misdemeanour on his part.'

There had already been one hell of a serious misdemeanour on Vincent Marshall's part. Now Carol realised she would have to decide how far to go with evidence for the prosecution. But in the meantime . . .

She stared in disbelief at Mr Chubb as he rounded off their meeting. 'The cash and annuities can be immediately put into effect, but some of the other things might take a little longer.' He forced a wintry, envious little grin. 'You can smile, my dear. Basically you're a considerably wealthy woman.'

Carol was too dazed to smile until she found herself walking back through the estate to her house. Then the sight of her neighbour cleaning the front windows released her broad smile. Crazy, but one of the most wonderful things about that news this morning was that it meant she could buy her council house and, like she'd always threatened, stick a bloody great flashing light in the window. Maybe a sign advertising Speciality Saunas.

A car horn beeped. Newall was leaning out of the driver's window, and in the back Liam's sallow olive face peered out at her. Already the money was working, giving her a new confidence as she strode across the street.

'Do you want to hear some good news?'

'Do you want to hear some bad?' Newall retorted. 'Hoyle's gunning for you.'

'Again?'

'No, not again. *Still.* You didn't think they were going to give up on you over that attempted suppression of evidence, did you? And now they've confirmed Rose Garrity's prints in Curly's car. Looks as if the pair of you were in it together. I'm telling you, Hoyle is an ambitious cow. She wants DI, and putting the pair of you away would be a big help.'

Carol was plunging down off cloud nine. 'What am I gonna do?'

'I'm driving back to Birmingham. We could go up to school, get your Emma out, and start again down there.'

'What, just leave everything?'

'Why not?'

'No.'

'Why not? I've been thinking of what you were saying about me getting off on you being a hustler. And could be you're right. What's only just clicked in my brain is that *you* were turned on because I was a copper. So I've got this idea.'

She wondered whether to interrupt and tell him how she stood now and why she didn't need to listen to him or anyone else. But he was going on, 'You hustle for me.'

'Piss off. You're joking.'

'No. I pay you the same as Curly paid you—'

'And what do you get for your hundred and fifty quid?'

He lowered his voice to a whisper so that Liam could not

hear. 'Sex. Whenever I like. Whenever I fancy popping round. Middle of the night . . . afternoon . . . When you're in the bath. If I see you outside, I can drag you off in my car, take you up on Baildon Moor and shag the life out of you.'

'Curly didn't get sex,' she said. 'He got nowt.'

'Well, that was Curly. I'm different.'

She had wanted to confront him with her news and watch his face. He was the one who had broken the story of the will and the money in that poxy station of his; but, like herself, he probably hadn't believed the story would really come true. It was going to make a hell of a difference. She needed to think over just what those differences would be.

'I'll think about it,' she said condescendingly, and marched towards her front door.

Smiley had told Tula not to worry. It would all be quite straightforward. She only had to stand by the information desk in Brussels airport, and somebody would come up to her. They would kiss her and hand over a teddy bear. She was booked on the next flight back, and could get a taxi home. Somebody would contact her for the handover of the teddy bear.

'Don't I get to see Belgium?' Tula had asked wistfully.

'Just the airport.'

'And when do I get me stuff?'

'When we get the teddy,' said Smiley.

It sounded simple enough. Tula relaxed on the plane over, feeling important. People were beginning to realise that she counted for something. She could move up in the world, do more courier jobs like this for them; take over from Tracy where Alfie was concerned.

But sweat was breaking out on her forehead as she waited in the echoing terminal at Brussels; and when the teddy bear was handed to her by a young man who kissed her and gabbled something in an affectionate tone of voice which she couldn't understand, she was sure everyone on the concourse must be watching.

The flight back to London was little different from the flight out. It hadn't been much of a break. Next time she would insist that Alfie and Smiley arranged things differently.

Sweat prickled again as she went through the Leeds and Bradford 'Nothing to Declare' channel. She had put the teddy bear with its head sticking out of her small haversack, as instructed, and was walking ahead of a middle-aged couple with a trolley carrying a couple of battered suitcases and two duty-free carrier bags.

Nearly there. And then a woman in blue uniform stepped forward, smiling pleasantly. 'Excuse me, madam, could you step over here?'

'What for?' Tula's voice came out in a high-pitched squeak.

'Would you mind if I looked in your bag?'

She found herself in a small, drab room with a couple of tables and a male Customs and Excise officer waiting for her. With an apologetic nod he took out the teddy bear, prodded it, and slit it open with a knife from an array of implements in one of the table drawers. Then he said 'Tut, tut' and shook his head at the sight of the teddy's stuffing – a mixture of cocaine and bicarbonate.

'Look,' said Tula desperately, 'it's all right, really it is.'

'Doesn't look all right to me.' The friendliness was evaporating.

'Ring DC Gregson at Turton Lane police station in Bradford. He knows all about this, he told me to go through with it so they could get their hands on the dealers at this end.'

The two officers silently consulted each other; then the woman left the room. It was an age before she came back. 'Never heard of you.'

'But that's crazy. Look, you lot are gonna screw everything up for the coppers if yer don't let me go soon. This pick-up bloke's supposed to be contacting me, and if he gets wind that you lot are on to me, he'll drop me like a hot potato. Gregson's wise to it, thanks to me. He's got to tell you.'

'I've spoken to DC Gregson direct,' said the woman, 'and I'm afraid he knows nothing about you or a teddy bear full of cocaine.'

'The lying bastard. He does know me. I've talked to him, I told him all about the Belgium trip, handed it to him on a plate!'

The other two exchanged glances which might almost have been sympathetic. The man said, 'You don't know anyone else who might have been involved? Somebody a bit more high-powered?'

Dimly it was beginning to dawn on Tula that she had been used. She had been all too obvious, set up to get caught while somebody else walked through unchallenged. So much for Alfie and his promises. And so much for the police, and what they were prepared to do for her after she'd done so much for them. And as for Tracy, who'd let her in for this . . .

Tracy sat on the sofa watching breakfast television. There was a phone-in session going on, and bits of it were very funny. From time to time she ran her hand through her hair. Sooner or later she'd have to have a shower and get rid of those knots of dried blood, but she felt too weak to bother right now.

Colette was going on at her. 'Tracy, it won't just go away. We're gonna have to do summat. Tracy, are you listening to me? What the hell are we gonna do?'

'Nothing.' Tracy turned the TV volume up. 'We don't have to do nothing.'

'We can't just leave him down there.'

'Why not? He liked hanging about.' That made her laugh. It was almost as good as the crack the television interviewer had just made. If only Colette would stop nattering.

But Colette couldn't stop. 'I can't believe yer just cut his throat like that. I thought yer were going to knee him in the bollocks or summat.'

'You said when you saw blood you felt alive,' Tracy reminded her.

'I meant my own blood.' Colette turned her right wrist upwards.

The movement tore Tracy away from the screen for a moment. 'Promise me you won't do that any more. Promise you won't cut yourself.'

'Yer off yer head! What yer worried about me for? What about yourself? They're going to lock you up, Tracy, yer gonna do serious time for this. We're not talking six months in a detention centre.'

'I don't give a toss. He got what he deserved.'

She was hurt that Colette just didn't understand. Not just about Dez bashing her with a rock so that she ended in hospital. It was everything that went before it. How he had picked her up when she first got here from Harrogate – picked her up at the railway station and took her to his house, and gave her money and bought her clothes. Said he would look after her for ever and ever. Until one day he said he needed some money for a deal, and asked her to do a trick. Just one. And like a fool she had believed him, and when she had finished he picked her up in his Merc and kissed her, told her she was his babe, gave her a little lifter, and they laughed all the way back home.

Only the next day he wanted her to do it again. And when she said no, she'd done it once and didn't want to go doing it again, he had grabbed her face so hard she had bruises on it for a week. She stood on the Lane until her legs were blue and her feet were numb. Smiling at cars like a frigging hyena, when all she wanted was for him to tell her he loved her again.

All she'd ever really wanted was love.

'We could dump his body somewhere,' Colette was urging, 'and clean things up down there. Did anybody see him come here?'

Before Tracy could decide whether to bother answering this, there was a sharp knocking at the front door. Colette let out a little moan of fear. When Tracy switched off the television and headed for the door, Colette put out a hand to stop her; but Tracy wasn't frightened, she'd stopped being frightened after proving just what she was capable of. She opened the door to find a burly man in a heavy tweed overcoat on the step.

He looked her up and down, not sure that he liked what he saw. 'I'm booked in,' he said uncomfortably. 'I rang the other day, spoke to your . . . er . . . personal secretary. A full body massage with relief. Am I a bit early?'

Colette edged out into the hall. 'She's not well. She'll have to cancel, won't you, Tracy?'

Tracy had been debating how she might get out of this booking, but Colette's interference settled it. 'I think I can manage all right. What's yer name?'

'Denis. Denis Harvey.' He was a hefty, overpowering type, but now he was looking unsettled. 'You haven't got the flu, or anything? The wife's susceptible to these things. She's a bit on the delicate side.'

'No, it's not the flu. Come in.'

'I don't believe it,' Colette muttered.

'It must have been Anita who booked you in,' said Tracy sweetly. 'Top of the stairs, first door on the right.'

She gave Colette a taunting smile as she followed Harvey upstairs and closed the bedroom door behind them. Five minutes later she heard the slam of the front door below as Colette stormed out somewhere; but by then she was hard at work kneading the man's tightly stretched belly and working her fingers expertly down to give him the relief that was part of the deal.

They were words Rose had never expected to hear from Colette: not words like this, and not the pleading tone of voice.

'I need yer to help me. Please, Rose.'

She stood in Carol's living-room, shrunken and despairing, vulnerable and no longer the aggressive bitch. But what she had to say turned Rose's stomach more than anything Colette had ever snarled at her in the past.

Not Colette. Hannah . . .

Her daughter, telling her an incredible story of bloodshed. And then throwing herself on her mercy. 'I came to you 'cos I didn't know where else to go, who else to tell. And I know you love Tracy, so yer won't tell on her, will yer? I promised I'd never hurt her . . . I promised . . .' She broke down, plunging her face into her hands.

Rose ached to hold her but did not dare make a move. It wouldn't do for both of them to break down, and she wouldn't trust herself once she had the girl in her arms.

'It's all right, it'll be all right,' she said breathlessly, without knowing how the hell it could be made to come all right. 'We'll sort something out.' She flinched at the sight of the weals and bruises on Colette's arms and the edge of her shoulder. 'Who did that to you?'

'Just a bad punter,' said Colette dismissively. All she was interested in was Tracy. 'I knew you'd help us. Look at you – near to crying, same as me. We know she's not like that really, don't we?'

Rose was not ready to tell her – not yet – who her tears were really for. She forced herself to say, 'You sure you saw her do it?'

'I was with her. I helped her put his hands in the manacles. She said she wanted to get even with him. I couldn't believe my bloody eyes when . . . when she just stuck the knife in his neck and pulled it across. I keep seeing her do it, over and over again.'

'She knows you've come to me?'

'Not frigging likely. I only got out because she were doing a punter. Can you believe that? As if nothing had happened.

But once he's paid her and cleared off . . . look, we've go
to get round there. You've got to come.'

There was silence in the house when they opened the doo
and went in. Rose looked round, plucked at by memories
Tracy and Colette ran the place now, but she still remembere
it as her own.

'Tracy!' Colette called up the stairs. 'Are you there
Tracy?'

There was no reply. Colette made her way up step by
step, as if afraid of wakening someone – or afraid o
something worse.

'Tracy! Guess who I bumped into on the Lane?'

She pushed the bedroom door open. Tracy was lying o
the bed, her eyes wide open, staring at the ceiling. When she
turned her head and saw Rose at Colette's elbow, she pushe
herself up.

'I don't want you here. I don't want anyone here. I wanna
be left alone.'

'Listen.' Colette was advancing warily towards the bed.
'Rose and me are gonna wait till it gets dark, and then—'

''Rose and me? So it's Rose and Colette now, is it?'

'Tracy, we want to help you.'

'I don't need any help.'

'You do need help. And yer can trust Rose.'

'So when did you two get such big buddies? I thought you
hated each other.' Tracy's fragile voice grew angrier. 'Or do
you love her now, and you're dropping me just the way she
dropped me—'

'I love you,' said Colette fervently. 'I've always loved yer,
since the first time I clapped eyes on yer. We're gonna sort
this out, then pack the whole lot in. We're gonna stop hustling
and stop smoking and get you right.'

Rose thought Tracy was going to keep up her defiance.
Instead, she let herself slump back on the bed, turned on to
her side, and put her thumb back dreamily in her mouth.

20

Joyce had left Rose's place puzzled by what was going on there. Because something had definitely been going on. Rose was red-eyed, utterly absorbed in a photograph she shielded from Joyce's glance, and Carol had been too wrapped up in her own problems to pay any attention to anyone else's.

Joyce made her way home and was setting about a mid-morning tidy of her bedroom when she heard a faint movement downstairs, followed by the unmistakable squeak of Michelle's pushchair. She tossed a pillow back on to the bed and went cautiously down to the hall. In the living room, Steve was loading some toys and a torn paperback into the pushchair basket.

'How did you get in?' Joyce demanded.

'I used Gina's key. Just came to pick up some of the kids' things.'

'Where's our Michelle?'

'At home. She's still asleep. I left her with Lisa,' added Steve awkwardly.

'I'll have that key of mine back, if you don't mind.'

'Look, you didn't want me to lie to you, did you?'

'I don't want you to do anything.'

Steve fished a wad of notes out of his back pocket. 'There's a hundred and twenty there. To see to things for your dad.'

'Keep it. I don't want your money.'

'So what you gonna do, Joyce?' Steve was exasperated into sarcasm. 'Ring the social, fill in the form?'

'It's my problem, so I'll sort it out. He's my family, not yours.'

'He was Gina's grandfather, he's my family by marriage. You'll get nothing for a headstone or a plaque. A coffin, a car and a spray of flowers is all you'll get.'

Joyce knew this was true, but said doggedly, 'He's going to get a proper send-off, don't you worry.'

'So take the money. If I had any more I'd—'

'I don't need it. I've decided I'm gonna get a loan.'

'Oh no, you're not.'

She went on wildly building up a fantasy, anything to keep him at arm's length. 'I might get this place decorated, as well. High time it was done, and bloody Bob could never stir himself to do anything. And while they're doing it I might go on a bit of a holiday.'

'On a loan? You know what happened to Gina.'

She overrode anything he was trying to say. 'I might go abroad somewhere. Yeh, I think I'll have myself a bit of a life while I still can.'

'What the bleeding hell are you talking about, Joyce?'

She was deliberately goading him, 'You never know, I might pull myself a nice toy-boy.'

'I can't believe you're saying all this,' Steve groaned.

She flung it in his face. 'And I can't believe you've got another woman in our Gina's house.'

Carol was taking her coat off as she went along the hall. There were two things she had to tell Rose: the good news and the bad news. It was hard to decide whether the benefits of the money were going to outweigh the problem of the police closing in on them about Curly's still unsolved murder.

Anita came fussing out of the kitchen, bubbling over with the urge to spread her own bit of news.

Carol was in no mood for Anita's flapping and chattering. 'Where's Rose?'

'Up at Tracy's. You'll never guess what's happened.'

There was no point in guessing, when Anita was bursting to blurt it all out. She had happened to be passing the door when she heard Colette and Rose – 'Yes, honest, *Colette* and Rose' – talking about what Tracy had done. Cutting her ponce's throat, that was what. That Dez – tying him up and cutting his throat.

Carol slipped her coat back on and headed for Rose's old place. She could have done without company, but Anita was teetering along beside her and was determined to be at the scene of the crime.

She had to knock four or five times before Rose cautiously opened the door a crack and stared at Anita. 'What do *you* want?'

'She's heard it all,' said Carol curtly, 'and she's told me everything. Or as much as she can carry in her head.'

'Like I said, the Mersey bleeding Tunnel!'

They went through to the kitchen. Carol broke the news about the police, but Rose was too concerned with what she had just found out about Tracy to concentrate on this other trouble. They'd soon have to consider both problems, though: another corpse in the lives of Carol Johnson and Rose Garrity wasn't going to improve relations with the law.

'Where is she?' Carol asked.

'Upstairs with the duvet over her head. Colette's with her. She won't let anybody else in the room. You'd better stay down here. If she knows you're here, it might freak her out even more.'

'And where's . . . he?'

'Him that was, y'mean. Still strung up down there.'

Anita was looking helpless; and Rose had been hit by too many things these last few days. Somebody had to make decisions. Carol said, 'So what's the plan? What are we going to do?'

'How do you plan for summat like this?'

'Have you been down there?'

'No.'

'And I'm not going down,' Anita whimpered. 'I had nightmares for years after I saw my father laid out.'

Before they could make any decisions, Colette came hurrying down from upstairs. She glared at them all. 'You'll have to go.'

'Look, I know what she's going through,' said Carol carefully. After that breakdown last year when she had maimed Curly, she knew what it felt like. 'I know what I'm talking about. I can help her.'

'She won't talk to anyone but me,' said Colette.

'He must have pushed her something deadly for her to go—'

'She said she were stringing him along to get her own back. She asked me to help her. I thought she were gonna knee him in the bollocks or summat, I didn't know she were gonna kill him.'

A thought occurred to Carol. It was monstrous, but once it had reared up in her mind she couldn't just slap it down. 'You don't think she's . . . done it before?'

Anita stared. George Ferguson? But Tracy wouldn't have had any reason to carve Ferguson up, any more than she would have wanted to track Curly down and slit his throat.

Rose was saying, 'No, it's a one-off, has to be,' when Tracy appeared in the doorway like a ghost. Carol had not realised until this moment just how far downhill Tracy had gone in a matter of months. She had been a young, pretty girl with a babyish complexion: just the sort of dim baby doll some punters went for. Now the ravages of crack showed on her face, her hair was in a bloody tangle, and she was shaking uncontrollably.

She looked straight at Rose. 'I did it for you.'

'What? I don't get it.'

''Cos he was trying to get the contract off you.'

Rose went pale. 'What are you talking about, love?'

'He were evil. He wanted to hurt you.'

'Who did?'

'George,' Anita whispered. 'She's talking about George Ferguson.'

It dawned on them one after the other, like a poisonous ripple spreading around the room.

'You loved that company,' Tracy went on. 'You worked all the time for it, it meant everything to you. Didn't it?' She was daring Rose to deny it. 'Didn't it?'

'You killed him for me?'

'And he put all that crap in the papers about yer being hustlers, and Anita ended up in hospital 'cos he wanted to teach her a lesson. Well, I thought it was about time someone taught *him* one.' She was looking eagerly from one face to the next for a sign of approval and gratitude.

'Tracy.' Rose was trying to keep her voice very calm. 'Do you understand you can't just go round killing people?'

''Course I understand that,' said Tracy patiently. 'I've not gone barmy all of a sudden. I've not flipped, y'know. I'm only doing what other people do all the time.'

'What d'you mean, other people? What are you talking about?'

'I'm doing what I want. I want to make things better, and I am. You see, when I killed me dad I knew he could never do to our Laura what he did to me.'

Carol felt a chill of horror stabbing down her spine. 'You killed your dad?'

'Yeh.' Tracy looked so innocent, unable to understand why they didn't understand her. 'He came to Carol's. He was looking for me, and I knew the only thing I could do was—'

'Hang on a minute,' Carol faltered. 'Your dad came to my house?'

'Yeh.'

'When?'

Tracy groped for dates and times, but they had slipped away into a haze. The main memories were clear enough, though, like all her memories of her father. Dates meant nothing. It had gone on for so long; and then, just as she'd thought she'd escaped him altogether, there he was, up to his old tricks and some new ones.

She was sitting on the sofa, while her father sat in the armchair looking at her and beginning to lick his lips. He was saying something about a Chinese takeaway waiting in the oven, if she wanted some. He was quite pleased when she said she didn't much go for Chinese. 'Haven't got a lot of time.' She remembered him saying that. And then he asked her to walk up and down in front of him, in her black stockings and black shoes. 'I'll give you fifty quid.' That was different anyway. It wasn't a matter of new trainers this time. When she hesitated, not knowing what he was up to or how he had found his way to Carol's house, he made it a hundred quid.

'She shouldn't be long, but if you'd just walk about a bit . . .'

She had walked up and down, rustling her stockinged legs together at every four or five paces. His marigold gloves began going nineteen to the dozen, and he was gasping, 'That's it . . . oh, yes, good girl, that's it. Good girl.'

She watched her father's hands and what they were doing. And the way he said 'Good girl' brought it all flooding back. He'd always said that when he had his hand down her knickers. And now he was asking her to go round the back of the chair. Once she was there, looking down on her father's head, she knew straight away what she had to do. It was dead easy. She just took her knife out of her bag and leaned forward and cut as hard as she could, and felt better. This time she had really finished her father off.

'It wasn't your father,' Carol croaked. 'It was Curly you killed.'

'No,' said Tracy confidently, 'it were me dad.'

The others exchanged glances. They knew now that they had a psychotic on their hands.

Carol said, 'It was you in my house, walking. It was you that Curly's nephew saw. Your dad didn't come to my house.'

'He did.'

'What were *you* doing there, in the first place?'

'I thought Rose was with you. I thought she'd run out on me, I wanted to talk to her and . . .' Tracy's voice faded as she turned towards Colette and smiled lovingly, already discarding Rose.

Carol sighed. When the police got round to dragging her and Rose down to the nick yet again for bumping Curly off, how would it sound telling the coppers it was all a mistake, and it had really been Tracy's dad all along? They'd got fingerprints of both of them on the car; they knew that Curly had been in her house; and it was obvious that she and Rose had tried to get rid of the body. And when it came to Ferguson, who knew both Curly and Ferguson? Us, she thought, that's who. She and Rose were the link. And now there was this latest killing. It was bound to look as if the two of them were working together, knocking men off like there was no tomorrow. Just when her life had shown signs of beginning to sort itself out, things were all going wrong.

Rose had moved closer to Tracy. 'Let's face it. You've killed three men.'

'You're a mass murderer,' breathed Anita.

'All right, Anita, we can do without that.'

'I tell you what, I think we should call the police, tell 'em we found him down there.'

'No police!' Tracy was panic-stricken, twisting round and clawing Colette's shoulder. 'Yer promised me.'

'Nobody's ringing the police.' Rose glared at Anita. 'Right, we'd better get down there and see what's what.' She looked in a quite different way at Colette. 'Do you want to stay here and keep an eye on Tracy?' she asked tenderly.

Colette's was resolute. 'I'd better come with you. I'll have to find the key for the manacles. I think I dropped it on the floor.'

'I don't mind staying with Tracy,' said Anita, as though conferring a great favour.

The others approached the cellar door with growing apprehension. When Rose opened it, the smell that rose to meet them made Carol retch. One after the other they went down the steps. The only light came from the high cellar window, casting an exaggerated shadow of the half-hanging, slumped body of Dez across the floor. Carol looked at another shadow, made by a vast bloodstain. She had thought Curly had leaked enough of the stuff, but this had spread far further.

Colette went down on her knees and found the key to the manacles. When the corpse's wrists had been freed and he was toppling slowly forward on his face, Carol said, 'Right. So what do we do next?'

'An irish jig,' growled Rose. 'What d'you think?' She picked her way round the sprawled body, and scuffed her foot in the litter of mortar and loose brickwork. 'Hang on. I think I've cracked it.' She sprang into action, dragging an old carpet from a dark corner of the cellar. 'And you two,' she ordered, 'widen that hole. Colette, have you got a ladder anywhere down here? And a hammer or something nice and heavy?'

When they had smashed a larger hole in the wall, they rolled Dez up in the carpet and set about heaving it up to the gap. Even with a rickety stepladder it was a tough proposition. Rose on the ladder stooped to take the weight on her shoulder as Carol and Colette struggled to tilt the body in the carpet towards her. When Rose had got it balanced, Carol gave a wild shove that despatched Dez into the wall cavity, leaving a cloud of dust behind him.

They began tidying up the mess on the floor. The dungeon was no less gloomy, but was beginning at least to look reasonably tidy, with the cross moved out of the way and the raw edges of the cavity evened out.

None of them heard anything from above until Anita opened the cellar door and called down, 'Colette! Your carpenter's here.'

'Shit.'

'I tried to get rid of him, but he—'

'I've come to put your cross back up,' Bill said from the top of the steps. 'I didn't come yesterday because I didn't have the right rawlplugs.'

Colette and Rose exchanged fearful glances; but Carol brightened. She waved at the blank hole in the wall, and silently mouthed at Colette that she should let Bill come down. A large piece of plasterboard would cover the gap. Unless he climbed in – which they could make sure he wasn't tempted to try – he would never know what had fallen through to the bottom of the cavity. Let him go ahead, replacing the cross and covering up everything else. Plaster and make good, and Dez could rot away in there without anyone ever suspecting.

Bill came down, giving a quizzical glance at the women's dusty faces but venturing no more than a 'Business must be a bit dead' and 'Filling in the time with your own DIY?'

Rose stretched her aching arms and shoulders, and climbed the cellar steps on her way to wash off some of the white dust and grime. Colette stayed watching Bill until she could be quite sure that he was plodding unsuspectingly through his work.

Anita met Rose halfway along the hall. She was twittering, making up excuses before she had even explained what had happened. 'I only turned my back for a few minutes – what with getting some soapy water to bring down to you lot, and letting that carpenter in, and then—'

'What are you on about?'

'She's gone,' wailed Anita. 'Tracy's gone.'

21

Colette was feverishly prodding digits on her mobile phone. Tracy's own mobile must be switched off: there was no reply. 'She'll have gone to find Rabbit for a smoke.' But Rabbit was in no mood to help. He suggested bitterly that Tracy could be with that arsehole of a ponce she'd picked up with again. Colette had the presence of mind to say, 'No, we've tried him,' before trying Tracy's own number again, still without result. She might have picked up another punter. Or might have done something desperate.

Carol, thinking wretchedly of the way they'd had to dispose of yet another dead body, and of losing Emma yet again, only this time maybe forever, urged Rose and Anita out on the streets with her, leaving Colette to settle with Bill and get him off the premises.

'There must be places where you can send people like Tracy,' Anita fretted. 'I mean, hospitals and that, where you can get them fixed.'

'She's gone mental,' said Carol. 'You can't fix that.'

'They fixed you, didn't they?'

'I cracked up, I didn't go mental, for Christ's sake.'

They were wandering aimlessly, getting nowhere. Rose's old affection for Tracy, who had once been so dependent on her, drove her at a quickening pace down the Lane, into the pub and out again. Had anybody seen Tracy? They tried to keep it casual, but Carol was terrified that somebody would sooner or later pick up the strain in their voices, and when the police started asking questions the net would tighten and there'd be no way of slipping through it.

Suddenly it struck her. 'You don't suppose she's gone back home?'

'Home!' Rose stopped dead. 'That's it! That's where she'll have gone, home to her dad's.'

'But she thinks she's already killed her dad—'

'Or after what we said, she's beginning to have doubts. About Curly, and about her dad still being alive—'

'We've got to get to Harrogate,' said Rose.

'I'm not going to no Harrogate.' Carol thought of Emma waiting to be picked up from school. And what was she going to tell the coppers who might be waiting for her when she got home? 'I'm warning you right now, if it comes to me going down for this or Tracy going down, it's not gonna be me.'

She turned away from Rose's pleading, reproachful face and went off. Emma came first.

Carol was not the only one hurrying to the school gates. Joyce was there just ahead of her, already opening her mouth to say something. Carol had no time right now for Joyce's woes and lamentations about the cleaning company or anything else. More important, Newall's car was parked twenty or thirty yards down the road. Carol pretended not to notice it until Emma had come running across the yard to grab her hand; and then led her towards it. She did not wait for Newall to lean out and say whatever he had to say, but opened the passenger door and the rear door.

'Get in the back, Emma. That's Liam. We're going for a little ride.' She closed the rear door and slid into the front seat beside Newall. 'That's right, isn't it? You're taking us for a drive.'

'Where to?'

She directed him up the hill and over the ridge, and down to the house set back behind its low stone wall and guardian trees. He slowed in by the kerb, but Carol waved him on between the brick gateposts with what might have been a ıythical bird but looked more like a chicken on top of each ne. The gates were open, and the open doors of the garage eyond showed that it was empty. They both knew that it ıust once have housed the car which finished up in a shop vindow with the owner in the boot.

When Liam and Emma had been let out, to rush without esitation into the grounds sloping gently down from the atio, Newall took a deep breath of what might have been nvy or disbelief. She knew how he felt. She was still only ıst getting used to the idea that all this was really hers.

'So his nephew didn't contest the will?' said Newall at ast.

'You know bloody well his nephew's still waiting to ppear in court on a charge of kidnapping.'

'Which you'll be pursuing?'

'I . . . don't know. Not exactly.'

'Anyway, all this is yours, is it?'

'And the business and everything else. She did me a avour.'

'Who did?'

'Whoever killed Curly.'

Too late she realised her mistake. He was still the copper, till alert for the fatal giveaway. 'You said *she*.'

'Did I?'

'Yeh, you did. You know who it is, don't you?' He was eaning fiercely towards her. 'You know who did it.' When Carol moved away from the car and pretended to study flowerbed, he got out and came round the bonnet to tand beside her. 'Come on, you can tell me now. I'm off he case.'

'You're still a copper. You'll never shake it off.'

'Was it Rose?'

'No.' He was getting too close. She moved further down he slope. 'So you see, I don't need your hundred and fifty week.'

'But do you need *me*?'

'No,' she said without looking at him. 'I don't nee anyone, except Emma.'

Under the shade of the tall hedge at the bottom of th garden, Emma and Liam were rolling happily about lik brother and sister. A squeal of laughter like a flurry c birdsong echoed up the slope.

Newall wasn't one to give up easily. 'Who killed you sugar daddy?'

Carol tried to cut round the end of the flowerbed on t the patio, staring up at the rear windows of the house *her* house.

'Look at me, will yer?' He was shouting loudly enoug to make the kids look round for a moment. 'Look, know you.'

'You know nothing.'

'And d'you know how I know you?' He grabbed her fac between his hands and was forcing her to look at him; an those brown eyes weren't pathetically dog-like any longe but burning and insistent. 'Because I'm like you, we'r two of a kind: two pathetic bastards, struggling to ge one over on each other so that we feel better. I look a you and I see me. And you don't like this because you'r staring at yourself.' He held her head steady. 'Kiss me Go on.'

She tried to shake her head, but was held too firmly in hi grip. 'No, I can't.'

He let go. 'So we're finished, then?' When no reply came he said, 'Well, have a nice life, with your house and you chicken factory and your secrets. Thanks for the private viev of the premises, anyway.' He raised his voice again. 'Com on, Liam, we've got to be going.'

Both the kids protested.

Carol felt a sudden panic. She wanted to clutch Newall' sleeve and hold on to him until she could decide . . . decid what? For a mad moment she thought of offering him a jo as security officer for the Durkin Chickens factory. She coul imagine the furious response. He still wanted to be in charge, to dominate.

'All right,' she said. 'I'll take your hundred and fifty quid and see you Thursdays.'

'That's not what I want.' He walked away, beckoning Liam to join him.

'It's not what I want either.' As the father and son walked along the drive to the car, she cried, 'Do you really want to know who killed Curly?' Anything to keep him for a moment, to show that there were things in which she was way ahead of him. But they had reached the car. 'I'll tell you, if that's what you want. But one thing you've got to understand. I can't . . . I can't love you!'

Emma came up beside her. 'Where's Liam going, Mam?'

'Home.' Carol fumbled in her bag for a handkerchief, and then for the bunch of keys Mr Chubb had provided. 'Do you want to look inside the house, see all the nice things?'

The house was so full of nice things. All for herself and Emma. Yet Carol felt empty, utterly empty.

Joyce's progress with Michelle in the pushchair was hampered, as usual, by Joanne trying to help but tending to lean too heavily on her end of the bar and twist them all sideways. They were going slowly uphill when Steve caught up with them.

'What d'you think you're doing, Joyce?'

'What's it look like? I'm taking them home with me.'

'You're bloody not.'

'You just try stopping me. They're staying with me till you get that sour-faced bitch out of our Gina's house.'

'She's not going,' said Steve.

'Because you're sleeping with the whore, aren't you?'

Steve glanced apprehensively at Sarah, who had fallen into step with him. 'It's none of your bloody business what I'm doing,' he said in a fierce undertone.

'It is my business when my grandkids are living in the same

house. Well, they're not going to. They're staying with me til
she's gone.'

Joanne was catching the discord now. 'What's the matter
Nanna?'

Steve held out his hand to her.

'Don't you touch her,' Joyce growled.

'She's my kid, for Christ's sake. Mine and Gina's. So don'
you tell me not to touch her.'

'You don't bloody deserve her.' Joyce couldn't contro
herself, or the pushchair. They came to a halt. 'You don'
deserve any of 'em. You're not fit to look after them, going
off two minutes after they'd lost their mother.'

They were attracting curious glances from other mothers
and their children catching up on the way from the schoo
gates. Steve kept his voice down. 'Going off? I went to ge
a job and some money. Because you told me to.'

'I didn't expect you to come back with some slut, though.

'Look who's bloody talking.'

'Don't you dare speak to me like that. Who the bloody hel
d'you think you are?'

'I'm their father, that's who. Just trying to live my life.'

'Well, go off and live it. Go on, piss off to Blackpool with
your woman and leave me and the kids alone.'

Sarah caught the magic word but wasn't sure about the
turmoil of the argument. 'Are we going to Blackpool again
Nanna?'

'Is that what all this crap's about?' Steve demanded. 'You
think I'm gonna run off to Blackpool. Joyce . . .?'

That was what she was dreading. How else did he expect
her to feel? She used to have two cleaning jobs and her
father to see to, and Bob and Gina and the kids. She had
been run off her feet; there'd never been enough hours in
the day to fit it all in. Now there were too many empty
hours. She looked at what she was left with, and was
terrified.

'Everything's gone,' she burst out. 'If you take the kids

away, I'll have nothing. Don't take them away from me, please.'

Steve's face crumpled. Realisation was dawning on him. 'But I'm not going to do that, Joyce. Not for Lisa, not for anyone. You're their nanna, for Christ's sake, how could I take them away from you? They need you.' He squeezed her arm, and she didn't fight him off. 'They need you, I need you. I'll never take them away. I swear it – on Gina's memory.'

Joyce wavered. But he meant it, she could see that. She looked down at Joanne. 'Go to your dad, go on.' Joanne reached for her father's outstretched hand. Sarah, troubled by the row, looked uncertain. 'Go on, Sarah,' Joyce urged her. 'It's just your nanna being silly. Your daddy loves you, go on. Go to him.'

Steve's other hand was held out. Sarah's hand slipped timidly into it.

Tracy had waited until she heard Anita and the carpenter going down the cellar steps, then she slipped silently out of the front door. The pricklings of an awful doubt were beginning to scour the edge of her mind. If she could get her hands on some crack right away, she could numb all that. Everything would come all right again. But without it, she was thinking impossible things. Of course what Rose and Carol and the rest of them said had to be crazy. She knew what she'd done, and why she'd done it. But they were friends, you wouldn't expect them to make things up just for the hell of it.

She needed something to soothe her, drive the nightmares away.

On the corner of the Lane she took out her mobile phone and dialled the Harrogate number. It was the first time she had rung home since home had ceased to be home. When Laura or their mother answered, she would have to tell them about killing daddy. They must surely know about his death already, but couldn't have the faintest idea how it had happened.

She had not even begun to think of the way she would break it to them when the phone at the other end was lifted, and her father's voice said: 'Hello. Tim Richards here.'

Tracy stopped on the edge of the kerb. The lane seemed to tilt for a moment; a gulf opened at her feet and then she was clear-headed again – staggered, but knowing there was only one thing to do now.

'Hello.' He was impatient, as he always was when kept waiting. 'Who is that?'

'Is that you, daddy?'

'Naomi?'

'Yes, it's me. I'm coming home.'

She had made a terrible mistake. There was only one thing she could possibly do to put it right.

The taxi driver looked at her dubiously, and she realised she had still done nothing about her matted hair. But when she showed him that she had plenty of money on her, he shrugged and agreed to take her all the way to Harrogate. He tried to make spasmodic conversation along the road, but Tracy was sunk in the past. She heard Dez saying, 'Smile baby,' and her own voice echoing it. And her father pulling her close until one hand could slide down inside her knickers and he'd be making a jokey secret of it by murmuring, 'We don't have to tell Mummy everything, do we?' And Daddy wanting her to prance up and down in front of him, with his hand doing other things, this time to himself, not to her. Only they said it hadn't been him, but Curly.

She checked that her cocaine knife was still in the front compartment of her little haversack.

Mr Richards must have been sitting in the front window waiting for the taxi to arrive. He was on the step as it drew up, and hurried down the drive to greet her. He was even waving aside her attempts to pay the driver, and thrusting notes on the man. Then he was holding her arm and bundling her indoors.

'You look so different, I can't believe it. I suppose you've grown up. You'll always be my little girl, though.' He took the haversack from her and put it on the hall table. 'Is that it? No other bags?'

'This is all I need,' she said in her most precise, polite voice; the sort of voice that went with this house.

'I kept telling your mother, one day she'll just pick up the phone, and I was right. You've done it. I'm so proud of you.'

How could a dead man burble on so?

'And when she gets home tonight,' he was going on, 'we're going to go out and celebrate. Such a pity that Laura's away at school, or we could have had a proper family meal like we used to.'

'So we're all by ourselves, are we?'

'That's not going to be a problem, is it?'

'No, not at all.' The phone in the hall, beside her haversack, began ringing. Instinctively Tracy felt that this might be Colette, or Rose, or any of them, guessing where she was. 'Can I get it?' She moved towards the receiver. 'It might be Mummy.'

'Go ahead. Tell her I'm making us a drink to celebrate.'

It was Rose's voice. 'Is that you, Tracy? We've been—'

'I'm sorry, you've got a wrong number.' Tracy put the phone down, then lifted it again so that it was off the hook.

She went to join her father in the living room.

He was full of pitiful eagerness to wipe out the missing years and months, cancelling them out by producing photograph albums of the great times they had had together when she was little, the happy family they had always been until she chose to break it up. She drank the sherry he had poured, and longed for something else that might take a lot of finding round this neighbourhood.

'Do you remember Malta?' He turned a page. 'That's you and Laura, and the other girl you palled up with.'

'Janine,' Tracy recalled.

Her father was delighted. 'That's right. She was a nice

girl.' He pointed at a window in a block behind the three figures. 'I think that's the apartment we stayed in. Look how brown the pair of you were.'

Tracy looked at his lips working away around a load of nonsense, and said, 'Did you ever do it to Laura?'

'It was a nice holiday. We were there for about three weeks, I think.'

'Did you?' asked Tracy implacably.

Her father struggled on. 'It wasn't the sort of place you want to go back to, though, was it?'

'She said you never did, but she might have been covering for you.'

He was flipping over the pages. 'And here we all are together at Grandma and Grandpa's fortieth wedding anniversary.'

She was staring at him, not at the dead, meaningless photographs. 'You can tell the truth. There's nobody here.'

'It would be nice if you went to see them. They're always asking about you.'

She felt much older than him, and knew a hell of a lot more than he would ever know; yet there was still one thing she had to know. 'Tell me!'

He looked helplessly at the album, and pushed it aside. Reluctantly he met her gaze. 'No, I never touched Laura.'

'Why me, then? Why?'

'You . . .' The words were not going to come easily. 'You were different. You looked at me sometimes . . . in a certain way. I can't explain.'

'Try.'

'Like you knew . . . like you were . . . oh, I don't know.'

'Like what?'

'Like you wanted me to.'

'I was eleven.'

'I know.' Her father spread his hands in an appeal to someone who was never going to answer it. 'I'm not trying to excuse what I did. I just . . . well, I was going through some shake-ups at work, and your mother and I were going through a bad patch . . .'

'So you thought you'd take it out on me?'

'No, it wasn't like that. It was the opposite. You were the only good thing in my life, the only person who . . . well, seemed to like me. You did what I said. Everything else was slipping away, but *you* made me feel . . .'

'What?'

She wondered how he would say it, what he would come out with, whether it was loving her or whatever. All at once it was important, more important than anything she had craved from Dez, Rose, Colette, or the demons that had driven her for so long.

'Say it!' she cried.

He was sagging into a chair before her. And all he could whimper was, 'I suppose . . . powerful.'

So that was it.

'I'm going upstairs,' she said.

Bill assured Colette that he would put the cross back when its new varnish had dried, but more securely this time. He was wrapping up when Rose said urgently, 'Colette, I was right. She's there. But she's left the phone off the hook, won't talk to me.'

'There with her dad?'

'And what'll she make of him still being alive?' Rose turned to Bill. 'That's your van outside?'

He wasn't happy about driving them to Harrogate. He had better things to do, couldn't see what the rush was, and he was supposed to be picking his wife up from the supermarket in half an hour. And as to someone being likely to get killed if they didn't get there fast, he was afraid that they'd all be killed if they expected him to drive any faster than the van was used to. But Colette's terror got through to him. Rose felt that if they didn't get their way, Colette would somehow crack just the way Tracy had cracked.

Bill grudgingly let them pile into the seat beside him, and headed for Harrogate.

He stopped in the middle of the town so they could find a town guide and the telephone book and the address. Rose felt panic gripping her throat like a deadly fever. She remembered Mr and Mrs Richards at the hospital way back; and didn't think they'd be glad to see her again – unless they were just in time to stop Tracy from finishing her deadly campaign.

When they reached the Richards' front door and hammered on it, Rose was convinced that it would be Mrs Richards answering, maybe in hysterics.

Instead, Mr Richards stood there. 'Yes?'

So he was still alive. They were in time.

'Is Tracy here?'

He eyed them suspiciously. 'Nobody called Tracy lives here.'

'All right, then, Naomi. You're her father.'

'Yes. And who are you?'

'Her friends from Bradford. Is she in?'

'She's having a rest upstairs at the moment,' said Mr Richards frigidly. 'Can I give her a message?'

Rose's relief at seeing Mr Richards alive was robbing her of the wild energy that had forced them here. But Colette was suddenly the hysterical one. 'I've got to talk to her.' She tried to push past Mr Richards.

'Who the hell do you think you are?' He pursued her towards the staircase. 'You can't just walk into people's houses like—'

'Tracy! Where are yer, Tracy?'

Rose dashed up behind her. Mr Richards was reaching for the phone by the hall table. 'I warn you, I'm ringing the police.'

Colette threw open a bedroom door. It was obviously a girl's room, but very pink and white and tidy: not Tracy's . . . or even Naomi's. The next one was a large double bedroom, with a bathroom door half open. Colette was sobbing as

Rose passed her and reached the next one, on a corner of the landing.

'She's here!' breathed Rose thankfully. She took a couple of steps into the room, with Colette edging in beside her. 'Tracy.'

Colette leaned forward. 'Tracy . . . you asleep?'

Tracy's face was pale and tranquil above the burgundy duvet cover pulled up to her neck. It was only when Rose tiptoed round the end of the bed that she saw the darker red stain seeping from below the duvet in a thick, steady drip on to the carpet.

'Tracy, what have you done? What have you . . .'

Hearing Colette's anguished wail, she pulled the duvet to one side. The sheet below was soaked in the blood from Tracy's wrists, with her cocaine knife an inch away from her red, sticky, lifeless fingers. Colette threw herself to the bedside, but Rose was there before her, lifting Tracy and cradling her in her arms.

'Tracy, you didn't have to do that.'

'The police are on their way—' Mr Richards, bristling and officious in the doorway, stopped talking as he saw what lay on the bed and what was draining away on to the carpet.

22

Noise in The Hustlers' Arms was reaching its usual level for that hour of the morning. A quarter of an hour from now, around noon, a few seedy businessmen might look in, buying a hasty drink and making a quick arrangement with one of the girls. Not, today, with any one of the sombre group in the corner. They sat in silence nursing their drinks. All of them were dressed in the darkest, most sober clothes they could root out of their wardrobes. With Colette, that amounted only to the least provocative black leather jacket and skirt she could find. Dark brown was the best that Rose, close beside her daughter, could manage. Carol had wondered whether to buy a completely new dark suit for the occasion; but in the end felt that it might look too much like showing off her new wealth in front of the rest of them.

Anita, who had spent the night with a battery of rollers in her hair, was patting repeatedly at the results. 'They might all be wearing hats,' she said out of the blue. 'It's Harrogate. They wear hats in Harrogate.'

Carol shivered. 'Bloody Harrogate, it's always freezing there.'

'It's cold in any graveyard.' Joyce, who had announced that she would not be coming with them, stared into her drink. 'It's her mother I feel sorry for. She'll never get over it.'

Rose stole a glance at Colette, who was shakily lighting another cigarette.

'Do you remember when she used to stand outside here?'

Carol recalled. 'I used to give her a couple of quid when I was flush.'

'I used to give her a hard time,' said Rose. 'Tell her to go home to her mammy. Mind you, she used to give as much back. I thought she were just a cocky little kid. I let her down.'

Colette shook her head, and reached out to squeeze Rose's hand.

Looking at the two of them, Carol wondered how long it would take for that new intimacy to be soured by events. Like the police trying to involve as many of them as possible in the three deaths. The killer was now known, but only to her closest associates. Mr Richards, reluctantly, would have to tell as much as he knew; but that was precious little. He still hadn't grappled with the idea of his daughter and George Ferguson, or his daughter and Curly, and the burden of sorting out the facts would all fall on Carol and Rose. Dez wouldn't be missed; but there were still so many loose ends to be tidied up regarding the two others. Money, thought Carol. Wasn't that what money was for – to pay for a good lawyer, to try suing the police for harassment and wrongful arrest as a counterbalance to whatever they flung at her and Rose? Whatever it cost, she would be in a position to pay. Money fixed everything. There would have to be a way of buying them off or fighting them off. She was rich. She'd show them.

There was the peep of a taxi horn outside. They looked at one another as if summoning up the courage to go to their own execution.

'Right.' Carol was on her feet. 'See you later, Joyce.'

'I'm sorry I'm not coming with you. I just couldn't face it, two funerals in a row.'

'It's all right, there's enough of us.' Carol stopped at the door. 'Look, when we get back we've got to have a talk. If that loony Brenda really does have something legal from George Ferguson, maybe you could get Scrubbit going again under a different name. If not, you've got the know-how to start from scratch again.'

'Legal?' scoffed Anita. 'George Ferguson?'

'Anyway,' said Carol, 'I'm going to need a cleaning company for the chicken factory. Interested?'

Joyce looked hopefully at Rose as she drained her glass and got up from the table. 'We'd be interested, wouldn't we? We could take it on.'

'Too bloody right.' Rose looked down at Colette, who was still sitting there, trembling. 'Come on, love.'

'I can't go. It's no good, I can't do it.'

''Course you can. We'll all be together.' Rose held out her hand. The taxi horn beeped again; and slowly Colette put her hand in Rose's and allowed herself to be lifted to her feet. 'I'm here for you,' said Rose softly.

She put her arm round her daughter. 'Come on . . . let's go and say tara to Tracy.'